John Parker Anderson, Roden Berkeley Wriothesley Noel

Life of Lord Byron

John Parker Anderson, Roden Berkeley Wriothesley Noel

Life of Lord Byron

ISBN/EAN: 9783337057510

Printed in Europe, USA, Canada, Australia, Japan

Cover: Foto ©Raphael Reischuk / pixelio.de

More available books at **www.hansebooks.com**

LIFE

OF

LORD BYRON

BY

THE HONBLE. RODEN NOEL.

————

LONDON

WALTER SCOTT, 24 WARWICK LANE

1890

PREFATORY NOTE.

A LL available authorities known to me have been consulted for this little book. Moreover, I have conversed with persons likely to be able to throw new light upon the facts; and to their courtesy I am indebted, although they elect, for reasons, to keep back the main part of their special information at present. My thanks are due to Mr. S. McCalmont Hill for kind permission to publish a hitherto unpublished MS. poem in his possession, called "The Monk of Athos," by Lord Byron. It is a fragment only, is in the poet's hand-writing, and descended to Mr. Hill from his great-grandfather, Mr. Robert Dallas, to whom Lord Byron gave it. Only three stanzas of this have I printed, however, because the rest of the poem seemed hardly worthy of Byron's reputation; and when an author has presumedly laid aside a work as unworthy of publication, it appears to me scarcely decent for another person to publish it, merely on account of the celebrity of that author's name. Concerning the date and occasion of this unfinished piece I find no record. The stanzas here given have, I think, a certain fine, characteristic, rhetorical roll of descriptive verse.

I have ventured also to reprint a poem at the end of the volume from my own "Songs of the Heights and Deeps," which was written after a pilgrimage to Newstead and Hucknall, since this condenses my general impression and feeling concerning the great Anglo-European poet so much better than I can do it in prose.

Certain grave charges against Byron one might not have cared to touch upon here, had they not already been publicly discussed all over the world, so that no biography of him, however brief in compass, could now pretend to be fair and full without some sifting of the evidence relating to them.

R. N.

CONTENTS.

CHAPTER I.

CHAPTER II.

CHAPTER III.

CHAPTER IV.

CHAPTER V.

CHAPTER VI.

LIFE OF BYRON.

CHAPTER I.

THE biographies of literary men are not usually very interesting, except to those who are interested in the record and analysis of their works; they are mostly uneventful. But in some cases men combine action with contemplation. And in certain instances it is difficult to separate the man from his work; he puts so much of himself into it; it is so identified with his own experience. His contemporaries feel as much fascination in his personality as in what he writes. Then is there difficulty in following the counsel of Tennyson to keep silence about a poet's life :—

> " No public life was his on earth,
> No blazon'd statesman he, nor king.
>
> He gave the people of his best ;
> His worst he kept, his best he gave.
> My Shakespeare's curse on clown and knave
> Who will not let his ashes rest ! "

But neither Shakspeare, Dante, Tasso, Milton, nor

Spenser lived recluse student lives like Wordsworth.
And for my own part I wish we knew a great deal more
of Shakespeare's private history than we do. We should
probably find a great deal of human nature in him,
seeing that we find it in his work—in the sonnets, for
instance. But ought we therefore to be very much
shocked, and desire to hush all the falls and errors up?
"No one is a hero to his valet, but that's the fault of
the valet." There is no use in feigning that the hero
of your biography was a bloodless, featureless monster
of abstract perfection. I am disposed to think indeed
that, in *every case*, the life and work of a considerable
writer are capable of throwing light mutually upon one
another. In certain salient instances there can be no
doubt at all that it is so. Who would wish to consider the Rowley poems apart from Chatterton, "the
marvellous boy"? And Burns, can we sever *his* character and career from his poetry? But no doubt the
personality of some artists is recognized for something
more than their art—I do not say greater, but more—
while that of others (usually the "impeccable" artists
perhaps) appears less. Mere thinking-machines—philo-
sophers, mathematicians — are not usually picturesque.
But Byron, like Rousseau, was one who wished us to
know a good deal about him, and took care that we
should: he put himself forward. Emotion, imagination,
the roving Berserker nature, Bohemianism, give colour.
And he was possessed of a fascinating, arresting personality, of what Goethe called a "demonic personality."
Here was more than an author; here was a man;
whereas "mere artists are often man kins." One must

look generously, and with human sympathy, at the errors, not denying that they were such, or covering them up, but admitting fully the virtues also, and discerning that the specific quality, or idiosyncrasy, of such a man's creation is vitally related to his errors and weaknesses, even as also to whatsoever of strength and goodness belong to him.   To deal thus with a great man's faults and vices is not to " disturb his ashes " in the spirit of "clown or knave," nor to cater (except accidentally) for the "many-headed beast's " unhealthy appetite for gossip and scandal ; it is rather to try and understand a man who has done great things for his country and for Europe.   Whether the influence of this poet has been for good or evil will always be a debated point.   But on Eckermann's doubting whether there is " a gain for pure culture " in Byron's work, Goethe replies : " There I must contradict you.   The audacity and grandeur of Byron must certainly tend towards culture.   We should take care not to be always looking for it in the decidedly pure and moral.   Everything that is great promotes cultivation, as soon as you are aware of it."   And again he says profoundly : " Greatness is always formative"; or, to *adapt* a happy phrase of John Nichol : Byron "keeps the soul alive, if he does not save it."   But death is the dreadful thing, not life ; while there is life there is hope. He is, like Burns, the poet of youth and passion, of enjoyment, of intense, vivid, physical life ; that is one main element in his immense popularity.   He tells simple tales in verse, before the epoch of novels.   He also clearly, and with unequalled vigour, expresses the *average* thought and feeling of his time, setting them

to facile music; he does not soar over people's heads
into some astral ether, like Shelley, nor dive into calm
profundities beyond their cognizance, like Wordsworth.
And then nothing succeeds like success. The bookseller, the editor, the *Brummagem* critic, and the general
public are in love, not with the popular man, but with
his popularity, that is, with the echoes of their own
"sweet voices." It then becomes a question of fashion
only, and birthday presents to lie on drawing-room
tables. But such a degraded view of Byron as Leigh
Hunt took is manifestly absurd, because it fails to
account for the *poetry*, *i.e.*, for the main product and
staple of the man's own inmost self. No true poet is
a mere mechanical medium for inspiration from without. He *co-operates* with it, and is at his highest in
producing. Lady Byron never showed her essential
incompatibility with her husband more than when she
said he "feigned enthusiasm." Nor could Trelawny
penetrate behind his *persiflage*, which his own tone drew
from Byron, little as he suspected it. When the Guiccioli (after becoming Madame de Boissy) wrote to prove
him a sheer seraph and saint, we need to put the hostile
representations of his wife and others together with
this, and those of his friends, to get an adequate portrait.
"*Angel or demon?*" Lamartine asked. I answer, a
little of both. For seven years he must have turned the
angel side of him toward Theresa Guiccioli; and we
ought to give weight to what she tells us of his many
virtues, while allowing for the partiality of love.

There is, undoubtedly, nourishment for the lower, as
well as for the higher, faculties and desires of human

nature, in this poetry. But that coinage is the more adapted for general circulation whose gold is tempered with alloy. Byron, indeed, is one of the poets whom Plato might have banished from his ideal republic. For Pride, Resentment, Anger, Lawless Pleasure have their niches in that temple, and serve to strengthen the dominion of earthly impulse over us. But then there is so much more. There is the joy in all that is strong, energetic, brave, and determined—delight in "life, the mere living," joy in all beautiful and sublime things, pathos, and reverent love for external nature; hatred of and battle with the tyrant; pity for his victim, for the feeble, the outcast, and oppressed; scorn of hollow conventions, cant, and mere seeming propriety; withering satire, winged Apollonian shafts for the lay-figure virtues of our cruel English respectability. But here the warrior and troubadour are one as of old, singer and doer. If this man sings to you of Greece and her woes, he also takes up arms in her cause, he dies in her defence; and so the active function harmonizes with, and adds fresh lustre to the contemplative. There is the same turbid, troubled, impure element also in the poetry as in the life. The cynic, the man of the world, are appealed to by a writer who was a little of both, and derived strength from contact with his mother earth. The epigrams, the witty couplets and stinging sarcasms of one who could not always, I fear, appropriate to himself that noble boast of a yet greater poet,

> " J'ai fait peur aux petits hommes,
> Jamais aux petits enfants ! "

have fascinated and amused cynical men and women of
the world; and these were sometimes literary echoes
from certain baser traits of his own character, certain
muddy passages of his own experience. Young people,
too, were taken by the romantic guise of the poet, by
the mystery he affected, as also by his beauty, high birth,
and becoming sadness. The young can be sad for very
wantonness. Nothing so dainty sweet as lovely melancholy! Byron "posed" charmingly in his stories; he
obtruded sentimentally his private wrongs, and angled
with alluring baits to secure public sympathy. But
much of all this popularity was essentially factitious and
illegitimate; and much was accidentally begotten of the
poet's circumstances, and fashionable personality as peer
and *parti*, put *en evidence*. This has faded with the
man, and the hour. Newer, and flimsier literary fashions
are now in vogue.

It was, on the whole, a credit to our anti-poetical
English race that it took to Byron; though most of us
perchance have been graciously pleased to condone his
merits for the sake of his faults. Assuredly certain
"lewd fellows of the baser sort," foul-feeders, feed upon
the offal he provides "for the general" along with
caviare for the few. How refreshing to the clumsy
speculative intellect of the average Anglo-Saxon, which
is all thumbs, that joke of Byron's about philosophic
idealism :—

> "When Bishop Berkeley said there was no matter,
> 'Twas no matter what he said."

" That's just what every fellow has always thought, don't

you know, put so pat! What clever fellows we are after all, and Byron quite agrees with us!" "Don Juan" has been belittled by the foolish praise of little men. Yet a great proportion of the work was sincere and enduring. Much of the scathing satire is legitimate, destructive to mean and evil things; much of the serious verse is elevating, ennobling, making for truth and justice, enlarging our outlook, quickening sensibility, intensifying, deepening, widening experience, bracing and nerving men to noble endeavour; while the book also provides them with abundant humour, with inexhaustible stores of wit and buffoonery—no despicable boon this in our heavy spleenful atmosphere of suicide-provoking fogs, for men treading their dull treadmill of daily work-wearying rounds !

"No genuine good thought," says Carlyle, "was ever revealed by him to mankind." Yet Goethe observed to Eckermann, "A character of such eminence has never existed before, and probably will never come again; I did right to present him with that monument of love in Helena" (he is *Euphorion* in the second part of "Faust") —"I could not make use of any man as the representative of the modern poetic era except him, who is undoubtedly to be regarded as the greatest talent of our century." But then Goethe also remarked, "He is a child when he begins to reflect." Doubtless it is this very absence of profound original thought which suffers him to be carried along so lightly and freely, like a thistle-down, over extensive plains of the average mind, which is not a soil congenial to the germination of ideas—the average mind, which neither forgives, nor comprehends original thought. But we must observe that Byron was the most eminent representative and mouthpiece of his age, which was an age of scepticism, denial, unrest, uprooting of established beliefs and institutions, as also of what the Germans call " world-sorrow," despair with oneself, and with the world around, in the absence of that faith which had heretofore afforded men firm foothold amid overwhelming waves. All things were questioned by the all-dissolving human reason, and such a general mood needed—needs even now—expression; the more powerful the better. Questioning and denial are the inevitable condition of future synthesis, of larger comprehension, more pregnant reaffirmation of what had been denied. Byron is a great iconoclastic voice breaking upon contented and comfortable slumbers, as with the sound of a sea bursting barriers; shattering cherished idols—troubled and turbulent as the sea—the poet of revolt. From a child he loved to breathe the breath of battle. And Carlyle ignores that Byron, with Rousseau and Chateaubriand, sent us to the contemplation of Nature, was the chief hierophant for Europe of that sacred cult, which is distinctive of modern times. As I have said elsewhere, " his burning words of passionate admiration kindled our boyhood to behold and worship; his magnificent music, sonorous with storm and ocean, with all that is free, illimitable, and enduring, thrilled to the very heart of Europe, compelling it, as at a god's command, to bow down once more, when the angels of Faith and Hope seemed to be deserting for ever the desecrated shrines of mankind. In a time when all secrets were at length supposed to be laid bare before man's microscopic understanding, all superstitions exploded, all mysteries explained; when the universe, emptied of ancient awe, seemed no longer venerable, but a hideous lazar-house rather, made visible to all human eyes in every ghastly corner of it; before the Circe-wand of materialism, love metamorphosed into a sensation, and man shrivelled to a handful of dust; when the body of God's own breathing world was laid with familiar irreverence upon the board of a near-sighted professor to be dissected—then the prophet-poets, Rousseau and Byron, pointed men to the World-Soul, commanding men once more to veil their faces before the swift, subtle splendour of Divine Life in nature." Yet, indeed, Wordsworth was purer, profounder, more subtle and delicate in his appreciation of nature, as well as Byron's precursor in the same cult.

Before telling briefly the story of his life, I shall quote testimony of another kind, coming from a source which every good and true man should respect. "The day will come," says Mazzini, "when Democracy will remember all that it owes to Byron. England, too, will, I hope, one day remember the mission—so entirely English, yet hitherto overlooked by her—which Byron fulfilled on the Continent; the European *rôle* given by him to English literature, and the appreciation and sympathy for England which he awakened among us." (For he was, in fact, European rather than English in his own sympathy.) "He led," adds Mazzini, "the genius of Britain on a pilgrimage through Europe." "I know no more beautiful symbol of the future destiny and mission of art than the death of Byron in Greece. The holy alliance of poetry with the cause of the people—the union, still so rare, of thought and action—the grand solidarity of all nations in the conquest of the rights ordained by God for all his children—all that is now the religion and the hope of the party of progress in Europe is gloriously typified in this image."

All which cannot be set aside by any pedantic, intemperate, microscopic cavils about the occasional shortcomings of this swift, spontaneous, full-blooded, long-and-strong-flighted eagle in rhythm and rhyme, too often slovenly, over-colloquial, and aristocratically careless in the use of his native tongue. But they who prefer the clothes. to the man may say *ditto* to such foolish depreciation. His words are "open to criticism," and they are also "above" it. "The magic still works," as Mr. Morley says. There are worse faults—coarseness, commonplace, ribaldry, occasional want of subtlety and distinction in thought and phrase, as well as in music; above all, monotony of subject and treatment—a tendency to theatrical "pose," and enthronement of the anti-social, aggressive, insatiable, impatient individual. Yet the measures are often sonorous and masterly, the sentiment rouses to high moods, like a clarion, in language, vigorous, limpid, terse, memorable—though to the *voces, et praeterea nihil* of our day, Byron will never commend himself. Where there is such weight and originality of substance, combined with so much effective expression, minute verbal criticism of technical details is impertinent when offered as a sufficient reason for refusing the bays, or for dethroning a great poet, upon whose claim Europe and posterity have pronounced their verdict.

"He was," says the eloquent Spaniard, Castelar, in his splendid eulogy, "like one of those Greek heroes—youthful, resplendent, as skilful with the sword as with the lyre—beloved by a beautiful woman, conqueror alike in sports as in battles; and yet condemned from the cradle by a cruel destiny to the infernal deities. Byron never gained a heart without afflicting it, or himself. All the sweetness of his rich fancy turned to bitterness at the presence of reality." "Men know not that all extraordinary virtue, all surpassing merit, is born of a disproportion between human faculties." "Demand of the Creator why the eagle sings not like the nightingale. All supernatural genius is an internal infirmity. Genius is a Divine infirmity, a martyrdom. The poet cannot go into the fire without being burned; cannot enter the thundercloud without receiving the shock of electricity. They feed the splendour, burning in the lamp of their own brain, with tears from their eyes, and with blood from their hearts." "The sea falls like a drop of gall, and the earth like an atom of powder, into the unfathomable abyss of desire. Every poet feels that which is called in common language home-sickness — the sorrow of exile, the longing after things higher and holier. Every great poet is like an exiled angel." "In Virgil, Petrarch, Raphael, it is a gentle melancholy; in Michael Angelo, Dante, Byron, an abandonment of grief, which borders on despair, like the roaring of a hurricane . above the foam of the ocean.

Many men of genius console themselves by unfolding their souls in their works. Michael Angelo secluded himself, and peopled the roof of the Sistine with prophets, sibyls, sublime Titans, that cost him the most profound emotion. All of them are the produce of his soul's agony." "This great genius lived to repeat the aspirations of all peoples." "We enter on the truth by scepticism, by despair, as we enter into life by sorrow, with tears in our eyes, and sobs in our bosoms. The age which doubts not is an age which asks not ; and we should importune the truth with questions, as we should come to God with supplications."

The poet was very proud of his descent both on the father's and mother's side. The Byrons are an old Norman family, whose ancestors came over with the Conqueror. Some of their number fought at Cressy; others at the siege of Calais and at Bosworth. Henry VIII. granted Newstead Abbey, on the dissolution of the monasteries, to one known as "Little Sir John of the great beard." The Sir John of Elizabeth's reign was illegitimate. At Edgehill there were seven Byrons in the field. For his services at Newbury another was created Baron of Rochdale in 1643. Of the rest, Admiral Byron, called "Foul-weather Jack" for his misfortunes by sea, and the "wicked Lord Byron," who married a daughter of Lord Berkeley, grand-uncle of the poet, who succeeded this "wicked lord" in the peerage, are the best known. Admiral the Hon. John Byron wrote a spirited account of his own adventures by sea, which were many, alluded to in "Don Juan," whose hardships were

" Comparative
To these related in my granddad's narrative."

"He had no rest on sea, nor I on shore," says the grandson. The "wicked lord" is celebrated for his irregular and savage duel with his neighbour and kinsman, Mr. Chaworth—fought in the room of an inn by the light of a tallow candle. Chaworth was run through the body, and Byron was tried for his life, a verdict of manslaughter being returned; and though he was afterwards set free, he is said to have lived a solitary, spectre-haunted kind of a life at Newstead, generally avoided. All sorts of false stories were told about him, but he seems to have been a bad man, and half cracked. It is alleged that the crickets, whom he fed and chastised with straws, left the abbey in a body when he died. He hated his sons, and cut down the trees in the park to spite them. This man surely must, in part, have suggested Lara, and the poet's other gloomy heroes. "Mad Jack Byron," the poet's father, was a handsome rake, who seduced the Marquis of Carmarthen's wife (Lady Conyers in her own right), and married her after a divorce had been obtained. She was mother of Augusta, the poet's half-sister, who married Colonel Leigh, and had a numerous family. After his first wife's death he married Catherine Gordon, of Gight, an heiress, whose fortune he soon ran through. She was very proud of her descent from James I., through his daughter Annabella and the second Earl of Huntley. Shortly after the poet's birth in Holles Street, January 22, 1788, the father, being pressed by his creditors, abandoned mother and child, leaving them with only £150 a year, and died at Valenciennes in August, 1791.

Mrs. Byron, early in 1790, settled with her child in a small house in Aberdeen.   There her husband rejoined her for a while; but their incompatible tempers soon compelled a definite separation.   Yet when the wife heard of his death in France, her shrieks of despair are said to have disturbed the neighbourhood.   (Sir Walter Scott relates that, *before* her marriage, she was carried out of the theatre, when Mrs. Siddons was personating Isabella in Southerne's "Fatal Marriage," screaming, "O my Biron, my Biron!")   Byron told Harness that his father died insane and by his own hand; but this has been generally assumed to have been a fib. There is no further evidence that it was true.   The poet remembered the father lovingly, who used to waylay the child at Aberdeen, and play with him; for Mad Jack took lodgings for awhile, apart from his wife, in the same town, before the final separation.   And the father once took him home to spend a night with him there.   He was only three then, yet remembered this.[1] In his early poems he says:

> "Stern death forbade my orphan youth to share
>   The tender guidance of a father's care."

---

[1] Mr. Jeaffreson relates a story, not without evidence to support it, that the child, on approaching the old Brig of Balgonie over the Dee, together with another child, who was taking turns with him to ride on ponyback, insisted on riding over himself, though it was not his turn, because his companion was an only son as well as himself, and he knew the weird prophecy which ran—

> "Brig o' Balgonie, wight is thy wa';
>   Wi' a wife's ae son on a mare's ae foal
>   Down shalt thou fa'."

And in " Lara " :

> " Left by his sire, too young such loss to know,
> Lord of himself, that heritage of woe,
> That fearful empire, which the human breast
> But holds to rob the heart within of rest,
> With none to check, and few to point in time
> The thousand paths that slope the way to crime. "

What an utter incapacity in the man, even had he lived long enough, to guide a son's inexperienced footsteps, and such a son's! The mother!—sometimes a mother may almost make up by her affectionate and gentle wisdom for the absence of firm kindness and judiciously applied experience in a father. But here there was no such mother. What an irreparable loss! not to have learned to reverence woman in the celestial light shed upon her out of one's own sacred experience of Motherhood! Poor Mrs. Byron was a warm-hearted person indeed, truly fond of her son in her own strange way; but as one of the poet's schoolboy friends too candidly observed to him, "Byron, your mother is a fool;"—to which he could only reply, "I know it!" She was vehement, undisciplined, subject to fits of fury, hysterical, and, on the whole, would seem to have been appointed in irony to train this volcanic child of abnormal sensibility and genius. And her extraordinary conduct to him is sufficient to account for a trait, which would, had we not known the facts, have appeared very unamiable — his comparative want of affection for the poor lady, as shown in his letters to her, and otherwise. Now she would lavish caresses on him, and now blows, with little other justification than her own arbitrary whims and moods. The image of him as a child defending himself with the chairs from her, trying to fling the poker at him, remains in the memory of all who have read Lord Beaconsfield's "Venetia." On one occasion, after violent abuse, she finished by calling him "a lame brat!" His lips quivered, his face whitened, a fearful light came into his eyes, as he replied, "I was born so, mother!" The scene was in his mind when he wrote the "Deformed Transformed" at Pisa.

Such was the inheritance, and such the education provided for this poet. His own disposition as a child prophesied what he would be in after-life—"passionate, sullen, defiant of authority, but singularly amenable to kindness." On being scolded by his first nurse for soiling a dress, he tore it from top to bottom, as he had seen his mother tear her caps and gowns. But to his next nurse, Mary Gray, he remained always attached. To her is attributed his considerable knowledge of the Bible; he was, she said later, fond of putting puzzling questions about religion even as a child. To her he owed that profound tincture of Calvinism which he retained to the end. But there is one high and noble characteristic which he owed to his mother. While, on the one hand, overweeningly proud of her descent, and teaching her son to be so of his—Mrs. Byron yet avowed herself "a democrat," which implied at that time in England no small courage. She taught the poet to abhor tyrants, to pity the poor, the weak, the oppressed.

I ought not to proceed without mention of his lameness. For beautiful in person as he was, save for this

one deformity, he was so vain, self-conscious, and
morbidly sensitive, that it embittered his life from childhood forward.   As has been remarked, a clubfoot was
incapable of disturbing the serene nature of Walter
Scott.   But then, after all, Byron's seems to have been a
particularly painful, perturbing, and injurious kind of
lameness.   The right *Achilles tendon* was so contracted
that he could never put the foot flat on the ground,
wearing for it a boot made with a high heel, and a pad-
ding inside under the heel of the foot; indeed the
tendons of both feet were contracted; he had to walk
on the balls and toes of his feet; but the right foot
is said to have been so distorted as to turn inwards; yet
this probably was owing to the unskilful surgical treatment of some one who operated on the foot.   He used
to "hop about like a bird," Leigh Hunt assures us
rather spitefully.

This affliction prevented Byron from taking a healthy
and normal amount of exercise, aggravating thereby his
predisposition to corpulency.   No wonder that he
adopted all sorts of plans, more or less injurious to his
health in other ways, to keep himself thin.   Why he
should be sneered at for not wishing to look clumsy and
unwieldy, having been born with natural advantages of
face, figure, and complexion, I could never understand,
the contempt for bodily beauty appearing to me no
virtue, but an indication either of defective sensibility,
or of an immoral ascetic theory.   Besides, corpulency is
itself a painful disease, to be combated on the score of
health.   So he starved, and took frequent doses of
Epsom salts—a very weakening habit.   But his adop-

tion of a low and meagre diet, though persisted in for
long periods together, was somewhat fitful and irregular,
and he would make up for his enforced abstinence now
and again by orgies of eating and drinking. Although,
like Scott, Byron had a very insensitive palate, and was
no gourmet to distinguish delicate flavours, it can have
been no easy task for him to go so perpetually hungry,
"clapping," as he says, "the muzzle on his own jaws."
But by starving his body he thought he subdued his
animal nature, and kept his brains clear. No man had
brighter eyes, or a clearer voice. A child called him
"the gentleman with the beautiful voice." He lived
for days together on biscuits and soda water; then, half-
famished, would swallow a huge mess of potatoes, rice,
and fish, drenched with vinegar. Such a regimen, in
concert with the immense draughts of brain-work made
on his nervous energy, rendered his digestion in later
life a torment to him. He would roll on the ground in
agony with it, and could not sleep. As a rule, he was
very moderate in drinking; but occasionally went in
for a drinking bout with Moore, or some other friend.
"Why should I make myself more stupid than God made
me?" the boy Chatterton once observed, excusing himself for not eating; but needing, alas! soon little excuse
enough. In 1816, and at Venice, Byron took brandy
to excess, and was for some time a laudunum drinker,
chewing tobacco also to mitigate the craving for food.
But this was more or less exceptional with him. As for
exercise, swimming and riding were about the only forms
of it possible to him; boxing and fencing also, however, in
some measure, and even cricket. Yet of running he could

have done little, and his power of "roving over the hills" as "a young highlander," of which he speaks in his early poems, must ever have been limited.   This at least was usually done on pony-back.   " In early life," says Tre-lawny, " whilst his frame was light and elastic, he might have tottered along for a mile or two ; but after he had waxed heavier, he seldom attempted to walk more than a few hundred yards, without squatting or leaning against the first wall, bank, tree, or rock at hand, never sitting on the ground, as it would have been difficult for him to get up again."   "He won several fights at Harrow," says Jeaffreson, "but in every case he won them by rushing at his adversary with the *élan* of a French foot-soldier, and making a short business of each round by putting in quickly two or three blows with his singularly muscular arms.   When he could not snatch success in this manner he was beaten," on account of his weak feet.   He boxed with Jackson the pugilist, and his pupils, in the same manner.   He used to enter London drawing-rooms, in the height of his popularity, running rather than walking, and stopped himself suddenly by planting his left foot on the ground, and resting upon it.   " What a pretty boy George is ! " said a friend, to his nurse, when he was a child ; "what a pity he has such a leg ! "   On which he, cutting after him with a baby's whip, cried out, " Dinna speak of it ! "   He hated Harrow till he got high up in the school ; the brutal, big bullies there would put his lame foot into a bucket of water by way of a joke.   He used, later in life, to fancy that the beggars and street-sweepers in London were mocking his gait—though Lady Blessington says that his lameness was not particularly noticeable till he referred to it. In his verses called "The Waltz" he satirized dancing; and in "Lara" one recalls that picture of the stern melancholy man, leaning against a pillar, while the gay dancers footed it round him. At Matlock the poet had, indeed, watched his own love, Mary Chaworth, in the arms of other partners, while he himself could only look on. His lameness! ought he not to have minded it? Why even Mary Chaworth, the lady of his love, struck the last cruel blow upon his boyish passion in the contemptuous reproach he overheard when she said to her maid, not knowing he was near, "Do you think I could care for that lame boy?" Upon which he rushed out of the house that held her, and flew to Newstead. On his death-bed he refused to let mustard be applied to his feet, according to the doctor's order; though at last he allowed Fletcher, his trusty servant, to do it, after ordering every one else out of the room. This makes the indelicacy of Trelawny's *post-mortem* examination of, and report upon, his feet, to my mind considerable; for, according to his own account, he did not uncover the feet, which Fletcher had religiously covered, before sending the poor valet away to fetch him a glass of water! Still Trelawny's is a book to rank with Boswell's "Johnson," and the better for not being written by a professed bookman, in spite of its *animus* against Byron.

After passing through the hands of certain preparatory tutors, the poet was sent to the Aberdeen Grammar School, in 1794. There he showed no particular aptitude for learning the common tasks inflicted at our schools upon all boys, without any discrimination of their particular

bents; and he arrived at the top of his form in a
singular manner; for it was the custom there to invert
the proper order of the classes at the beginning of the
lesson, so that the most ignorant were for the moment
placed first; and more than once the master said, banter-
ing him, " Now, George, man, let me see how soon you'll
be at the foot!" But even then he was a reader of
books, and educated himself, while refusing the kind of
education provided for him by his adult inferiors. He
gives a surprising list of books read by him before he
was ten.

About this time, when he was in his ninth year, he
"fell in love" with his cousin Mary Duff, a little older
than himself. He says that he used to coax a maid to
write letters from him to her, and that when he was sixteen, on being informed by his mother that his cousin
was married, he nearly fell into convulsions. This
reminds one of Dante's passion for Beatrice in his tenth
year. He tells us also of his "silent rages and sullen
fits"—which Lady Byron found so unpleasant later on.
In 1796, after an attack of scarlet fever at Aberdeen, he
was taken by his mother to Ballater, and from this
period he informs us he dates his love of mountainous
countries. "After I returned to Cheltenham I used to
watch the Malvern Hills every afternoon at sunset with
a sensation which I cannot describe." In the "Island"
he says :—

> " The infant rapture still survived the boy,
> And Loch-na-gair with Ida looked o'er Troy,
> Mix'd Celtic memories with the Phrygian mount,
> And Highland linns with Castalie's clear fount."

3

His nurse denied that he ever did "climb the steep summit of Morven," as he boasts, but at any rate he wandered about the mountain in imagination as he gazed.

In May, 1798, on the death of his grand-uncle, the fifth and so-called "wicked lord," George Gordon, in his eleventh year, succeeded to the family title, having become the next heir when his cousin, the fifth lord's grandson, died in Corsica. And in the autumn of the same year, Mrs. Byron (having sold her household effects for about £75) set out for England with her son, who never re-visited Scotland. On passing the toll bar of Newstead in a post-chaise, Moore tells us that Mrs. Byron asked the woman in charge to whom the Abbey belonged, and on her replying that the late lord had died some time since, Mrs. Byron further inquired who was the next heir, to which the woman answered, "They say it is a little boy who lives in Aberdeen." Whereupon the nurse, Mary Gray, who was in the carriage with the boy, ejaculated: "And this is he; bless him!" But Mrs. Byron could not afford to live there, and took up her abode at Nottingham. The house, moreover, had been left in a very ruined and dilapidated condition by the late owner. The estate was already in Chancery, and the Earl of Carlisle—George Gordon's first cousin (once removed), son of Isabella Byron, sister of the fifth lord—was appointed his guardian. Mrs. Byron lived about twelve months at Nottingham, where she found for her son a certain tutor named Rogers, whom he regarded with affection. He suffered much here from a bonesetter called Lavender, who maltreated his foot, and put him to useless torture. On him Byron played a childish trick—arranging the letters of the alphabet in gibberish words he asked Lavender what language that was, upon which the man replied, "*Italian*," to the boy's huge delight.

When the poor little fellow was sitting, doing his lessons in much pain from his foot one day, the kind tutor said how it troubled him to see his pupil suffering. "Never mind, Mr. Rogers," answered the brave lad, "you sha'n't see any signs of it again." It is said also that here an old lady he disliked was the occasion of Byron's first verses—satirical ones. She believed that our souls would live in the moon after death, and having offended him one day, he suddenly exclaimed to his nurse that "he couldn't bear the sight of the old witch," and broke out into the following doggerel :—

> "In Nottingham County there lives at Swan Green
> As curst an old lady as ever was seen ;
> And when she does die, which I hope will be soon,
> She firmly believes she will go to the moon."

The following year, Mrs. Byron moved to Sloane Terrace, in London, having received a pension of £300 a year from the Civil List, and at Lord Carlisle's suggestion the boy was taken to Dr. Baillie (a brother of Joanna), who directed that a particular kind of shoe should be made for him, on the lines originally suggested by John Hunter, the well-known surgeon. Mary Gray, the nurse, now returned to Scotland. The child parted from her with affectionate sorrow, giving her the first watch he had ever possessed, which on her death-bed

passed to Dr. Ewing, of Aberdeen, who also received
from her some memoranda about the poet's early years,
and the child gave her a miniature of himself by Ray.
He was now sent to a school at Dulwich, kept by a Dr.
Glennie. Sleeping in the doctor's library, he was encouraged by him to read the books there, and these he
eagerly devoured. "In my study," says Dr. Glennie,
"he found, among others, a set of our poets from
Chaucer to Churchill, which I am almost tempted to
say he had more than once perused from beginning to
end." One of the books was the "Narrative of the
Shipwreck of the *Juno*," from which, almost word for
word, the picture of the two fathers in the shipwreck
of "Don Juan" is taken. Mrs. Byron would have her
son with her from Saturday to Monday, and interrupted
his education in various ways. Lord Carlisle, on Dr.
Glennie's appealing to him, exerted his authority against
these interruptions; but Mrs. Byron exhibited so much
temper on his remonstrating, that he said to the master :
"I can have nothing more to do with Mrs. Byron; you
must now manage her as you can." Dr. Glennie, though
fond of the son, has given a very unfavourable account
of the mother. After two years, she requested Lord
Carlisle to remove the poet to Harrow, where he accordingly went (1801) in his fourteenth year.

In his twelfth year (1800), the boy fell in love with
his cousin, Margaret Parker—a girl of an exquisitely
delicate complexion. "My passion," he says, "had its
usual effects upon me. I could not sleep—I could
not eat—I could not rest; and although I had reason
to know that she loved me, it was the texture of

my life to think of the time which must elapse
before we could meet again, being usually about twelve
hours of separation. But I was a fool then, and am
not much wiser now! My sister told me that when
she went to see her shortly before her death, upon
accidentally mentioning my name, Margaret coloured
through the paleness of mortality to the eyes, to her
great astonishment, she knowing nothing of the attachment." It was at Cheltenham that his mother was
much moved by the prediction of a fortune-teller that
her son should be in danger from poison before he
was of age, and should be twice married—the second
time to a foreign lady. Margaret Parker died of con-
sumption about two years after the poet fell in love
with her. On her he wrote his first serious verses, and
later the lines :

> " Hush'd are the winds, and still the evening gloom ;
> Not e'en a zephyr wanders through the grove,
> Whilst I return to view my Margaret's tomb,
> And scatter flowers on the dust I love."

Was this girl " *Thyrza,*" as Mr. Jeaffreson thinks?
I believe not. Moore says that Thyrza was a creation
of the poet's imagination, and that the poems addressed
to her were "the essence, the abstract spirit as it were,
of many griefs," *sorrow for the loss of Eddlestone, his
young chorister friend at Cambridge, being one of them.*
The verses seem to commemorate "a violent, though
pure love and passion," whose object is unknown, which
he mentions in his journal as having possessed him in
the summer of 1806, his first year at Cambridge, con-

temporaneously with his friendship for Edward Noel
Long, who was drowned on his voyage to Lisbon with
his regiment, in 1809. He writes of this to Mr. Dallas,
on the exact date of some of the lines to Thyrza,
October 11, 1811, saying, "I have been shocked with
a death, and have lost one very dear to me in happier
times, but 'I have almost forgot the taste of grief,'
and supped full of horrors till I have become callous;
nor have I a tear left for an event which five years ago
would have bowed my head to the earth." Several
years after, Lord Byron, being asked to whom the poems
referred, refused to answer, with marks of painful agita-
tion. At any rate, the lines commencing, "*And thou
art dead, as young and fair*," are probably as beautiful
and tender as any in our language. It is very possible
that "Thyrza" was the chorister friend—not only partly,
as Moore believes—probably because Byron had avowed
thus much—but solely;—only to avoid banter, and even
possible misconception, he gave his lost boy-friend a
female name, and to the language of the poems a turn
appropriate to the disguise adopted. If justification
were needed, one might refer to the Sonnets of Shakespeare, or even to "In Memoriam."

Byron was a Harrow boy from the summer of 1801
to that of 1805, and for some time he was under Dr.
Drury, of whom he was fond, and whom he never ceased
to respect, while the head-master was fond of his pupil,
and predicted his future greatness. He said to Lord
Carlisle, who was inquiring about his abilities, "He has
talents, my lord, which will add lustre to his rank."
And Dr. Drury, in his story of this episode, adds that

the guardian's only reply was the monosyllable "*Indeed!*" pronounced with an accent of surprise, which did not express all the satisfaction the good Doctor had expected. "We are left in doubt," says Nichol, "whether the indifference proceeded from the jealousy that clings to poetasters," (for the Earl had written indifferent verses, which his ward unkindly calls "the paralytic pulings of Carlisle,") "from incredulity, or a feeling that no talent *could* add lustre to rank." Of Dr. Drury Byron says: "He was the best, the kindest (and yet strict too) friend I ever had, and I look on him still as a father, whose warnings I have remembered but too well, though too late, when I have erred, and whose counsel I have but followed when I have done well or wisely." Yet till the last year and a half he hated Harrow—that is till he was high up in the school, and could lead. He was very unpopular at first, but though he was bullied when very young, he remained long enough to show the native energy and determination of his character, and become respected among his schoolfellows; yet he never did much schoolwork there. In 1805, Dr. Drury retired, and was succeeded by Dr. Butler, an appointment unpopular with the boys, who would have preferred Henry Drury, son of the former master. Byron, always famous for rows, was a ringleader of the boy rebels. He tore down the window-gratings before some of the Master's windows, "because they darkened the hall." He also set limits to the rebellion, however, when some of the wilder spirits would have burned one of the class-rooms, preventing this outrage by reminding them that so they would destroy the old desks, upon which their own fathers and grandfathers had carved their names when they were boys. One of Byron's schoolfellows told Moore that when Dr. Butler sent him an invitation to dinner as an upper boy, he refused to go, and on being asked for a reason, replied, "Why, Dr. Butler, if you should happen to come into my neighbourhood when I am staying at Newstead, I certainly should not ask you to dine with me, so therefore I feel that I ought not to dine with you." But Dr. Butler assured Moore that there was very little foundation in fact for the story; it is evident, however, from the terms of this disclaimer, that there was some. Byron apologized later for his rudeness; yet in "Hours of Idleness" he published some offensive verses about the Master, calling him "Pomposus of the narrow brain." "I soon found," says Dr. Drury, "that a wild mountain colt had been committed to my care. But there was mind in his eye. . . . A degree of shyness hung about him," (which indeed clung to him through life). "His manner and temper soon convinced me that he might be led by a silken string to a point, rather than by a cable—on that principle I acted." The master also relates that when the boy recited a written declamation, in common with some of his schoolfellows, he diverged with much fire and animation from what was written, bringing his oration to a successful conclusion, and coming back to the written theme, though unconscious that he had so diverged; and that his manner and delivery were excellent. Drury thought he would turn out a great orator. While Sir George Sinclair used frequently to do his exercises for Byron,

the latter more than once fought Sinclair's battles for
him with his fists. "He was pacific, and I savage;
so I fought for him; thrashed others for him, or
thrashed himself to make him thrash others, when it
was necessary as a point of honour and stature that he
should so chastise. . . . I fought my way very fairly;
I think I lost but one battle out of seven: my most
memorable combats were with Morgan, Rice, Rainsford,
and Lord Jocelyn, but we were always friendly afterwards." And here I may remark that I was told by
my grandfather (the same Lord Jocelyn, afterwards Earl
of Roden) about this "mill" with Byron. So far as
Lord Roden could remember, it was a drawn battle
(and therefore Byron cannot be said to have "*lost*"
it!) My grandfather was not intimate with his celebrated schoolfellow, but recollected him as rather a
rowdy, not particularly attractive boy, who amused
himself, at any rate on one occasion, by wringing the
neck of a duck (presumably one of those swimming
upon the water, called "duck puddle," at Harrow!)
This reminds one that the poet, who afterwards became
beautiful in face and figure, and was himself but too
conscious of a fact which the women did not allow
him to forget, appears as a schoolboy to have possessed
few personal attractions. He was described by Miss
Pigot of Southwell—a partial acquaintance—as "a fat,
bashful boy, with hair combed straight over his forehead,
and looking a perfect gaby." Moore learnt from several
quarters that he was by no means popular among girls
of his own age. Moreover, he was conceited, shy, and
awkward, with rough and odd manners. Yet thoughtful

moods must have characterized him even then, for we
hear of him reclining by the hour on the well-known
tombstone under the elm in the churchyard, from which
there is so beautiful a view, and near to which now
rests little Allegra, his beloved illegitimate daughter.
Later, he became so tender to animals that he repudiated field sports and fishing.   The list of books he
read, moreover, drawn up by him in 1809, is a remarkably long one—so that he must have done a fair amount
of reading even at Harrow, including much history,
biography, and some divinity.   Dr. Glennie says he
was greatly interested in talking over *religious* questions
with him at Dulwich.   "I read eating, read in bed,
read when no one else reads," he writes—and he had a
most retentive memory.   But his note on the passage in
"Childe Harold" on "Soracte and the Latian Echoes"
is worth transcribing here, as bearing on the system of
education which then prevailed, and has been modified
only to some degree since :—

"I wish to express that we become tired of the task before we
can comprehend the beauty ; that we learn by rote before we get
by heart ; that the freshness is worn away, and the future pleasure
and advantage deadened and destroyed at an age when we can
neither feel, nor understand the power, of composition ; which it
requires an acquaintance with life, as well as Latin and Greek, to
relish or to reason upon. . . . In some parts of the Continent young
persons are taught from common authors, and do not read the best
classics till their maturity."

"My school friendships," he says, in one of his
journals, "were with me passions, for I was always
violent ; but I do not know that there is one which has

endured (to be sure, some have been cut short by death) till now. That with Lord Clare began one of the earliest, and lasted longest—being only interrupted by distance." "I never hear the word 'Clare' without a beating of the heart even now, and I write it with the feelings of 1803-4-5—*ad infinitum.*" From Pisa (November 5, 1821) he writes about a chance meeting with this friend :

"I met him on the road between Imola and Bologna, after not having met for seven or eight years. . . . This meeting annihilated for a moment all the years between the present time and the days of Harrow. It was a new and inexplicable feeling, like rising from the grave to me. Clare, too, was much agitated—more in appearance even than myself, for I could feel his heart beat to his fingers' ends, unless indeed it was the pulse of my own that made me think so. . . . We were but five minutes together, and on the public road, but I hardly recollect an hour of my existence which could be weighed against them."

And this is the man whom his enemies represent to have had no feeling, to have been capable only of acting and simulating feeling ! One may laugh at it as " sentiment "; but he was so sensitive and affectionate that, as a Harrow boy, he wrote a letter to a friend, complaining that this friend had addressed him as " my dear " instead of " my dearest " Byron. Mr. Harness, with whom he was intimate, says " of his attachment to his friends no one can read 'Moore's Life,' and entertain a doubt. He required a great deal from them—not more perhaps than he, from the abundance of his love, freely and fully gave—but more than they had to return." Whatever evils might be incidental to this passionate and loving comradeship, it could haidly be otherwise than ennobling, especially among the formal, cold, calculating denizens of our northern clime, and Byron seems to have been a sort of apostle of friendship in his later Harrow career. It is certainly true that, made up as he was ever of strange, perplexing contradictions, he was at Harrow a curious combination of shyness, and meditative, almost feminine sensibility, with pluck, energy, and activity, even roughness and occasional brutality. His favourites were the Duke of Dorset, Lord Clare (whom he calls "Lycus"), Lord Delawarr ("Euryalus"—"Shall fair Euryalus pass by unsung?"), the Honourable John Wingfield, brother of Lord Powerscourt, whose early death by fever in Portugal he commemorates in a stanza of "Childe Harold" ("Alonzo"), Cecil Tattersall ("Davus"), Edward Noel Long ("Cleon"), Wildman, who bought Newstead, and Sir Robert Peel. The latter, afterwards so distinguished as a statesman, was born in the same year. A big bully claiming the right to fag little Peel, and the latter resisting, the big boy determined to punish him for his refractoriness; so twisting one of his arms round, he beat the little fellow on it severely. Byron was looking on with tears in his eyes, and though he knew he was too weak and small to fight the bully with success, he came forward, and asked in a voice trembling with indignation how many stripes the tyrant meant to inflict? "Why, you little rascal," returned he, "what is that to you?" "Because, if you please," said Byron, holding out his arm, "I would take half." When people with the modern detestation

of class distinctions rail at him for his rather comical
plea in favour of Lord Delawarr, whom Wildman was
going to thrash, on the ground that he was a "brother
peer" (which failed of course, as it deserved to do !),
they might remember the foregoing incident, as also the
following :—Young Harness, still lame from an accident
in his childhood, and just recovering from severe illness,
was rescued from another hulking bully by Byron ; and
the next day, as he was standing alone, Byron came up
to him saying, "Harness, if any one bullies you, tell
me, and I'll thrash him, if I can." They had not been
friends till then, but afterwards became the warmest.
"The child is father of the man," and this generosity
of spirit showed itself later in Italy and Greece. He
thrashed other bullies there. The cynic may sneer that
Byron liked to lead and to protect now, as later, from
vanity; and so also he may sneer that Nelson wished
for "a peerage, or Westminster Abbey." But human
nature is made up of selfish and unselfish elements,
difficult to disentangle, and thus the rough work of the
world gets done. Byron's pride of rank was no doubt
excessive. Since Thackeray (who owned himself a "snob")
we have agreed that rank may be made an idol, to
worship which is "snobbish." Yet there may be more
ignoble idols even than blood, or caste. At Dulwich,
Byron's ostentation of rank had procured for him the
nickname of the "Old English Baron." And on his
accession to the peerage, when his name was first read
out in school with *Dominus* before it, he burst into
tears from emotion. Byron cared much for beauty in
his friends, as is well known. Thus he mentions the

beauty of his friend, Delawarr. His own hair was auburn, his complexion very fair, his eyes large, blue-grey, and luminous, his lips voluptuous and well formed. Coleridge and Scott both agreed about the wonderful beauty of his face, and Trelawny, who often swam with him, mentions that, save for the defect in his foot, his body and limbs were of Apollonian symmetry and fairness—the delicate shapeliness of his hands being noticed by many, men as well as women. But he was not nearly so handsome at fifteen as he afterwards became, and his serious love affair at that age shows sufficiently that Mary Chaworth was insensible to whatever personal attractions he may then have possessed.

In the summer of 1803, Mrs. Byron was in lodgings at Nottingham, where her son came to spend the holidays with her. Lord Grey de Ruthven, the tenant under Chancery, and occupier of Newstead, made acquaintance with the young peer, and put a room at his disposal in the Abbey, which was to be his future home. The Chaworths, who lived near, at Annesley, also invited him to sleep there. At first he would not, but went back to Newstead in the evening, alleging that the ancestral Chaworths would come down from their picture-frames and take revenge on him for his grand-uncle's fatal and irregular duel with one of their race. But he afterwards consented to stay, and Annesley became his head-quarters during a part of the summer holidays. So he fell in love with the heiress—"the bright morning star of Annesley." Had she returned his love, the result would have been a union which, he said, "would have joined broad lands, healed an old feud, and satisfied at

least one heart." They went together to Matlock and
Castleton; at the former took place those dances to
which I have referred as making the lame boy jealous
and miserable; and at Castleton, let him describe what
occurred in his own words :—

"When I was fifteen years of age, it happened that in a cavern
in Derbyshire, I had to cross in a boat, in which two people only
could lie down—a stream which flows under a rock, with the rock
so close upon the water as to admit the boat only to be pushed on
by a ferryman (a sort of Charon), who wades at the stern, stooping
all the time. The companion of my transit was M. A. C., with
whom I had long been in love, and never told it, though she had
discovered it. I recollect my sensations, but cannot describe them,
and it is as well."

He was fifteen, but she two years older, and what a
difference this makes! To her he was a mere schoolboy—to him what was she not? He rode with her on
his pony about the broad lands of their fathers, he
listened to her playing and singing in the summer
evenings; but the Montagues and the Capulets were not
to be so united. Mary was a lively and pleasant girl of
some beauty, who preferred her pale, commonplace,
fox-hunting squire, whom she soon afterwards married ;
for her cousin was lame, and shy, and awkward, and had
not yet proved himself one of the master minds of
England; and who was she that she should divine his
greatness? or value it, even if divined? Nobody had
told her. Moreover, it was a greatness that burned
rather than warmed any on whom its beams might
chance to fall.

I have already related the manner in which the cup

of happiness he had dared raise to his lips was dashed
from them. A year later they met again on the "hill
of Annesley"—

> "the hill
> Crowned with a peculiar diadem
> Of trees in circular array, so fixed
> Not by the sport of nature, but of man."

That interview stands immortal in "The Dream," a
beautiful poem, written in 1816, at Diodati, "amid a
flood of tears." "I suppose," he said, "the next time
I see you, you will be Mrs. Chaworth" (her betrothed,
Mr. Musters, was to assume her family name). "I hope
so," she had replied. She only laughed when the boy-
coxcomb showed her a locket given him by an old
love, in order to kindle her own love to him! The
announcement of her marriage (August, 1805) was made
to him by his mother, with the remark, "I have some
news for you. Take out your handkerchief—you will
require it." When he heard what she had to say, he became pale, but assuming an air of forced calm, answered,
"Is that all?" and turned the conversation. Yet the
wound had pierced deep. How strange and how sad it
seems, to look back from this distance of time on it
all! She was unhappy in her marriage, was separated
from her husband, and her mind passed under a cloud.
She died in 1832, of a fright caused by a Nottingham
riot. "I have taken," said Byron, "all my fables about
the celestial nature of women from the perfection my
imagination created in her. I say created, . . . for," he
added cynically, "I found her anything but perfect." In
the following year he accepted an invitation to dine at

Annesley, and was much affected by the sight of the infant daughter of the woman he had loved. He sent her the lines beginning,

> " O had my fate been joined with thine ! "

And shortly after, when about to leave England for the first time, he addressed her in the verses :

> " 'Tis done, and shivering in the gale,
> The bark unfurls her snowy sail."

It was in one of these Harrow vacations also that he first learned to know, and love his half-sister Augusta, with a love never after to be dimmed by time or distance— a purifying and ennobling love—that inspired some of his tenderest poetry. It was the best and most abiding influence of his life, let Calumny lay harpy hands on it as she may. The children had been separated till 1802, for Augusta had lived with old Lady Holdernesse, her grandmother, but on the latter's death they came together. Augusta was four years older than her brother, and called him "Baby Byron," even after he had become a famous man, perceiving, with a kindly sense of humour, certain childish traits in him, which, methinks, were not the least amiable features of a complex character. This meeting took place at Brighton. His sister was rather plain than beautiful, but amiable, pious, and excellent in all the relations of life.

From Nottingham Mrs. Byron moved with her son to Southwell, a small country town with a fine old church, not far from Newstead. There occurred here many

furious hurricanes of wrath on the part of the mother,
which provoked her son's "sullen rages"; and such
was the estimate formed by each of the other's violence,
that mother and son went one evening separately
to the apothecary, and cautioned him against selling
poison to the other, should it be asked for.   The poker
or tongs having just missed him on one occasion, he
sought refuge in the house of a friend, and decided on
escaping to London, where he remained for some time
in Piccadilly.   Mrs. Byron pursued him, but they
separated eventually, and he went to Worthing for
awhile, rejoining her in August of the same year.

In the novel "Venetia," Lord Beaconsfield has
imitated these rows in the encounters he describes
between young Lord Cadurcis and his mother.   But
in one of his own. graphic letters to Mr. Pigot, a
Southwell acquaintance, Byron himself gives what, to
some of us who know all a mother may be, and has
been more than once, to an only son, must appear a
very grievous, though amusing account of these scenes;
with comments upon them.   Byron was a delightful
letter-writer, lively, graphic, nervous, vigorous, and
homely in style, never writing as if "for publication";—
but letter-writing is a lost art.

"His journal," says Beyle, "his familiar letters, all
his unstudied prose is, as it were, trembling with wit,
anger, and enthusiasm; since St. Simon we have seen
no more life-like confidences.   All styles appear dull,
and all souls sluggish by the side of his."   To me
the absence of bookishness, formal pedantry, airs of
professional authorship, is one of Byron's most distin-

guished charms.   He is no sapless, dry abstraction from humanity, and no literary *petit maître,* but a man ; hence he will ever be distasteful to the academic prig, and to the mere *littérateur,* who holds that his own ability to turn a sentence prettily places him at the centre and summit of creation, while any other kind of human function might so very easily be dispensed with altogether.   But he will always be dear to the men and women of Europe.   He says in "Beppo" :—

> " One hates an author that's all author, fellows
> In foolscap uniforms turned up with ink,
> So very anxious, clever, fine, and jealous,
> One don't know what to say to them, or think."

And he went to Greece partly to show the world that he could, as he expressed it, "do something better than 'write verses." He died dreaming in his fever heats that he was leading the Greeks to assault Lepanto. He cared as much for his fourteen-feet dives with Matthews into the Cam, to pick up coins and trinkets ; for his amorous adventures with the ladies in England, and darker orgies at Venice ; his sea-rovings in the *Bolivar,* and long swims with Trelawny or Ekenhead ; his travels with Hobhouse, and solitary communings with nature ; for his pleasant hours with young Eddlestone, the sweet chorister of Cambridge ; and the home-life with Augusta ; for Ada, and Allegra—cared as much for these as for the composition of "Childe Harold" or "Don Juan." There was the rather vulgar ostentation of rank to set off against these keen interests in life, the whim, or affectation, of wishing rather to be treated as

a lord than as a poet, which may have made him too
careless, or less conscientious than it behoves every true
artist to be in the technical finish of his art, which
ought to be sacred with him, the ideal wife, the queen
of all mistresses.   Still it was, I think, pure gain for
Byron to be no mere bookman, hide-bound in calf,
instead of human skin, and treating the universe as so
much docile material for such as he to make pretty little
things out of.   He was a Berserker, whose wild spirit
found vent in song, and his was a bleeding human heart,
even though he made of it "a pageant."   What he does
has the salt breath of impetuously moving sea, the thrill
of warm-blooded life ; his fervid voice has the living
accent.   It was not in order to write poems that he
conversed much with sea and mountain, or humanity ;
though these inspired him with the irresistible impulse to
write.   He mixed with men and women, helped them
or marred, eat, drank, and caroused with them.   But
nature and men were as much to him as the creations
they inspired, which, having taken their own resplendent
shapes in the high and solitary places of reflection and
imagination, issued therefrom, transformed and immortal.
It is mainly this rare and memorable combination of interest alike in action and contemplation which gives Byron
the eminent personality attributed to him by Goethe.
But, at the same time, it must be added that he lived
under a "plague of microscopes."   Every lesser person
who could gain a little reflected lustre by describing him,
noted down every least significant word, mood, look,
whim, gesture ; passing it, moreover, through the sometimes distorting medium of his own understanding, and

too often also through that of his own rancour or prejudice, heightening this trait, diminishing or ignoring the
other; so that we are left with a series of indifferent
photographs, which hardly enable us to do the man
justice. Who could come scathless out of such an
ordeal? And then, as Miss Blind says, in her excellent
introduction to his "Letters," he was all things to all
men, reflected chameonlike the character of his companions, or correspondents; he was many characters in
turn. So while all the sketches have a one-sided truth,
they need to be combined and modified into a portrait.

CHAPTER II.

IN October, 1805, the youth left Harrow and went to Trinity College, Cambridge, remaining there during three years of irregular attendance, taking his (honorary nobleman's) M.A. degree in March, 1808. He was never anything but a poor scholar, however, bestowing little care on the studies of the place. He formed there several strong friendships, and, as I have already told, a very warm attachment to young Eddlestone, a sweet-voiced chorister in the college choir, a pretty and amiable boy of seventeen, who gave him a cornelian heart, which was the occasion of some verses. He writes to Miss Pigot: "I certainly love him more than any human being"; and, in 1811, when he died, his sorrow was deep. The most extraordinary suggestion made by one biographer after another is that this attachment is accounted for by the fact that Byron wanted some one of an inferior social position to *patronize!!* Whatever Byron's failings, he was not quite such a snob as the lord-and-lady-loving Tom Moore would suggest when he remarks that the poet's alterations in the epitaph he wrote on the boy, and the omission of another poem about him from the "Hours of Idleness," were probably caused by his wish to sink the recollection of his friendship for one of the people (!!)

Edward Noel Long, who had come up from Harrow, continued to be his friend; they swam and dived together in the Cam. Harness also had come from Harrow. In a letter to Murray Byron gives an amusing account of Porson, "hiccoughing Greek like a Helot in his cups." One of the most distinguished of his Cambridge chums was Charles Skinner Matthews, son of the member for Herefordshire. He seems to have been a youth of rare promise. He was drowned while bathing alone among the reeds of the Cam in the summer of 1811. Byron told a good story of Matthews who had occupied his rooms at Trinity during his year's absence. Jones, the gyp, in his odd way had said in putting him in, ' Mr. Matthews, I recommend to your attention not to damage any of the movables, for Lord Byron, sir, is a young man of *tumultuous passions.*' Matthews was delighted with this, and whenever anybody came to visit him, begged them to handle the very door with caution, repeating Jones' admonition in his tone and manner. Scrope Davies was another man of whom the poet was very fond. After the break-up of his home he wrote to him, "Come to me, Scrope; I am almost desolate—left alone in the world. I had but you, and H., and M., and let me enjoy the survivors while I can." "Matthews, Davies, Hobhouse, and myself," says Byron, "formed a *coterie* of our own. Davies has always beaten us all in the war of words, and by colloquial powers at once delighted and kept us in order; even M. yielded to the dashing vivacity of S. D." He once lent Byron £4,800 in some strait—repaid one night when the pair sat up over champagne and claret from six till midnight, after which " Scrope could not be got into the carriage on the way home, but remained tipsy and pious on his knees.". Then there was John Cam Hobhouse (afterwards Lord Broughton), a very close and faithful friend, companion of the poet in his travels, the witness of his marriage, executor of his will, and lastly the veritable destroyer of the famous " Memoirs "— a destruction which has been generally ascribed to others —an able man, as his literary and political career alike prove, of mature and excellent judgment also in practical matters, and the vindicator of Byron's good name. Hobhouse admitted his faults, but loved him notwithstanding, as I, who, when a boy, heard him speak of his illustrious friend, can testify. He told me that the portrait of him as a young man standing by the boat, with flowing tie, neckerchief, and open collar, by Sanders (engraved in Moore's " Life "), was the likest thing ever done of him. Hobhouse was the poet's confidant all through his domestic troubles, and at every period of his life. " Part of his fascination," said Lord Broughton, " may doubtless be ascribed to the entire self-abandonment, the incautious, it may be said the dangerous, sincerity of his private conversation ; but his weaknesses were amiable, and, as has been said of a portion of his virtues, were of a feminine character—so that the affection felt for him was as that for a favourite and sometimes froward sister." He admitted that his selfishness was a serious blot on an otherwise noble and generous nature. But he adds, in reference to the charges against his friend, " Lord Byron had failings, many failings certainly, but he was untainted with any of the baser vices ; and his virtues, his good qualities, were all of a high order." On the other hand,

Byron said to Trelawny, in the course of one of their rides, "Travelling in Greece, Hobhouse and I wrangled every day. His guide was Mitford's fabulous history. He had a greed for legendary lore, topography, inscriptions; gabbled in *lingua franca* to the Ephori of the villages, goatherds, and our dragoman. He would potter with map and compass at the foot of Pindus, Parnes, and Parnassus to ascertain the site of some ancient temple or city. I rode my mule up them. They had haunted my dreams from boyhood; the pines, eagles, vultures, and owls, were descended from those Themistocles and Alexander had seen, and were not degenerated like the humans; the rocks and torrents the same. John Cam's dogged perseverance in pursuit of his hobby is to be envied; I have no hobby and no perseverance. I gazed at the stars and ruminated, took no notes, asked no questions. He said nature had intended him for a poet, but chance made him take to politics, and that I wrote prose better than poetry."

Anyhow, Byron always spoke of Hobhouse as his best surviving friend, and Madame Guiccioli tells us that when he unexpectedly walked up the stairs of the Lanfranchi Palace at Pisa, Byron was seized with so violent an excess of joy that it seemed to take away his strength, and he was forced to sit down in tears. The Rev. F. Hodgson was another friend, whose correspondence, edited by his son, contains interesting details about the poet. He recognized in the early Satire, and the first cantos of "Childe Harold," the promise of a great poet. The good advice he gave his turbulent and unorthodox companion seems to have been judicious and kindly, and

taken in good part. Even thus early Byron defined his
attitude towards religion, in a letter to Hodgson, "In
short, I deny nothing, but doubt everything." He was a
sceptic, what would now be termed an agnostic. But to
Gifford he says that he never denied the existence of God
—only doubted our immortality. Even this he scarcely
doubted later. On the other hand, he used to say to Lady
Byron, "The worst of it is, I do believe." And she in
vain tried to reason him out of the Calvinism of his
Scotch teaching—herself a Unitarian, and holding the
doctrine of Universal Restoration. Against that gloomy
creed of Calvin his reason and conscience revolted, yet
he could never entirely shake it off. He told his wife
that he had sinned too deeply for repentance, and the
possibility of salvation. "Calvinism was the rock against
which I was broken," she said. And this explains the
fierce hostility of his attitude toward orthodoxy (as he
knew it) in "Cain," and elsewhere. But "Cain" is
steeped in the idea of Predestination, Fate, Destiny,
against the injustice of which Cain rebels ; sin, suffering,
and death being involved. The wrath and vengeance of
Deity are deprecated in that poem, and in "Heaven and
Earth," where the angel lovers will not leave the doomed
mortals, even when summoned to their own blissful seats
in heaven. So Japhet will not leave Anah. This is a
revolt against the revengeful, tyrannical God, made in
the image of kings and priests ; but orthodoxy was
equally shocked with the later revolt of a great theo-
logian, F. D. Maurice, against the very same conception
—not certainly that of our Lord, who came to reveal the
Absolute Love as Father of all. Cain objects even to

the bloody sacrifice of innocent animals upon the altar of Jehovah; he is a humane man. In conversation Byron set himself against the dogma of everlasting punishment (see Kennedy's " Conversations," &c.)— though he may never have been able completely to throw off the idea, not having speculative grasp sufficient to conceive in his own way, and mould anew the eternal truths revealed through Christianity. And while believing in Destiny (thus Maddalo—*i.e.,* Byron—takes the Necessarian side in arguing with Julian—Shelley—in Shelley's fine poem), yet one who asserted *individuality* so strongly could not but admit likewise the modifying and directing energy of a man's own initiative, which is Free-will. It is possible that his wife's more liberal religious opinions may have exercised a favourable influence on Byron's convictions after all, without his being distinctly aware of it.

He is indeed very much akin to Burns, whose supreme song " survives," " deep in the general heart." Burns has the same wild irregular passion, the same humour, and intermingling of grave and gay, the same character full of contradictions. But, as in Burns there is an element of coarse commonplace, in Byron there is a certain gaudy charlatanry, blare of brass, and big bow-wowishness of the life, as of the poetry—that imposes on the vulgar, for ever insensible to the delicate, subtle warble of bird or brook, to the soullike tones of a master's violin. So Wordsworth, Shelley, Keats, and Coleridge waited, while Moore and Byron had their loud day. But Byron wrote up to them at last, giving the world his own distinctive song—though purely as a lyrical poet he is hardly equal to Burns. The writers of

"Tam O'Shanter," and "Don Juan," however, poured their own lives into song.

To no one did the poet more freely unbosom himself than to Hodgson, more freely abuse himself, betray his little weaknesses; to him were addressed those humorous and rollicking verses, "On board the Lisbon Packet," commencing "Huzzah! Hodgson." To him Byron, with his accustomed generosity, gave £1,000 to pay off some debts with. In a letter to his uncle Hodgson says, "Oh, if you knew the exaltation of heart, ay, and of head, too, I feel at being free from those depressing embarrassments, you would, as I do, bless my dearest friend and brother, Byron;" and he speaks of the exquisite delicacy with which the kindness was done. Then there was Henry Drury, Hodgson's brother-in-law, and Robert Charles Dallas, a connection by marriage of the poet. In the letter Byron wrote to him before they met, flippancy, bounce, brag, and the habit of posing as wicked to make people stare, are very pronounced; nor are they, one must unfortunately admit, uncharacteristic of the author—though now of course boyish in their crudity. He makes Dallas stare by telling him he is like the *wicked* Lord Lyttleton, Dallas having complimented him by comparing him to the *good* one! There was the taint of worldliness, of too much "Empeiria" about Byron, as Goethe affirmed; and Shelley spoke of the "canker of aristocracy," of "perverse ideas," that needed cutting out. It was partly a defect of nature, partly what the artificial and corrupt society of the Regency had made him. His conversations with Trelawny not seldom show him in his least amiable mood.

The constant affectation, or obtrusion of cynicism, is unpleasant. Though Trelawny was a fine fellow, he was a man of the world, and drew out the least elevated elements of conversational ability in this spoilt child—spoilt by too much petting, rendered bitter and cynical, moreover, by cruel injustice—though in the affairs of life Trelawny's influence over the poet was healthy and bracing.

Byron hated Cambridge. 'Their Alma Mater has often proved but a harsh and crabbed foster-mother to the children of genius, whom she has starved upon thin, sour milk from her all too ancient and venerable bosom.' Milton so hated the same university that he detested even the fields that environ it, and Gray spoke slightingly of it. Dryden has recorded his scant affection for this same Alma Mater; nor, as Moore says, must the names of Swift, Goldsmith, and Churchill be forgotten, to every one of whom some mark of incompetency was affixed by the universities whose annals they adorn; while Shelley was dismissed from Oxford with contumely. Of Cambridge, Byron sings, " Her Helicon is duller than her Cam."

In November, 1806, Byron first printed for private circulation his juvenile poems. They were printed by Ridge of Newark; and in March, 1807, he published the " Hours of Idleness " at the same press. In June we find him congratulating himself on his reduction in weight and girth. He had been very fat, and weighed over fourteen stone! This caused positive pain to his

---

¹ But one gladly admits recent improvements in the system of University education.

lame foot, Trelawny says; so he determined to keep himself down to eleven stone; which, by vapour baths, medicine, diet, and such exercise as he could take, he generally did. Sometimes he managed to weigh even less. In October he writes to Miss Pigot: "I have got a new friend, the finest in the world, a tame bear. When I brought him here they asked me what I meant to do with him, and my reply was, 'He should sit for a fellowship;' this answer delighted them not." The greater part of the spring and summer of 1808 he was at Dorant's Hotel, Albemarle Street, London. Here he went in for the dissipations so many young men indulge in, saying as little as possible about them. But Byron, *more suo*, trumpeted them abroad. The fact is, his imagination played about, magnified, and decked out for artistic purposes everything in his own experience, good and bad, as did that of Rousseau. This was all real, and strongly felt, only that in these men it grew into imaginative forms also. Byron was subject, from his volcanic and sensuous temperament, social position, and personal beauty, to great temptations, and he had no good or influential adviser. "My blood is all meridian," he said. He possessed, moreover, ample means wherewith to gratify his whims, and all encouragement from a loose-living society to do so. His habitual sombre melancholy, relieved by occasional outbursts of semi-hysterical, wild spirits, would favour the same result. Debauching women was then deemed stylish, and "manly" moreover; while Byron was half a slave, not only to his own passions, but to the opinion of that modish little world, self-styled "good society,"—imposed on by its airs of self-complacent superiority to the rest of the race—assumptions common to it indeed with the nation whose "smile is childlike and bland," with swashbucklers, bullies, and roughs of the New World, with literary æsthetes of modern London, and unwashed *sans-culottes* of Paris slums. Alas! so much the less poet he! The remarks of Beyle (Stendhal), who lived with him for several weeks, are to the point here. "In presence of beautiful things he became sublime. But on certain days he was mad" (so Lady Byron thought, till the doctor decided otherwise). "Petty English passions," says the continental writer, "pride of rank, a vain dandyism unhinged him; he spoke of Brummel with a shudder of jealousy and admiration." "But small or great" (this is *very* acute and significant), "the present passion swept down upon his mind like a tempest, roused him, transported him, either into imprudence, or genius." Yet Byron always averred that he had never seduced a girl, which is more than some of his loudest, and most jealously malicious, accusers could say. And seeing that he always made the worst of himself, we may well believe him. He gambled heavily, and keeping a carriage up at Cambridge with saddle-horses and servants, he soon became heavily embarrassed.

In the summer of 1807, Leigh Hunt noticed a respectable, manly-looking person watching something bobbing up and down in the Thames. This was Jackson the pugilist, with whom Byron was very intimate, looking on with keen interest while his patron swam for a wager from Lambeth to Blackfriars, a distance, including tacks and turns, of about three miles. By the way, the intimates of Byron through life were persons distinguished for their talents and wit, or else for their charm and goodness; or again, otherwise interesting people like Lord Clare, the sweet chorister of Cambridge, and the muscular professor of pugilism. Of course he liked to mix with his own set now and again. But he did not choose his friends among the mere supercilious inanities of rank and fashion—"tenth transmitters of a foolish face." His care for that kind of thing has been maliciously exaggerated by people whose susceptibilities he had offended, or who were unable to understand the feelings of well-born men and women.

The Rev. Mr. Becher, of Southwell, induced Byron to destroy the whole first issue of his "Juvenilia," because of an amatory poem in it he thought too warm. And now we come to the *Edinburgh Review's* smart, yet stupid critique upon the "Hours of Idleness," in which the author is sneered at for being a young lord, and advised forthwith to abandon poetry, for which he has evidently ,no vocation. The creature who spoke only spoke after its kind, and the thing would not be worth notice except for its effect. But as the irritating grit in the shell of the oyster excites the fish to fill the wound with pearl, so did the wound made by this poor thing rouse the fury of Byron to the satire of "English Bards." Whoever it was hid his ugly face ever after; and we do not *know* that it was Brougham, though Byron thought so. Mr. Jeaffreson's suggestion that it was a Trinity don, uncomfortable under the really rather promisingly amusing invective of the juvenile verses against Cambridge *Dondom*, seems to me a happy one. At the same time, had the writer made the faintest attempt at truth and justice (an attempt obviously impossible to persons of his calibre), there was much in the book which he might have worried, not only with the congenial delight proper to his species, but even with a good conscience. For never did a great poet produce an early volume that gave so little promise and contained so much doggrel, or weak, conventional, and bumptiously affected verse. Still "Loch-na-gair," "the Prayer of Nature," and some satirical things should have received kindly recognition. Byron is reported, just after reading this review, to have looked like a man who was about to send a challenge—he confesses to have drunk three bottles of claret the same evening—and he did *not* let himself be "snuffed out by an article." "What I feel is an immense rage for twenty-four hours," he said on a similar occasion, "I cannot understand the submissive yielding spirit." A Viking scald this, no Christian. Yet submission and self-control must be learned; he was learning; but "Cain" could not teach them. Byron never taught them. He is good to begin with, not to end with. The book was dedicated to Lord Carlisle, who acknowledged its receipt before reading it, and never wrote again. On coming to London from Newstead, moreover, in March, 1809, to take his seat in the House of Lords, he had to take it, contrary to his wish, without being introduced by any member of the Upper House; for he had written to his guardian announcing that he should be of age at the opening of the next parliamentary session; but instead of responding with a cordial offer to introduce him, the Earl only wrote a cold note, telling him what formalities

were necessary upon the occasion. And again when he
found that evidence must be produced as to the marriage
of his grandfather, Admiral Byron, which was difficult to
procure, the excitable youth became much alarmed lest
he should be unable to prove his father's legitimacy; for
Lord Carlisle, when appealed to for information that
might be of use, either could not or would not give
it. All this together made the poet furious; so that
whereas, on coming to town with his satire, the lines
about his guardian had been complimentary, he now
substituted an angry diatribe. But, well advised as ever
by his beloved sister, in " Childe Harold " he afterwards
made amends; in the glorious passage on Waterloo,
where he laments the " young, gallant Howard," Lord
Carlisle's son, introducing the line,

" And partly that I did his sire some wrong."

My grandfather told me that Byron wrote to *him* also,
asking if he could accompany him on this occasion, but
Lord Roden's absence from London made it impossible.
The young peer seems to have been under a misconcep-
tion as to what the prevailing *etiquette* required. Mr.
Dallas, however, happening to call just as he was going,
accompanied him, and has described what ensued.
"There were very few persons in the house. Lord
Eldon was going through some ordinary business. When
Lord Byron had taken the oaths, the Chancellor quitted
his seat, and went towards him with a smile, and though
I did not catch the words, I saw that he paid him some
compliment. This was all thrown away on Lord Byron,
who made a stiff bow, and put the tips of his fingers

into the Chancellor's hand. The Chancellor did not press a welcome so received, but resumed his seat; while Lord Byron carelessly seated himself for a few minutes on one of the empty benches to the left of the throne, usually occupied by the lords in opposition. When on his joining me I expressed what I had felt, he said, ' If I had shaken hands heartily, he would have set me down for one of his party; but I will have nothing to do with them on either side. I have taken my seat, and now I will go abroad.' "

A few days later "English Bards and Scotch Reviewers" came out. The first anonymous edition was exhausted in a month—the poet had studied his favourite Pope to some purpose. The work showed considerable vigour and point. But it was only a work of promise, pointing to the great satire of the "Vision of Judgment" and "Don Juan"; moreover, it was full of injustice and indiscriminate abuse. The writer regretted many of the allusions in after years. The last months of 1808 had been spent at Newstead, where he was busy in arranging a few rooms for himself and for his mother, who was to go there after his departure, not before. He had at this time two beautiful dogs— one a savage bulldog, Nelson, the other a Newfoundland, Boatswain, who died in a fit of madness at Newstead, his master wiping the slaver from the poor beast's lips, not knowing he was mad. On this dog he wrote :—

> " To mark a friend's remains these stones arise ;
> I never knew but *one*, and *here* he lies."

On the monument, in the garden at Newstead, I have

myself read the warm and well-written tribute to the
virtues of the noble animal which lies buried there. In
the earlier months of 1808 the poet had lived in lodgings
at Brompton with a girl, who used to ride about with
him dressed as a boy, and she accompanied him to
Brighton in the same attire, he introducing her to his
acquaintances as his "brother Gordon." A lady of
fashion, meeting them riding there one day, complimented her on the beauty of her horse; her reply
being, "Yes, it was *gave* me by my brother!" This girl
afterwards (May, 1809) formed one of the roystering
party at Newstead, and (with the doubtful exception
of a housemaid) was apparently the only representative
of those "Paphian girls" who are said, in "Childe
Harold," to have "sung and smiled" in the Childe's
ancestral halls before he left his native land! On this
occasion Byron entertained at Newstead, Matthews,
Scrope Davies, Hodgson, and Hobhouse; few of the
country gentry seem to have called, and none are named
as having been present at the ball given in honour of
his coming of age. But three or four of the neighbouring clergy came in now and then to join the young men.
These were "the revellers from far and near"! Yet
the party passed the time merrily enough. Rising late,
they breakfasted at noon, read, fenced, single-sticked,
rode, walked, sailed on the lake, practised with pistols,
and at dinner-time played the fool, as Byron always
liked to do: for he was a mischievous, fun-loving boy
(with a spice of the malicious imp in him) to the end.
They dug up a monk's skull in the Abbey garden, and
he had it polished into a wine-cup for Burgundy; he

dressed himself as the Abbot, and put his friends into monks' robes (crosses, beads, tonsures and all), and they had a wild time of it after dinner, no doubt. But these friends did not remain with him for long together at the Abbey, and Byron studied a good deal in the intervals. A wolf and the bear were kept chained at the chief entrance. While he was in London, he wrote to Mrs. Byron from St. James's Street, about the death of Lord Falkland, killed in a duel, whose family were left very destitute. He felt keenly for them, and in the most delicate as well as generous manner (notwithstanding his own difficulties), after reminding the widow that he was to be godfather to her infant, put a five-hundred-pound note into a cup for her, when he attended at the christening, so secretly that it was not found till after he had left the room. At this time he declared that he would never part with Newstead, whatever his difficulties. But he was then relying on the suit that was proceeding for the recovery of Rochdale, a property which had been illegally sold by his predecessor. The suit, however, was dragged through one court after another, involving him in heavy expense, and with no satisfactory result.

On the 2nd of July he sailed from Falmouth, with his friend Hobhouse, for Lisbon, and remained abroad for two years.

He writes with his usual affectionate sensitiveness at the slight he had suffered on leaving England from an old friend, who excused himself from bidding him farewell because he had to go shopping. He arrived at Lisbon about the middle of the month. Hobhouse wrote a prose account of their journey, while he composed the

early cantos of "Childe Harold," and his friend
furnished some notes for the same. The latter says that
Byron made a more dangerous, though less celebrated,
swim here than his passage of the Hellespont—crossing
from old Lisbon to Belem Castle. Byron thought
Cintra the most beautiful village in the world, and
praises the grandeur of Massa, the Escurial of Portugal.
Sending baggage and servants by sea to Gibraltar,
Hobhouse and he rode through the south-west of
Spain, about seventy miles a day. At Seville, they
lodged for three days in the house of two unmarried
ladies, and he gives a pleasant picture of them, as of
their rather free and easy relations with him. The
eldest embraced him with great tenderness at parting,
and cut off a lock of his hair, giving him one in return
about three feet in length ; her last words were: "Adios,
tu hermoso ! me gusto mucho !" ("Adieu, you pretty
fellow ! you please me much !") At Cadiz, he had also
fallen half in love with a beautiful girl, whom he accompanied to the opera. He speaks enthusiastically
of the dark beauties of Spain, surely with good reason.
For what can be more ideally lovely than a gazelle-eyed
Spanish brunette? To the younger of his two Seville
hostesses he made love by help of a dictionary, but
she asked him for a ring, which he wore, as a pledge
of affection ; and this he would not part with, which
offended her. He arrayed himself in a superb
scarlet uniform on state occasions. Having touched
at Gibraltar, he sailed to Malta, where he engaged in
a Platonic, but warm, flirtation with Mrs. Spencer
Smith, whom he addressed as "Florence" in "Childe

Harold," and also in the lines written during a thunderstorm on the road to Zitza. She was wife of our
minister at Constantinople. What he thought of Malta
may be read in the verses beginning *" Adieu ye joys
of La Vallette !"* Here he was on the point of fighting
a duel with an English officer. On September the 29th,
the friends left Malta in a man-of-war, and skirted the
coast of Acarnania, in view of Ithaca, the Leucadian
rock, and Actium. Landing at Prevesa, they journeyed
through Albania, visiting Ali Pacha, at Tepeleni, and
halting on the way at Janina, where Byron was supplied,
by order of the Pacha, with a house, horses, and all
necessaries, gratis, Ali himself being absent, besieging
Ibrahim, in Illyria. A few days after, they arrived at
Tepeleni, and were received by Ali in person. The
scene, on entering the town, recalled to his mind Scott's
description of Branksome Castle in the " Lay," and the
feudal times. Byron gives a lively account of his
reception in a letter to his mother. Ali received him
standing, and made him sit on his right hand, asking
him why he had left home so early, telling him he had
heard he was of a great family, sending his respects to
his mother, and adding that he—

" Was certain I was a man of high birth, because I had small ears,
curling hair, and little white hands. He told me to consider him
as a father whilst I was in Turkey. Indeed, he treated me like a
child, sending me almonds, and sugared sherbet, fruit and sweet-
meats twenty times a day. He begged me to visit him often, and
especially at night, when he was at leisure. . . . Two days ago
(proceeds Byron) I was nearly lost in a Turkish ship-of-war, owing
to the ignorance of the captain and crew. Fletcher yelled after his
wife ; the Greeks called on all the saints ; the Mussulmen on

Allah ; the captain burst into tears, and ran below deck, telling us to call on God. The sails were split, the mainyard shivered, the wind blowing fresh, the night setting in, and all our chance was to make Corfu, or, as Fletcher pathetically called it, 'a watery grave.' I did what I could to console him, but, finding him incorrigible, wrapped myself in my Albanian capote and lay down on the deck to wait for the worst."

" Unable," says Hobhouse, " from his lameness, to be of any assistance, he in a short time was found among the trembling sailors fast asleep." However, they landed on the coast of Suli. In November, he travelled, with a guard of fifty Albanians, through Acarnania and Œtolia, on his way to the Morea. The vivid description by Hob-house of a night scene round the camp fires, with back-ground of rugged rocks, in the Gulf of Arta, will be remembered by readers of " Childe Harold," among the notes to that poem, the wild Albanian soldiers dancing in the firelight, and singing fierce bandit songs, with the refrain κλεφτεις ποτε Παργα (*robbers all at Parga!*) On reaching Mesolonghi (where later he died), he dismissed all the Albanians excepting one, and, after spending a fortnight at Patras, he arrived at Vostizza, where first the grand peaks of Parnassus on the farther side of the gulf rose to view; riding along the mountain-side, he saw a flight of twelve eagles, which he took as a good omen. At Delphi, he wrote the lines about Parnassus for " Childe Harold." " The last bird I ever fired at," he says, "was an eaglet, on the shore of the Gulf of Lepanto, near Vostizza. It was only wounded, and I tried to save it, the eye was so bright, but it pined and died in a few days; and I never did since, and never will, attempt the death of another bird." From Livadia they went to Thebes; crossed Cithæron; and on Christmas day, 1809, near the ruins of Phyle, he caught his first glimpse of Athens. His first visit there lasted three months, and he made excursions to different parts of Attica, Eleusis Hymettus, Cape Colonna (where he narrowly escaped capture by pirates), the plain of Marathon, and to some caves beyond the Ilissus, in which he and Hobhouse were, by accident, nearly entombed. At Athens he lodged in the house of a lady who was the widow of an English vice-consul, and had three daughters. They were all, he says, good-looking, and the eldest of them was Theresa, "the Maid of Athens," whom he celebrated in those pretty verses with the Greek line at the end of each; but the affection he felt for her was very innocent and Platonic. Early in March, an English sloop-of-war took the travellers to Smyrna. There he finished the second canto of "Childe Harold," which he had begun at Janina. After visiting the ruins of Ephesus, the travellers sailed in the frigate *Salsette* to Constantinople, touching at the Troad, and roaming about the reputed remains of Ilium.

While waiting for a fair wind in the Dardanelles, Byron, landing on the European shore, swam with Lieutenant Ekenhead from Sestos to Abydos, not much above a mile, but the strength of the current made it three. He did it in an hour and ten minutes. Of this feat he talked a good deal, and it was indeed a good swim. Trelawny says he was subject to cramp; but a boat, I think, accompanied the swimmers on this occasion. Later he took some fine aquatic exercise

with Trelawny, who admits his indomitable pluck, and
even the excellence of his swimming, but still boasts
(rather ungenerously) of how he himself could beat him,
and avers that he gave in sometimes in their contests lest
the poet might be mortified by defeat; relating how the
latter was sick in the water one day when trying conclusions with him, swimming to and from the yacht
Bolivar—the fact being, of course, that Trelawny was a
man of iron physique and constitution, a first-rate
athlete, unexhausted by great drafts of nervous energy
on the brain, and by the excesses of a furious, hyper-
sensitive temperament. But it was the man of action this
time who would " bear no brother near the throne." It
should have been sufficient for the prowess of a poet to
win laurels on ideal fields, like Shelley !

When the English minister, Mr. Adair, obtained an
audience with the Sultan on taking leave, and Byron
with other travellers was to be presented on the occasion,
the poet is said to have insisted on his right to some
precedence in the ceremony; but the minister answered
him that none could be allotted, since the Turks would
only recognize official dignities. He, however, would not
yield the point until the Austrian internuncio had been
consulted, and confirmed the decision of Mr. Adair. It
hardly seems to me extraordinary that he should have
urged the claim till better informed—though certainly, if
the tale be true, about his not landing on his arrival at
Malta for some time because he expected a salute from
the forts, his pretensions on the score of rank must have
been extravagant and absurd.

It is related that, when he left Constantinople on

board the *Salsette*, walking the deck, he one day·took up
a yataghan, or Turkish dagger, and was overheard, while
gazing on it unsheathed, muttering to himself, " I should
like to know how a person feels after committing a
murder ; " and some one has conjectured with plausi-
bility that this little incident may have been the germ
from which arose the absurd story about his having
committed a murder ; a story accepted among others
by Goethe, who gravely surmised that " Manfred "
had been suggested by some such horrible experience.
At Stamboul he gathered much material for poetry—
from the slave market an episode for " Don Juan ;" while
the spectacle of a dead criminal tossed on the waves he
utilized for the " Bride of Abydos," and that of lean dogs
gnawing a dead body outside the palace of the Sultans
for "The Siege of Corinth." He and Hobhouse had
now agreed to separate, and the latter returned to
England, while Byron was landed on the island of Zea
with the Albanians, a Tartar, and his valet, Fletcher, of
whose squeamishness about the discomforts of foreign
travel and timidity he much complains. Soon after he
returned to Athens, where he renewed acquaintance with
his schoolfellow, the Marquis of Sligo, and made friends
with Lady Hester Stanhope, who saw him first bathing
under the rocks of Cape Colonna. In July, 1810, we find
him at Patras, staying with the Consul, Mr. Strané,
having passed through Corinth. At Patras he had an
attack of fever, not very unlike the last fatal illness,
which carried him off, a little way from this, at Mesolonghi ; and he rails at the doctors who attended him now,
as he was also to do in his last illness. "One of them,"

he says, "trusts to his genius, having never studied; the other to a campaign of eighteen months *against* the sick of Otranto, which he made in his youth with great effect." Byron's recovery at Athens was greatly retarded by his course of thinning diet; he took nothing but rice, vinegar, and water. He studied Romaic in a Franciscan monastery, where he conversed with a motley crew of many nationalities, and wrote notes for " Childe Harold," the " Hints from Horace," and " The Curse of Minerva," which fulminates against the removal of the Elgin marbles to the British Museum. Here occurred an incident, which suggested one in " The Giaour "—he rescued a young woman about to be thrown into the sea by a party of Janissaries for some intrigue with a Frank. Galt seems mistaken in stating that the intrigue was with Byron himself. He had intended to visit Egypt, Persia, and India; but Hanson, his solicitor, failed to send remittances, and therefore he set sail, on the 3rd of June, 1811, in the *Volage* frigate, for England.[1] On board he writes in very low spirits to Hodgson, having suffered from a tertian fever at Malta, "I am returning home without a hope, and almost without a desire." Naturally he anticipates no pleasure from having to settle his much-embarrassed affairs. He also declares he will write no more—though he had written about four thousand lines on his journey.

On Byron's arrival in London, Mr. Dallas called on him at Reddish's Hotel in St. James' Street. He wished the latter to see through the press his " Hints from

---

[1] Before leaving Athens, Byron had become much attached to a youth, named Nicolo Giraud, to whom he left in his will a sum of £7,000.

Horace," of which he himself thought highly. But they are in fact much tamer than the " English Bards," and Mr. Dallas was greatly disappointed, on reading them, to find that his Eastern travel had produced no more inspired result :—this he frankly avowed to the poet next morning. " Then Lord Byron told me," says Dallas, "that he had occasionally written short poems, besides a great many stanzas in Spenser's measure relative to the countries he had visited. They are not worth troubling you with, but you shall have them all if you like. So came I by 'Childe Harold's Pilgrimage.' He said a friend had condemned them, and he did not think much of them. Such as it was, however, it was at my service." That very evening Dallas wrote, "You have written one of the most delightful poems I ever read. I have been so fascinated with 'Childe Harold' that I have not been able to lay it down."

Dallas, though a little narrow-minded, was a shrewd man ; he saw that the poem was likely to succeed, took the risks of publication, put the MSS. into Murray's hands, and made a good profit out of it—Byron being at that time unwilling as a peer to make money by his writings, which was considered *infra dig.* Murray submitted the work to :Gifford, the most feared critic of the day, contrary to Byron's wishes, who did not care to seem to curry favour with the literary set—in the disposal of whose patronage too often merit might claim to have the casting vote, if only no other more influential suffrage should intervene. He would lick no man's boots—nor be concerned in any of the backstairs intrigues, delusive dodges, and hidden wirepullings of literature.

It will have been noticed that Byron, though his relations with his mother were necessarily strained and painful, yet wrote to her dutifully and often, having also made sedulous arrangements for her comfort at Newstead. Here he was on the point of joining her, when he received the news of her sudden death, brought about, it is said, through excitement, caused by an extortionate tradesman's bill, telling on a natural weakness of heart. She had observed to her maid, when he announced his intended visit, " If I should be dead before Byron comes down, what a strange thing it would be ! "

All the old natural affection for one who had, after all, nursed him tenderly in childhood, as well as little Augusta, his sister, seems to have returned, and he quotes Gray to a friend: " I now feel the truth of Gray's observation that we can only have one mother ! Peace be with her ! " He got down too late to find her alive. Her maid one night, hearing a sound of sighing in the room where the body lay at rest, found Byron by the bedside, who, when she spoke to him, burst out crying, and said, " O Mrs. By, I had but one friend in the world, and she is gone ! " I know few more arresting incidents than that of this young man watching the funeral move away from the Abbey door—why he did not follow it who can say?—and then calling to young Rushton, a favourite servant, to spar with him, as usual—but silent and abstracted all the time. As if from an effort to get the better of his feelings, he threw more violence, Rushton thought, into his blows than was his wont, till at last, the struggle seeming too much for him, he flung away the gloves, and retired to his room.

She had taken, poor woman, much interest in her son's literary career, and he had tried to comfort her when the unfavourable review of his book appeared. Peace be with her! She loved him in her way. But what a legacy of violence, sullen rage, and unrestraint had she left him! He addressed her as "the Honourable," a title to which she had no claim, and in their moments of fun called her "Kitty Gordon," or "the Honourable Kitty." Young Eddlestone had died also before his return to England, and he now lost in succession two more of his friends, Charles S. Matthews (whose pronounced religious scepticism must, from his remarkable intellectual power, have strongly influenced that of Byron), and the Honourable John Wingfield. "Matthews," he says, "has perished miserably in the muddy waters of the Cam, always fatal to genius." He writes as none but a man of the warmest, most affectionate heart could write to his surviving friend, his "dearest Davies": "Some curse hangs on me and mine—my mother lies a corpse in this house; one of my best friends is drowned in a ditch. My dear Scrope, if you can spare a moment, do come down to me—I want a friend. What will our poor Hobhouse feel?" "The blows," he says to Hodgson, "followed each other so rapidly that I am yet stupid from the shock, and though I do eat and drink and talk, and even laugh at times, yet, I can hardly persuade myself that I am awake."

At this time he made a will, appointing Hobhouse and Davies his executors, and directing that he should be buried in the vault of the garden, at Newstead, without any religious ceremony whatever, and with his dog

Boatswain. Soon after, he became acquainted with Moore, whose letter, seeking an apology, or satisfaction for a passage in the "English Bards," had not been forwarded abroad to Byron by prudent Mr. Hodgson, who had undertaken to send it. Moore now wrote again, but more mildly; and the correspondence ended in the two poets meeting and dining together, with Thomas Campbell, at the house of Samuel Rogers. From that time they became fast friends. Moore speaks of the beauty and pallor of his face, as also of his curling picturesque hair; and Lady Caroline Lamb, when she first met him, exclaimed, "That pale face is my fate!" Every variety and shade of feeling passed over his mobile features in turn.

On the 27th of February, 1812, he made his first speech in the House of Lords, on the Nottingham Frame-breakers Bill, and received the congratulations of distinguished statesmen; the speech was voted a success. "I have traversed," he said, "the seat of war in the Peninsula, I have been in some of the most oppressed provinces of Turkey; but never, under the most despotic of infidel Governments, did I behold such squalid wretchedness as I have seen since my return in the heart of a Christian country." Reprobating the severe measures proposed against the poor starving mechanics who broke the looms that deprived them of food, he proceeded, "Is there not blood enough upon your penal code, that more must be poured forth to ascend to heaven, and testify against you?" Thus ever was he on the side of the oppressed. Two other speeches he made in the House, one on Catholic Emancipation; but these were thought somewhat mouthing and theatrical.

Two days after, " Childe Harold " appeared. The pre-
sentation copy to the Honourable Mrs. Leigh was in-
scribed, "To Augusta, my dearest sister and my best
friend, who has ever loved me much better than I
deserved, this volume is presented by her father's son,
and most affectionate brother, B."

The result was electric, sudden, startling, dazzling.
" I awoke one morning," he says, "and found myself
famous." " Childe Harold " and " Lord Byron " became
the theme of every tongue. " At his door," says Moore,
" most of the leading men of the day presented themselves—some of them persons whom he had much
wronged in his satire. From morning till night the most
flattering testimonies of his success crowded his table—
from the grave tributes of the statesman and the philoso-
pher down to what flattered him still more, the romantic
billet of some *incognita*, or the pressing note of invitation
from some fair leader of fashion ; and in place of the
desert which London had been to him but a few weeks
before, he now not only saw the whole splendid interior
of high life thrown open to receive him, but found himself among its crowds the most distinguished object ! "
Byron had actually called his hero *Childe Burun* in the
first draft of the poem, and yet he deprecated identifica-
tion of that hero with himself; though it was quite
obviously the story of himself, and of his travels, with a
few embellishments thrown in, chiefly to make the chief
personage look more "Satanic." Moore had told the
author that he feared it was too good for the age. Yet,
as Mr. Nichol observes, its success was due to the fact
that it was just on a level with the age. If it had been

6

on the level of the poetry he wrote later, its success would probably have been less immediate. It was graceful, beautiful sometimes, new in subject and manner, faithful in description, the revelation of an interesting personality on the spot to confirm the impression, written by a peer, and a "curled darling" of society, fascinatingly sad, gently, not too boldly and vehemently sceptical or defiant; it was also very intelligible, not in the least too thoughtful for the multitude. The same criticism may be made on the "tales" that followed; they accorded with the taste of the fashionable and gentle world. But they were, one may say, a *legitimate* success, like that of Burns, Tennyson, Longfellow. Byron's early success was deserved, if exaggerated. There is really good art, as well as really bad art, which appeals to popular taste, and that immediately. Subject and treatment alike may appeal to the people; the work may even be first-rate of its kind, as in the case of Burns, Beranger, Dickens, Thackeray, Scott. Byron's earlier works indeed were hardly first-rate, yet they were true poetry.

The works he poured forth in abundant succession, written easily and with haste, had originality, individuality, the one essential element in literature. They opened up a new vein of genuine ore. It is the mere extravagance of reaction and fastidious caprice to deny their value, monotonous as they were, and imitated as they have been *ad nauseam*. But, while it met a want of the hour, this poetry, save in snatches and fragments was hardly powerful, or subtle and piercing enough for permanence. There were indeed exquisite passages concerning Greek nationality and aspirations, concerning

death and passion, the beauty and frailty of women, their
lovely fidelity, their devotion ; graphic pictures also of
fierce wild life, and of external nature, in the "Corsair,"
"The Giaour," the "Bride of Abydos," "Parisina,"
"Lara," the "Siege of Corinth," which should not
perish. All these, moreover, contain self-portraitures of
a gloomy, unhappy, restless, remorseful, unbelieving, still
unsatiated and insatiable soul. The misery of the lines
"To Inez," in "Childe Harold," is surely not affected ;
nor the sea delight of "O'er the glad waters," in ."The
Corsair"; the fervent sympathy with freedom of "Here-
ditary Bondsmen !" in "Childe Harold"; the pathos
of "He who hath bent him o'er the dead," in "The
Giaour"; and that of the Dark Page watching dying
"Lara." But still, the greater Byron is not here—the
volcanic force and fire ; the defiance, the immense dis-
dain of all mortal things, including himself; those Thor-
hammer strokes resounding in "Don Juan" and "The
Vision of Judgment"; the haughty and headstrong rebellion of elect individualism, or genius in "Manfred," a dis-
organizing, aggressive, anti-social individualism ; the more
Promethean, though still selfish, ineffectual revolt of
"Cain"; the highest *ethical* note of his lyre being struck in
"Prometheus." But all this was in embryo here. It was
the young Heracles strangling snakes, not the adult
hero slaying Lernæan Hydras of orthodox and political
tyranny, clearing Augean stables of English hypocrisy.
The poetry is too much one of melodrama and pose, of
"how interesting the women will think me"! Still,
Walter Scott generously felt that Byron had gone beyond
him in the lyrical rush and swing of these verse stories ;

while even the critics relented, wanting a new toy, since they had elected to pass with insolent silence, or else had honoured with their contempt, the greater poetry of Wordsworth, Shelley, and Coleridge.   Perhaps public enthusiasm, for once enlightened, carried even their stolid conservatism away from the cold, classical elegance of Rogers and Campbell to the fitful splendours of this young champion of a new Romantic era.

In London society the poet's demeanour with strangers is thus described by Lady Caroline Lamb : " A studied courtesy in his manner, a proud humility, mingled with a certain cold reserve" (see the self-conscious description of "Don Juan" in England, cant. xv.).   He was con-. stitutionally shy, and could be haughty to men whom he disliked, which was visited upon him when they got the opportunity.   "But," says Moore, "nothing could be more amusing and delightful than the contrast which his manners when we were alone presented to his proud reserve in the brilliant circle we had just left.   It was like the bursting gaiety of a boy let loose from school, and it seemed as if there was no extent of fun or tricks of which he was not capable."   "The women suffocated him," Lady Caroline Lamb writes, " with their adulation in drawing-rooms."   Lady Jersey brought Lady Caroline up to him, to be introduced, not *vice versa*.   She, turning on her heel, hardly bowed to him, and in her journal set him down as " mad, bad, and dangerous to know."   Nevertheless, she was determined he should love her, and this conduct was calculated to pique him into paying court to her.   She was pretty, and eccentric to the last degree, a leader of fashion, wife of the

Honourable W. Lamb, afterwards Lord Melbourne.
When Byron first called on her, she was in her riding
habit, talking to Rogers and Moore, but she flew to
beautify herself on his being announced. He afterwards
called frequently, and sat with her of a morning, sometimes nursing her child; but she quite certainly threw
herself at his head, at length even coming to his chambers in male disguise, the valet having been directed to
refuse her admittance, since he wished for no scandal or
"scene." A friend of her mother-in-law, Lady Melbourne,
who had warned him of what she might do, he had no
desire to go the lengths the lady would have gone in
her infatuation. Then the *spretæ injuria formæ* turned
against him at last (Lady Melbourne having made up the
match between him and Miss Milbanke, Lady Caroline's
cousin, in order to separate her from Byron), and she
vented her wrath in the novel "Glenarvon," a mere
caricature. But the poor flighty woman never really got
over her infatuation. Her husband having repudiated
her, she met years after, driving out in her carriage,
a funeral, which, upon inquiry, turned out to be that of
Byron; on hearing which she fainted, and always on
the verge of insanity, her mind and health gave way.
She died reconciled, however, to her magnanimous
husband.

What Murray thought of Byron, and what to the
bibliopolic mind constitutes "great" poetry, may be
learned from Trelawny's reported conversation with
Murray, which is most amusing. "This morning,"
says Murray, "I looked over my ledger, and I find that
£75,000 has passed over that counter from Lord Byron's

pen alone. Can any one in the trade say as much? And then look at the time it was done in—ten years—*I think that proves he was a great poet!*" The last sentence is delicious! "This quiet street was as thronged with carriages and people as Regent Street, and this shop was crowded with lords and ladies and footmen, so that the trade could not get near the counter to be served. That great man with his pen could alone have supported a publishing establishment, and I was bereft of my senses to throw it away. But his friends said the people in good society were shocked at the low tone he had fallen into, and they bothered me into remonstrating with him, and I was fool enough to do so in haste, and have repented at leisure of my folly"—for why? *Risum teneatis?* "Mr. Gifford, and others who knew, remarked, even after reading the later cantos of 'Don Juan,' how great" (and that to the bibliopolic mind, as we have just seen, means how saleable) "a poet Byron was. They talked of his immoral writings," continued the publisher—"there is a whole row of sermons glued to my shelf. I hate the sight of them. Why don't they buy them?" Trelawny answered, "That is what Byron tells you is the cant of the age." He might have added that the present conversation was one of the choicest specimens! In fact, John Hunt published the later cantos of "Don Juan," and other shocking things, which the more fashionable bookseller shrank from publishing. Still Murray was a good and true friend to Byron after all. He offered him timely help when cash difficulties obliged him to sell his books, and he might have made much money by the notorious "Memoirs," which yet, at the request of both Lord and Lady Byron's friends, he destroyed.

However, 14,000 copies of "The Corsair" were sold in one day! Such success was, of course, intoxicating, and intoxication is perilous. It stimulated the wilful arrogance of Byron, and his unhealthy craving for immediate popularity at any price, disposing him to unfaithfulness toward his art, the instant and noisy success that was dear to him being obtainable only at the price of writing down to popular taste, and to that of the literary persons who cater for it. This he admitted later in life with bitter regret and self-scorn.

"'The Giaour," "Bride of Abydos," "Corsair," "Lara," "Ode to Napoleon," "Hebrew Melodies," were published during the years 1813, 1814, and 1815; the "Siege of Corinth," and "Parisina," in the spring of 1816, though written previously. Some of the "Hebrew Melodies" have a very distinguished and delicate beauty. The "Waltz," a poorish satire, was published anonymously April, 1813; and the author very disingenuously disavowed it. But Byron appears much more likeable for his suppression of "English Bards" in its fifth edition, being ashamed of its spitefulness, and sorry for the pain it had given to those who were now his friends. Scott, among others, remonstrated with the writer. But his remonstrance resulted in their meeting, and liking each other cordially ever after, each paying warmest tribute to the genius of the other. Such a spectacle is admirable and rare : the irritable race do not as a rule appreciate one another, nor bear a brother near the throne. Byron apologized for "the evil works

of his nonage," and Scott asked him to Abbotsford,
requesting also to see more of his poetry. The former
again presents a copy of "The Giaour" to Scott,
calling him the "Monarch of Parnassus," and later, in
Italy, terms him "the Ariosto of the North." They met
in London, during the spring of 1815, almost daily in
Mr. Murray's drawing-room. "At heart," Scott says,
"I would have termed Byron a patrician on principle;
though he sometimes expressed a high strain of what is
now called Liberalism." In truth, his inherited, native,
aristocratic, and fastidious pride was at war with his conscience, reason, and sympathy with men and women as
such, that is, when deprived of their rights, or treated with
cruelty. This last proviso has to be made. He could
not be "hail fellow well met" with every one, whoever
he was, as one born among the people, like Walt Whit-
man, can be.

His genius and human sympathies fired him to transfix
with winged shafts the immoral and ridiculous pretensions of mere aristocracy, and wealth, accidentally, or
by superior cunning, "be-consoled up to the chin,"
especially when these were blasphemously propped by
tables of stone from Sinai, or Bibles later and holier
—thus sheltering selfish human greed under the protecting shadow of Divine Sanctuaries. Yet his heroes are
haughty and exclusive aristocrats; so that Hazlitt, and
Gabriel Sarrazin, one of the most eminent among younger
French critics, can even name as the "note" of Byron's
poetry, its feudal and lordly tone (see the latter's admirable
critical volume, "Renaissance de la Poésie Anglaise");
and personally he was sometimes proud and reserved in

demeanour, "letting" his acquaintances "up or down,"
as the mood seized him. Leigh Hunt, the Radical,
thought his aristocratic assumptions insufferable—but
Hunt did not happen to suit Byron. Not self-consistent,
he professed a scorn like that of Coriolanus for the multitude, and yet breathed in as sweet incense and wholesome nutriment the rank breath of their unwise applause.

Scott says :—

"Like the old heroes in Homer we exchanged gifts; I gave
Byron a beautiful dagger, mounted with gold, which had been the
property of the redoubted Elfi Bey. But I was to play the part of
Diomed in the 'Iliad,' for Byron sent me some time after a large
sepulchral vase of silver, full of dead men's bones, found within the
land walls of Athens. He was often melancholy, almost gloomy.
I think I also remarked in his temper starts of suspicion, when
he seemed to pause and consider whether there had not been a
secret and perhaps offensive meaning in something that was said to
him. In this case I also judged it best to let his mind, like a
troubled spring, work itself clear, which it did in a minute or two.
What I liked about him was his generosity of spirit as well as purse,
and his utter contempt of all the affectations of literature. He
liked Moore and me, because, with all our other differences, we were
both good-natured fellows enjoying the *mot pour rire*. . . . I have
always reckoned Burns and Byron the most genuine poetic geniuses
of my time."

In 1812, Moore and Byron visited Leigh Hunt in
Horsemonger Lane Gaol, when he was there for having
called the Prince Regent "a fat Adonis of fifty."
Byron at this time declares his intention to have
done with literature, and publish no more; but he published nevertheless. He met frequently Madame de
Staël, and Sheridan, whom he praises as "the author of
the best modern comedy, 'School for Scandal,' the best
farce, the 'Critic,' and the best oration, the 'Begum

Speech,' ever heard in this country." One night, coming out of a tavern with "Sherry," he relates how both found the staircase in a very "corkscrew" condition. The address on the re-opening of Drury Lane Theatre was written by Byron at Lord Holland's request, the other addresses sent in for competition being found unsuitable,— which gave rise to the "Rejected Addresses," a series of clever parodies by the Brothers Smith. And for a time he was on a committee for the management of this same theatre. He was now trying to sell Newstead, though he had intended never to do so; but his affairs were much embarrassed. A Mr. Claughton offered £140,000; failing, however, to complete the agreement, he was to forfeit £25,000; and this he did, the estate remaining with Byron.

The tide of popularity was turning. The avowal of the verses, "To a Lady Weeping," roused the fury of that portion of the press which was favourable to the Prince Regent, and so they proceeded to declare that Lord Byron was a scribbler of poor verse, to be placed low in the list of minor poets; that he was a venal poetaster, capable of pocketing large sums of money for his verses; that he had eaten his own words, in order to curry favour with the powerful persons he had libelled in his satire, &c., &c.; and lastly, that he was no less deformed in mind than in body. But, as Dryden says, one would be unaware of the existence of certain little creatures if they did not bite. The frightened Murray wished to withdraw the lines, but the poet would not yield. There also began to be an outcry against him as a pernicious influence in religion, morals, and politics.

CHAPTER III.

I NOW believe that we have erred in regarding the poet's marriage as merely a *mariage de convenance*, without affection. Miss Milbanke had a fortune of about £10,000, with a prospect of a little more when her father died, and some expectations from her uncle, Lord Wentworth. But the latter could dispose of his wealth as he liked, and he had other nephews and nieces, besides natural children. The money, whatever it was, would first go to her mother, Lord Wentworth's sister, who was only sixty-one. So that Miss Milbanke was *not* a great " catch " for an embarrassed peer.

Lord Broughton, who knew, always affirmed that his friend did not marry for money. Nor do his own expressions at the time of his engagement warrant the idea. The story, in Medwin's conversations, of his mistaking Miss Milbanke for a humble companion, when he first met her, seems to be pure fiction. Neither does the story Moore tells (from imperfect recollection of the destroyed " Memoirs ") appear much more probable. He says that Byron, by the advice of a female friend, made an offer to another lady between his first and second proposals to Miss Milbanke, and that, on receiving a refusal, he sent his second proposal to the latter, the friend having observed "it was such a pretty letter, 'twas a pity it should not go."

This is very likely a malrecollection of something in the "Memoirs;" but I fear we must admit, on a careful review of Byron's life, that when he once took a hatred to a person, he was, like some women, and like Shelley, predisposed readily to believe anything to his discredit; might even make statements to pain that person, which, if founded on fact, were certainly highly coloured in passing through the ardent medium of a hostile and injured imagination. That "The Dream" contains some such semi-fabricated illusions calculated to wound Lady Byron—written as it was after he had heard of her cruel confidences about him—so far as concerns his alleged absorption in the image of Mary Chaworth, when he stood before the altar with his bride—seems to me extremely probable. And yet I quite believe he only *heightened*, in the glamour of bitter retrospection, a feeling that may verily have invaded his mind even at the moment of his marriage, on comparing the actual happening present with an ideal, which appeared such because it had never passed into the reality of experience, and remained a fair possibility only. But he emphasized this in order to mortify the implacable woman who had left him. For the passages of his journals and letters to intimate friends which relate to his engagement, and earlier period of his married life, seem quite inconsistent with the notion that he merely married for money, and appear even to prove that the union was one of mutual—though surely not ardent—

affection, in spite of its unfortunate and speedy termination. Engaged in September, 1814, the poet was
married in January, 1815. In October, 1814, he writes
to a friend, from the Albany where he had bachelor's
apartments, " I am very much in love, and as silly as all
single gentlemen must be in that sentimental situation.
She has no fault, except being a great deal too good for
me, and that I must pardon if nobody else should."
To Henry Drury he writes : " I am going to be married,
and have been engaged this month—an old, and, though
I did not know it till lately, a mutual attachment."

In the midst of the honeymoon he wrote gaily to
Moore from Halnaby Hall : "So you want to know about
milady and me? I like Bell as well as you do (or did,
you villain !) Bessy—and that is, or was, saying a good
deal." And so it was. Byron knew well how Moore
liked his wife ; and on his return to Seaham next month
he writes to him : " My spouse and I agree to admiration. Swift says no wise man ever married; but for a
fool I think it the most ambrosial of all possible future
states. I still think one ought to marry upon lease, but
am very sure I should renew mine at the expiration,
though the next term were for ninety-and-nine years."
Augusta Leigh again writes to Hodgson :—

"I have every reason to think that my beloved B. is very
happy and comfortable. I hear constantly from him and his *rib*. It
appears to me that Lady B. sets about making him happy in the
right way. I had many fears. Thank God that they do not seem
likely to be realized. In short, there seems to be but one drawback
to all our felicity ; and that, alas ! is the disposal of dear Newstead.
I shall never feel reconciled to the loss of that sacred, revered

Abbey. Lady B. writes me word that she never saw her father and mother so happy ; that she believes the latter would go to the bottom of the sea herself to find fish for B.'s dinner."

Byron, indeed, says he was rather bored with listening after dinner, over the wine, to "that damnable mono-logue (of his father-in-law) which elderly gentlemen are pleased to call conversation."

Anne Isabella was the daughter of Sir Ralph Milbanke, Bart., and Judith Noel, daughter of Viscount Wentworth. She was attractive-looking, philanthropic, clever, learned, unaffected, though rather stiff, prim, and formal ; was regarded as a "paragon" of virtue at home, an only child, who had always got very much her own way ; a spoilt child, like her husband, and probably a bit of a female prig. She refused Byron's first offer, but they kept up a correspondence, and his regard for her, judg-ing by his journals, evidently deepened. In March, 1814, he jots down : "A letter from Bella, which I answered. I shall be in love with her again, if I don't take care." That he was despondent before his mar-riage, as Moore assures us, is likely enough, for he must have seriously questioned his own ability to "reform," and make his bride happy, as he announced his intention of doing, and doubted whether she was not "too good for him," as he also expressed it ; moreover, he feared that the bailiffs were likely to be in his house ere long, his creditors pressing him for payment on the strength of his marriage and expectations, which is indeed what eventually happened.

He had agreed to make a large settlement on his wife, whose trustees would have control over £60,000 of the capital that should come from the sale of Newstead. Her own fortune of £10,000 was also settled upon her. This Lord Broughton made clear in an article in the *Westminster Review.*

They were married in the drawing-room at Seaham, Sir Ralph's place, Hobhouse being best man; after the ceremony they drove to his other place, Halnaby, near Darlington (the bridegroom having made the ominous mistake of calling his wife *Miss Milbanke* after the ceremony). Hobhouse handed her into the carriage, her parting words to him being: "If I am not happy it will be my own fault." Medwin says Byron told him that a lady's maid sat between them, much to his disgust. This is one of the fibs Hobhouse wrote to contradict. But whose was it? Byron's, or Medwin's? It seems that it was at that time the fashion to "*bam*" people, that is, to tell them ridiculous stories with little or no foundation, for the sake of "greening" them, if one may use a modern slang term in order to explain an old one. Thus George IV. used to relate gravely that he was Commander-in-chief at Waterloo. It was a very silly fashion; but some people, no doubt, are tempting subjects for such an operation, gossips, and curiosity-mongers especially. And Byron's impish love of practical joking was excessive all through life. This "bamming" fitted into his reprehensibly garrulous habit of talking about himself and his affairs to many who had no sort of claim to his confidences, especially when they involved the reputation of others. Byron and Shelley, moreover, versified their own experiences a great deal, of course embroidering fanciful inventions upon them:

but they seem to have imagined or invented more or less, also, in recalling their experiences to themselves, and relating them to others. Then there was the infantile, half-malicious delight, in shocking very "goody," precise, and conventional people. The greater part of "Don Juan" is "chaff," let ponderous moralists remember. It is said that Byron dressed the statues in Neville's Court, Trinity College, up in surplices; and it is certain that he popped with pistols at the statuettes opposite his windows at Mesolonghi, till all the old women came howling out to remonstrate. Other old women—grave moralists—remonstrated with still more emphatic howls at other more serious examples of his buffoonery in print, and in daily life.

"No boy cornet," says Trelawny, "enjoyed a practical joke more than Byron." He relates that on their sea-voyage together from Genoa to Greece, the captain wore a scarlet waistcoat, and, as he was very stout, Byron wished to see whether it would button round both of them. He got hold of it, and while the captain was having a siesta, he, standing on the gangway, with one arm in the garment, said: "Now, put your arm in, Tre; we will jump overboard, and take the shine out of it," and so they did, the geese and hens, which Trelawny had released, and the two big dogs swimming about with them. All the crew were laughing at the fun, till the captain, hearing the row, came on deck, and seeing what was up, roared out: "My lord, you should know better than to make a mutiny on board ship! I won't heave to, or lower a boat; I hope you will both be drowned." "Then you will lose your *frite*" (for so the captain pronounced the word *freight*), shouted Byron. But they pacified the skipper later on.

So that one really must not be too serious, too ponderous, precise, and matter of fact to enter into a Byron, or a Heine. He was seldom quite serious in company for five minutes together; and those who can't see a joke are likely to regard him as a "malignant," and a "fiend"—names actually applied to him by stern censors. I admit fully, indeed, that his jokes were often in the worst taste, and very much out of season. And so, as Sir Walter Scott, the great, generous, large-hearted judge observed, he was his own worst enemy; for remember that Scott did not change this opinion, even after reading the destroyed "Memoirs." Thus Lady Byron, not in her stern and merciless letter to Lady Anne Bernard about her husband, but in conversation with that lady, stated that he informed her in the carriage on their very first drive to Halnaby, "with a malignant sneer," how "it was enough for her to be his wife for him to hate her." "If you were the wife of any other man, I own you might have charms," &c. ; and he added that he only married her out of revenge for her having refused him ! She told him it was a bad jest, that he was not in earnest, and he laughed it off when he saw that she was hurt. "Then I forgot," she added, "what had passed till forced to remember it." If he, indeed, spoke so, and this was not said in anger on another occasion, which is far more probable, it *was* a bad jest, an inconceivably bad one, hardly consistent with sanity, as uttered by one claiming to be a gentleman to his young bride. Later on he used to tell her that he wedded her for her

name and fortune, and that she had wedded him only to
have the glory of reforming him. She spoke of the
"coldness and malignity of his heart," and of his
"acting derangement," in order to screen his vices.
But what will an irritable man goaded to anger not say?
And what could be more coldly cruel than such a judgment on him coming from such a quarter? Did he ever
say anything worse of her in his maddest rages? Only,
he had no self-restraint, and "posed." He lived too much
in the world's eye, and so published what he felt and
thought at the moment, taking, after the fashion of all the
"sentimentalists," the public into his confidence—while
she was colder, more controlled, with far more of dignity
and prudence. But there is no doubt that he did fear
madness, and that he *was* strange at times—he speaks
of a certain occasional incoherence in his ideas; there
is quite as little doubt that his enthusiasm was real,
not "feigned," as his wife was good enough to affirm.
Would not a person like Lady Byron be apt to think *all*
enthusiasm "feigned"?

The lady was evidently too serious herself, too simple,
and wanting in humour, for all her talent and self-
attributed skill in reading character, to make allowances for so volcanic a temperament, for a man of so
many varying, complex, and swiftly succeeding moods,
sincere and strongly felt though each one of them was
at the moment. And he was malicious enough to
delight in teasing her all the more that she was so
terribly in earnest, took him always so gravely. Had
she but chaffed, bantered, and laughed at him, it would
have been much better. He was obstinate, and would

go his own way, could not be lectured into better behaviour, but, like a naughty boy, would roll himself more thoroughly in the mud the more his nurse, or his governess, called to him to come out of it; so as a baby he had torn up the frock another preceptress scolded him for soiling. Yet the fact remains that he was not faithful to her, and that he often behaved cruelly to boot. She had therefore some justification for leaving him, and even for refusing to return. You do not blame a collier's wife for seeking to get away from a man who kicks her with big clogs—though when she tries to shield, excuses, and elects to stay with him, you cannot help admiring her. But surely a woman has the same right to live her own life out undisturbed and uninjured, even if the husband happen to be a half-bad and half-noble madman of genius. Lady Byron was a clever woman, a philanthropic one. But she was not very magnanimous, not a heroine,—not the kind of woman to influence so divergent a character as the man she married, partly hoping to reform him. Strangely matched!—fire and snow—erratic comet and cold, chaste moon—the stony pillar, half a woman, looking back to embrace some lurid fume from doomed cities, now buried under Dead Sea waters—forming together what the husband wittily calls "that moral centaur, man and wife." Her virtue was conventional and rigid. It is enough to know that she made his nervous affection on seeing Kean act "Sir Giles Overreach" one of the suspicious circumstances to be laid before Dr. Baillie as proof of his insanity, and another the fact that he broke a watch in a fit of fury on occasion of an execution in his house, which indeed were very frequent at 13, Piccadilly Terrace, where they resided during their stay in London, in the months before the wife's departure. This is enough to show how incapable the lady was of understanding her husband, and therefore of influencing him for good.   At first, indeed, all went smoothly, even happily. She was interested in his poetry, and copied it for him ; she was not only philosophical, and mathematical, but wrote fair verses herself, and showed them to Byron.   His money difficulties, however, were driving him to distraction ; his health was seriously impaired by drinking bouts and orgies, alternating with fasts ; his liver became so diseased that he had an attack of jaundice at the period when he was guilty of the worst offences that could be charged against him; and he now took laudanum habitually ; so that, with a highly-wrought nervous organization trembling in the balance between sanity and madness, he could hardly have been accounted fully responsible for his actions at this juncture.   His conduct must have been very bad and unkind at a time when peculiar tenderness and attention were due to a young wife—latterly, he never took his meals with her, and he was out "late o' nights."   But was Lady Byron quite reliable in her statements as to details? Women in a delicate situation sometimes get strange fancies. May not the delusions of such a time occasionally remain with them, or recur later?   Might this *partly* account, I wonder, for what Lady Byron so many years after told Mrs. Stowe ?   But keeping loaded pistols in the room— one of the grave charges — was not necessarily very "mad" or very "bad" !—though perverse and unkind, if she objected. Byron had not, like Burns, married a Jean Armour—worse luck for him.

Subsequent to the separation, some additional statement was made to Dr. Lushington by Lady Byron when she came to town again, a fortnight after Lady Noel, her mother, had seen the lawyer, and laid the wife's case before him ; for he then had judged that, though there was serious cause of complaint, a reconciliation was not out of the question. But Lady Byron affirmed that she had deliberately withheld part of her case from the knowledge even of her parents. Why, and what was it ? That is the question. *One* cause of her resentment was her husband's expressed resolve to travel in the East, or in Italy and Spain again, either with or without her, she preferring to remain in England. It appears, however, that the couple had no serious disagreement till August. In March they went to visit Colonel and the Hon. Mrs. Leigh at Six-mile Bottom, their place ; and it is certain that the two ladies "took to one another" greatly. Byron himself had never seen much of his half-sister before. But now the trio called one another by pet names. Augusta called him " Baby," he calling her " Goose," and his wife " Pippin," because she had rather a round face, while her diminutive for Byron was " Duck." In London husband and wife drove about and went to parties together, though, from money difficulties, they entertained and went out little. In April, Lord Wentworth died, leaving the bulk of his property, £7,000 to £3,000 a year, entailed on his sister, Lady Milbanke, with remainder to his niece, Lady Byron, and her issue, on condition that the Milbankes should assume his

name, Noel.   They, having taken up their abode at Lord
Wentworth's seat, Kirkby Mallory, offered Seaham to
the Byrons.

Early in August Byron showed his affectionate care for
his wife,—whom very soon after he began to treat so
strangely—by asking her to invite her mother to Seaham,
to be with her in her confinement.   And the poet
announced to his wife that he had made a will, which
contained provisions for Augusta and her children, on
account of her husband, Colonel Leigh, having suffered
pecuniary losses, and this communication was most
sympathetically received by Lady Byron.   At the period
of their differences, George Byron, the poet's cousin,
who succeeded him in the peerage, and his sister herself,
sided very much with Lady Byron, and were inclined to
think that the poet might be out of his mind.   He used
latterly, his wife said, to scowl at her, and look down on
the floor when she approached.   On one occasion, when
she came into his room, while he was meditating on his
embarrassed affairs, and asked him if she was in his way,
he replied, "*damnably!*"   But what trifles to hang so
irrevocable a severance on!   Can human forgiveness
indeed go no further?   He and Hobhouse arranged to
go abroad together in the spring.   He told her, probably
in a fit of rage, he had never cared for her, and would
free himself from the "unendurable bondage of matri-
mony."   All this may have been enough to justify her
in leaving him; for every one is not called upon to
follow "counsels of perfection," least of all great saints
mated to great sinners; though she might, perhaps, have
given him a rather longer trial than she did!   Hard

measure may have been dealt out to her by the poet's partisans. But it remains, nevertheless, that she fore-went the high privilege and honour that might have been hers for all time, could her virtue, less self-conscious and self-regarding, have risen to the height of magnanimity, forgiven till seventy times seven, and remained to save a human soul, which she supposed herself to have loved, and which had felt love for her—though whether their temperaments were not too hopelessly unsympathetic for mutual toleration and benefit is a serious question. One admits that they *may* have been better apart, as she believed.

Lady Byron was glad to welcome to Piccadilly Mrs. Clermont, known *par excellence* as "the mischief-maker," her old governess, concerning whom her husband wrote the very Popean, and too vindictive "sketch." Augusta Ada, "the child of love, though born in bitterness, and nurtured in convulsion," was born in December, 1815, and named after Mrs. Leigh, her godmother (note this, O calumny!). "Ada, sole daughter of my house and heart," eventually married the Earl of Lovelace,— the remarkable Lord Ockham, who died, the present Lord Wentworth, and Lady Anne Blunt being her sur-viving children. All through this wretched time kind Mrs. Leigh was there, comforting and nursing the poor wife, even taking her part, yet a true and affectionate friend to her brother also, one, moreover, never afraid to tell him the truth about his conduct. He wrote to his wife requesting her to leave London with the child as soon as possible, and go to her mother; so that Lady Byron was wont to say that she did not desert him, but that he sent her away. Yet the house was certainly no place for her, besieged as it was by bailiffs and dunning tradesmen. She entreated Augusta to stay in Piccadilly, though the latter wished to go home. Lady Byron assured her that she had been her comforter and best friend throughout. She could control her brother better than any one else; from her the wife expected to receive at Kirkby Mallory reliable news about what passed in Piccadilly; yet, according to Mrs. Stowe, she believed the story she told about Augusta *before* she left London; indeed, she declared that she had ocular evidence of the alleged crime, which Byron, moreover, had justified to her! Now the mere freedom and familiarity of which she speaks in the demeanour of brother and sister toward one another was obviously no sort of evidence at all, except to a prudish and perverted imagination. Indeed the very openness of this conduct was its own all-sufficient defence. But in a person like Byron, with an almost insane and childish desire to shock proper people, and pose as a terribly wicked man ("inverted hypocrisy" Harness calls it), the temptation to "bam," to accuse himself of something exceptionally bad, and defend it with sophistry, may well have proved irresistible, when his wife was so absurd as to let him see what she fancied, and broke out into shrieks of virtuous horror, which were perfectly uncalled for. I am simply taking the *ipsissima verba* of the widow, as Mrs. Stowe repeats them; and Lady Byron can really have had no better evidence than this — unless we except some (possible) malicious insinuations of the "mischief maker" as better evidence ! Of course he had put himself into his wife's power by such damaging self-accusations. Yet "there is no one whose society is dearer to me," she writes on leaving her husband in Augusta's care ! In after years, when she quarrelled openly with Augusta—partly on account of a difference about trustees, but chiefly no doubt from the resentment long rankling at her husband's printed glorification of his sister, at her expense, the full extent and force of which she only realized on reading Moore's life, where verses appeared which had hitherto been withheld from publication—her strong suspicions recurred with the force of certainty. And prejudice envenomed them, so that she could even accuse Augusta of fanning the discord between her and Byron, which wounded the sister sadly ; for her influence had been quite in the opposite direction, as her brother ever testified, and his wife herself had formerly fully admitted. Ah, poor human nature ! But ostensibly they quarrelled about the appointment of trustees of the marriage settlement, provided for under the poet's will, Augusta, as we have seen, being interested in the will. In that instance (see the correspondence published by Mr. Jeaffreson between the two ladies) Lady Byron certainly showed herself " wanting one sweet weakness, to forgive "—even harsh and implacable.

It seems clear, however, that the subject of incest had a certain fascination both for Shelley, and also for the poet who wrote "Cain," "Manfred," and the original version of the "Bride of Abydos." This experience of his—this accusation by his wife, together with his own peculiar warmth of feeling, wherein passion and affection seemed to blend, and his wanton, defiant adoption of the wife's suggestion—may have been the very circum· stance that induced his morbid imagination to brood over the subject with a certain unhealthy pertinacity, when he threw himself repeatedly into the situation of one whose guilt should be counted abnormal. So far as one can judge, this seems a probable explanation of that dark element in some of the poems, as also of the mysterious hints he was wont to throw out concerning the composition of "Manfred,"—though indeed neither Ford, nor Shelley, was accused of participation in the guilt they imagined for their poetry.

The strange thing is that when Lady Byron left London with Ada on January 15th, and wrote on the road the playful fond letter to her husband, beginning "Dear Duck," and signed with her pet name, she certainly left with the hope of having him with her again at Kirkby Mallory very shortly! Lady Noel in the kindest terms invited him, and Augusta was to persuade him to go. Byron himself expressed his resolve to join her there; for both he and his wife were in hopes of a son and heir being born to them, as a result of that future meeting. But, if so, how could she *then* have regarded her husband with so much aversion as she fancied in after years she had done? She affirmed, indeed, that she supposed him mad, and that the doctor had advised her thus writing in a pleasant strain. Lady Noel and Mrs. Clermont came up to London shortly after, to lay all the facts Lady Byron had told them before Dr. Baillie and Dr. Lushington. Dr. Baillie and a lawyer were also instructed to pay Lord Byron a visit that they might judge of his mental state, after doing which they reported that he was not out of his mind. Then Lady Byron decided never to return to him.

> " For Inez called some druggists and physicians,
>   And tried to prove her loving lord was mad,
>   But as he had some lucid intermissions
>   She next decided he was only bad ;
>   Yet when they asked her for her depositions,
>   No sort of explanation could be had,
>   Save that her duty both to man and God
>   Required this conduct—which seemed very odd."
>
> (" Don Juan," c. 1.)

It appears that Mrs. Clermont (either with or without his wife's orders) broke open Lord Byron's private desk, and, finding some compromising letters to a married lady (written before his own wedding), she, or his wife, actually sent them to this lady's husband ! This was amiable, certainly ! But her ladyship seems to have been very miserable at Kirkby Mallory after her decision was arrived at, ·for the ill-assorted couple had some affection for each other after all ; else would he so persistently have sought a reconciliation, which her immense sense of what was due to her own dignity, and also her inevitable, perfectly just indignation at his conduct towards her, in publishing the " Farewell," which · appeared in April, forbade her to entertain? Although indeed those verses were full of affection, and the MS., Moore says, was blotted with his tears. Moreover Mrs. Clermont, the mischief-maker (Mr. Jeaffreson says, though a writer in the *Quarterly* answering him denies it) had

informed Lady Byron of her husband's *liaison* with
Jane Clairmont.[1] This, however, had not commenced
till after Lady Byron left her husband's roof, though
she may well have been told and supposed otherwise.
Byron met Claire at Drury Lane, where she had applied
to him (one of the managing committee) for employment
as an actress; and the result was that the mercurial
poet and she conceived a passion for one another.
There is, indeed, no sort of proof that Byron's relations
with any actress there were immoral, though he had
been accused falsely of too close a connection with Mrs.
Mardyn, who by the virtuous British public was hissed
off the stage on the strength of this utterly mythical
intimacy, when they espoused his wife's cause, and
turned with so indiscriminate, undiscerning a fury
against him. He at first refused to consent to sign
the private agreement to separate insisted on by Sir
Ralph Noel, but on its being intimated that the Noels
would take the case into court, he consented. And it
is alleged that this shows his conscience must have
accused him of some terrible sin like that of Mrs.
Stowe's story. But surely it is more probable that he
shrank from a public exposure of his many petty acts of
unchivalrous discourtesy, perhaps cruelty, towards a
young, irreproachable, and affectionate wife, so un-
befitting, alas! a noble gentleman, celebrated for his
fine aspirations after the ideal. Yet he could scarcely
have foreseen how many scandalous charges of all kinds
would be brought against him, and all the more from

---

[1] "Claire,"—the daughter of William Godwin's second wife, a
widow, Mrs. Clairmont, and therefore Mary Godwin's stepsister.

the very silence Lady Byron, till some years after his death, was *supposed* to have maintained concerning the causes of their separation,—which he once told a gentleman were "too simple to be found out." The storm indeed broke heavily; the re-action to execration was proportionate to the poet's recent exaggerated popularity. He was advised not to go to the House of Peers, lest he might be mobbed. "I was accused," he says, "of every monstrous vice by public rumour and private rancour; my name, which had been a knightly or a noble one, since my fathers helped to conquer the kingdom for William the Norman, was tainted. I felt that if what was whispered, and muttered, and murmured was true, I was unfit for England; if false, England was unfit for me." The capricious public was now for whipping and breaking its adored idol. People of his own class avoided him, and Lady Jersey was one of the only old friends who did not fall away from him, but invited him to her party on the eve of his leaving the country. Yet even that effort in his favour was a failure: the guests cut him, or treated him with marked coldness. Years after, he wrote with satirical amusement of the behaviour of his quondam friends that evening! The men were wreaking their vengeance on the man whom they disliked: first, because their women liked him; secondly, for not taking more port wine and beefsteak, like his fellow-Britons; then for being a great poet, instead of an ordinary partridge-killing seducer, who—commendably free from the eccentricities of that uncanny thing called "genius," veneering his vices with a seemly show of

decorum, conformity to established religion, and the
politics of privilege, throwing his pinch of incense on
the altar of the great goddess Grundy, whose image
is so well known to have descended from Heaven—
might be received with condoning eyes, and deferential
smiles, into the bosom of the most respectable families,
therefrom to carry in triumph the fairest and purest
virgin to his den. In England the fault lies in being
found out. But this man was also a satirist, who had
made enemies of the literary set, not only by his lashing
satire, but by the sterling and original excellence of
his verse. Without one scintilla of proof he was forthwith compared to Nero, Heliogabalus, Tiberius, and
other celebrated criminals, while his misconduct at
home was mercilessly and monstrously exaggerated by
rumour. Far worse men than he, ready to commit any
crime in the interest of their own caste, or their private
property—men of the world, as well as intolerant Phari-
sees—made a queer sort of vicarious atonement for
their own vices by an immoderate and unjust condem-
nation of his. He became their whipping-boy. So he
left England, and from the Continent pealed forth the
melodious wail of his wounded, wrathful, sullen genius,
with compass immeasurably fuller from opposition, desertion, and despair. Still, there can be no doubt that
he himself was largely responsible for what took place.
He had charged himself in public, truly or untruly,
both directly and indirectly, with great, remorse-haunted
crime, and then professed angry surprise when people
took him at his word; while the religious scepticism he
avowed was generally associated in the popular mind

with immoral conduct. Only it did appear to the poet himself somewhat absurd that the notorious holiness of English high society under the Regency should profess itself so "much offended," he having sat cheek by jowl, and knee to knee with it, inevitably forming his own conclusions about the soundness of its pretensions to sanctity. Moreover, he was condemned unheard. But he avenged himself in the English cantos of "Don Juan."

I have it on the best authority that documentary evidence exists (it may probably be published some day) to prove that, after the separation, Byron for awhile spoke of his wife with the utmost affection and regret. But it is not borne out by this body of evidence that the opinion of the doctors was so decided against the supposition of the poet's temporary insanity at this juncture, which had been entertained, not only by the wife, but by the sister also. Mrs. Leigh's letters by no means confirm the full assurance of his complete sanity, by which the wife justifies her inflexible resolve to leave him. The *Quarterly Reviewer*, answering Mrs. Stowe, (vol. 128, p. 227), had access to some of this very important evidence when he asserted, "it is quite clear that the notion of her quitting him for ever had never so much as crossed his mind when they parted." If he spoke of her after awaking from fits of gloom, it was to inquire for her, to express deep affection for her, and to exhibit marked impatience for her return. He became so agitated on the arrival of a letter from her that he told his sister to open it. When made aware of her intention to separate, he was so terribly shaken that his sister expected him to go mad outright, or to commit suicide, and wrote adjuring Lady Byron to pause, lest the most terrible of all responsibilities should devolve upon her! Lady Byron had seen enough to convince her that the picture was not overcharged, that the danger was real, and that the sister was rather for her than against her in this emergency. But she was incapable of the amount of self-sacrifice demanded, and shrank from the painful task which she described in a letter written shortly after her departure from Piccadilly—" If these (the symptoms of mental derangement) should not become more convincing, they have been so apparent that I might hereafter adduce them to justify the inter-mediate measures if it were necessary to take a different line of conduct on different grounds; and it could only be attributed to a patient and persevering affection that I did not immediately seize the advantage, when the only reward of delay would be the privilege of a melancholy attendance on hopeless suffering." Surely there is something hard and unloving about this! As to Mrs. Stowe's assertion that he was only acting a part when he expressed a resolve under certain circumstances to institute a suit, it seems sure that in January, 1817, he sent positive instructions to his solicitor, Mr. Hanson, in this sense; but it was only to be, if some specified charges were not disclaimed; and *formally* they appear to have been disclaimed. Lady Byron in one letter (February 24, 1816) says, "My resolution is therefore such that, if my father and mother were to implore me by every duty to *them* to return to my husband, I would not." But the argument is very strong that had Dr. Lushington been able to say truthfully that this was *not* the specific charge brought by Lady Byron against her husband at the time of the separation, he would have said so after the publication of Mrs. Stowe's book, for the sake of the honour of the families concerned. And the story had certainly got about, even in 1816. How, and to whom was it traceable? Karl Elze pertinently asks, whence the change in Byron's tone toward his wife, whence the new and excessive bitterness in his poetry, which began to show itself when he was in Switzerland, unless he had then heard that this story affecting his sister had been circulated by Lady Byron? Only, how explain her *apparently* undiminished confidence in, and affection for, Augusta—which lasted so long after the separation—unless one imputes interested and sinister motives, which one is very unwilling to do? For since the story was told to her intimates, it could not have been to shield her sister-in-law's reputation.

It would seem that other charges of abnormal irregularities were made against him at this time ; but all appear to rest either on the wife's stories, and his own morbid self-accusations, or on malignant gossip—a very insecure foundation. But these environed the poet with a subtle atmosphere of poisoned reputation, which could not be faced or fought, like open, honest, definite charges. Yet "the significant eye, that learns to lie with silence," and "the moral Clytemnestra" lines, are very severe, and should never have been published. Some women, however, would shield the beloved person, even though he were a murderer! *She* constituted herself his judge, and sometimes spoke even as if she were his

Heaven appointed executioner. But then he posed before her as an unrepentant criminal. Mrs. Leigh, indeed,
continued to put such full confidence in Lady Byron
that she submitted the contents of her brother's letters
indiscriminately to her—frank and unguarded in their
statements about his goings on as they always were.
With respect to the calumny affecting Mrs. Leigh, when
Lord Broughton (by assuring her that her brother himself
had latterly expressed a strong wish that the " Memoirs"
confided to Moore should not see the light) had induced
her to assent to their destruction, Lady Byron also con-
curring, the wife was represented at the burning of the
MS. in Murray's drawing-room by Mr. Wilmot Horton,
the same gentleman who, on behalf of Lady Byron, had
expressly disclaimed every conceivable calumny, one
after the other, in 1816.   Nor in Lady Byron's correspondence with her advisers as to what her answer to the
statements about the separation in Moore's Life of Byron
should be (1830), is there the smallest mention of the
charge in question.   At any rate, the story *was utterly incapable of proof.*   Even if Lord Byron had written a
confession of its truth (Lady Byron asserts that he *made*
such a confession to her verbally), there would still be
no more proof than there is of the truth of the self-
accusations of innumerable morbidly-disposed persons
that *they* were perpetrators of crimes, which they
have not committed.   Why, this very eccentric man
of genius is even said to have libelled himself in
continental journals by sending to them sensational
narratives of his own imaginary misdeeds, and in one of
his journals he not obscurely hints that he was himself

engaged in piracy, like Conrad, at one time of his life! But who in his senses would accuse himself of crimes counted abominable by his own age and country, *if he had really committed them?* Yet there is a form of monomania which persuades a man that he has been guilty of certain crimes, though, except in imagination, it is not so. And therefore the wife should not have told the unverified story to her intimates, involving such terrible consequences to the persons concerned. Far less should she have told it, with so fearful a personal application, to the unfortunate girl Medora Leigh, or repeated (after quarrelling with Augusta about money matters) the additional and monstrous calumnies circulated by this poor unreliable girl against her own mother! It is indeed very difficult to know how far we may trust Lady Byron's later impressions as to what really did take place earlier. Mrs. Leigh was clearly not supposed by Lady Byron to be a weak woman under her brother's control, though she is said to have told this to Mrs. Stowe; the whole tone of the correspondence between the sisters-in-law forbids us to accept such a version of the situation. If the wife believed what she declared about the crime, then she condoned it by entreating Mrs. Leigh to remain in London, and her mouth should have remained sealed on the subject— whether or not she thought her husband might be mad.

William Howitt relates that a schoolmaster, warmly recommended by him, was dismissed suddenly by her ladyship, with no reason specified, and that she never could be got to name one, so that Howitt wrote to the master, "remember Lord Byron; if Lady Byron

has taken it into her head that you shall go, nothing
will turn her"; and he adds that, while charming and
amiable one day, she could be hard, cold, and frozen
the next. In these moods she would take strong impressions against people, which nothing could ever
remove. Some of her acquaintances always thought
her hard; though it is fair to remember that others
had a very different impression. *If* she told Mrs.
Stowe that Mrs. Leigh had repented at the last under
her good influence, this, to put it charitably, must have
been a sheer delusion! For it is proved (through papers
belonging to Mr. Morison, of Fonthill, and by others
in the British Museum, first published in *The Athenæum*,
and then reprinted by Mr. Jeaffreson) that the sisters-
in-law quarrelled in 1830, and kept up no sort of
intercourse, except in the shape of a very unsatisfactory
parting interview at Reigate in 1851. If, again, the
"haunts of vice" Byron went to at night from Piccadilly
were only the late dinners with poor "Sherry," and
such folk, one can hardly wonder at the buffooning
pantomime the wife relates him to have acted before
her, when he pretended to implore her forgiveness on
his knees, after she had bored him with her somewhat
uncalled-for display of virtuous indignation, on his
return home. In his rejoinder to her curt refusal to
read and correct any misstatement in the destroyed
"Memoirs," Byron quotes Dante :—

> " E certo
> La fiera moglie, più ch'altro, mi nuoce."

CHAPTER IV

BYRON sailed from Dover to Ostend on the 25th of April, 1816, with Fletcher, young Rushton, and a Swiss servant, accompanied also by that too pretentious, inflated youth, Dr. Polidori, who had to be dismissed in the course of the journey, and later committed suicide. The poet travelled through Europe *en grand milord*, in a rather cumbrous and luxurious carriage (made after the model of Napoleon's taken at Genappe), through Flanders, and by the Rhine to Switzerland, visiting the field of Waterloo, and gathering materials for the third canto of "Childe Harold." He wisely resolved, about this time, to take the money for his books, which Murray was willing to pay, and received £4,000 for "Childe Harold" (third and fourth cantos) and "Manfred." Indeed, he made his 'cute publisher give larger sums than he offered, and became more and more particular about money matters the longer he lived; although he never stinted his benevolences, which remained always munificent. At Geneva, he first took up his abode at the Hotel Sécheron, with the Shelleys, and Claire; but, being annoyed by the intense curiosity of English tourists, he moved to

another villa, where, however, he could not escape
them, for the landlord of the Sécheron obligingly
provided the tourists with ´telescopes, through which
they were still able to survey the wicked poets and
their lady loves. So Byron again moved to the Villa
Diodati, at Coligny, and Shelley to a house near. It
was at Geneva that the two poets first met, and
formed an intimacy which remained unbroken till
Shelley's death. Touring on the lake together, ´they
were nearly wrecked in a squall off the rocks of
Meillerie, famous for the same kind of adventure
recorded in Rousseau's " Nouvelle Heloïse." The incident was a striking one ; for Shelley (who could not
swim) being anxious lest Byron should be drowned in
trying to save him, caught hold of the seat and declared
he would "go with the pigs (of iron) to the bottom,"
while Byron expressed his resolution to save him, if
possible.

Late into the night they would sit in the Villa Diodati,
holding high converse ; for Byron was always at his best
with Shelley ; that strange, volatile, yet ideal-loving, and
ethereal spirit touched the robuster and earthlier soul
of his great brother to finer issues, so that he became
more serious and thoughtful in this companionship.
Indeed, the influence of Shelley (as well as of Wordsworth, whom Shelley made him read) is to be felt in the
subtler touches of the later " Childe Harold," especially
in the stanzas about Switzerland ; but the pantheism that
appears here is far less intelligently felt and expressed
by the more popular poet. He was now falsely accused
in England (probably by these same veracious tourists

—perhaps to prove their own superior sanctity by false witness—the lie being repeated with gusto by Southey) of living in promiscuous intercourse with "two sisters," *i.e.*, Mary Godwin, and Jane Clairmont. The same story was later told also about Shelley. Byron's daughter by Claire, Allegra, was born when the mother returned to England with the Shelleys in 1817.

Byron visited Madame de Staël, at Coppet, in July. There a lady novelist, of mature virtue and maturer years, fainted on his Satanic presence being announced! Genevese society in general declined to receive him. On one occasion, when rain confined the friends to their villa, they agreed to write ghost stories, the best of these being Mary Godwin's "Frankenstein"; Byron's sketch, "The Vampire," was afterwards expanded by Polidori, and published by him as a work of Byron. When the Shelleys left, Byron made an excursion with Hobhouse—whom he snowballed—through the Oberland—by the Col de Jaman and Simmenthal to Thun, and the Staubbach—thence over the Wengern to Grindelvald and the Rosenlaui Glacier —by Berne and Friburg, back to Diodati. In his journal he says—

"The glacier like a frozen hurricane—starlight beautiful, but a devil of a path. Passed whole woods of withered pines, all withered, trunks stripped and barkless, branches lifeless, done by a single winter. Their appearance reminded me of me and my family. . . . In the weather for this tour I have been very fortunate. I was disposed to be pleased. I am a lover of nature. But in all this the recollection of bitterness, more especially of recent and more home desolation, which must accompany me through life, have preyed upon me here; neither the music of the shepherd, the crashing of the avalanche, the torrent, the mountain, the glacier, the forest, nor the cloud, have for one moment lightened the weight upon my heart, nor enabled me to lose my own wretched identity in the majesty, and the power, and the glory, around, above, and beneath me."

Detained by bad weather at Ouchy, he wrote in two days "The Prisoner of Chillon," with its glorious introductory sonnet to Liberty. This tale is a very beautiful composition, having unity, graphic description, tenderness, and pathos. Now he also finished the third canto of the "Childe," and part of "Manfred," the monody on Sheridan, "Prometheus," the stanzas to Augusta, and other things. At the instance of Madame de Staël, he made overtures from Geneva to Lady Byron for a reconciliation, but she was obdurate; indeed, if the reports circulated in England by the tourists reached her ears, who can wonder at it? He was furious at her refusal, and revenged himself by writing "The Dream," the cruel *Incantation*, afterwards forming part of "Manfred," and the lines commencing—

"I am too well avenged! but 'twas my right."

These lines were not *published*, however, till after his death. Then there were the prayer for vengeance in the fourth canto of "Childe Harold," and the sarcasms about his "moral Clytemnestra," and "Miss Millpond" in "Don Juan." So vindictive and incontinent of his fury was he! Yet he had said to Moore, *just after the separation*—

"Don't attempt to defend me. If you succeeded in that, it would be a mortal, or an immortal offence. The fault was not—no, nor even the misfortune—in my choice—unless in choosing at all—for I do not believe—and I must say it in the very dregs of all this bitter business—that there ever was a better, or even a brighter, a kinder, or a more amiable and agreeable being than Lady Byron. I never had, nor can have, any reproach to make her while with me. Where there is blame it belongs to myself, and if I cannot redeem, I must bear it."

His detractors assert that he was a conscious hypocrite, only writing thus to curry favour with her, and induce her to relent. But he was incapable of this; he was too volatile and mercurial in his tempestuous and varying moods; a creature of impulse, true to each while it lasted. The savage denunciations were equally true to him when he wrote them—and evidently he had a much graver incentive to wrath against his wife now.

"Manfred" is one of the poet's finer works. I cannot conceive the kind of critical mind which discovers in Byron's tales, or in "Manfred," only the fantastic and insincere presentment of a sombre, theatrical lay-figure, now happily outworn. It was quite evidently the man himself—in one stern, unhappy, remorseful mood—notably so was "Manfred." I have already explained what I believe about its motive. The gloom and remorse of a solitary spirit, gathered into a dark cloud of miserable individual self-absorption, aware with semi-sympathy of the free unfettered glories and splendours of external nature, intellectually, even emotionally alive to them, yet undelivered from its prison, were never more powerfully presented—neither was passionate affection, nor the pathos of frantic grief for a beloved person, lost in death, with the damnation of whose soul the lover upbraids himself. But the dealings in magical arts of this proud Baron, shut alone in his castle, are not described with the power of Goethe in "Faust," which partly suggested "Manfred." The scenery, however, is very fine, notably the passages about the Alps and the Coliseum at Rome. The poem is virtually a monologue, though a hunter appears, and an old abbot. The passion of the invocation to lost Astarte is immense. This poetry is the expiring groan of self-centred individuality, that has not yet found freedom and happiness in ministering to others.

How profound and grandly expressed in the later cantos of "Childe Harold" are sympathy with, and absorption in, Nature! And those noble stanzas on the battle of Waterloo! "Childe Harold" is a record of travel over scenes familiar to all—made memorable by the presence of great men, and consecrated by noble deeds; it most felicitously combines glowing, and faithful, natural description with the record and retrospect of illustrious and world-famous historic actions, while it erects monu·ments of radiant beauty to the heroes who have taken part in them. Rome, Venice, Florence are enshrined in immortal verse; and there is a certain unity of mood maintained from the pervading presence of one reflective, restless, melancholy mind, in which all is mirrored. The nothingness and vanity of man, the eternity of nature, the hollowness of all earthly things, ay, even of the ideal, if sought for in the concrete individual object, that is the recurring theme; nothing satisfies, all passes. It is the modern Ecclesiastes.

But a grave defect of Byron's, and of Shelley's poetry alike, which shows itself in their lives also, is certainly the glorification of inconstant love. Philistinism, and Puritanism apart, this must surely be conceded. · So far indeed as their poetry made for love fuller and more inclusive than the ordinary domestic ideal provides, that was good and wholesome; but so far as it made for the repudiation of one, taken into the heart with deliberate responsibility, for the sake of a newer fancy, or even of an alleged more ‘complete "affinity," the tendency was degrading, because fatal to continuous harmony, and reliabllity of character, as also to all generous, protecting, self-mastering consistency in human life. For we are men and women, not mere ephemera of a moment. Thus Byron deserts Claire, and Shelley Harriet. Cruellest of all aristocracies that of intellect ! Shelley's may, or may not, have been a rather larger soul than Harriet's; but, after all, even the latter was presumably *human*. No true democrat would have acted so. If his *was* the larger soul, hers required the more protection from him. The good little grisette wife, and nurse of Heinrich Heine hardly knew that he had written poetry; but he didn't act the sulky cry-baby, or merciless prig with her on that account; he loved her as she deserved. Truly, the Ideal is not in one individual; yet the Ideal is not best approached through unfaithfulness to individuals, or neglect of common duties. To him who is faithful in the least things shall be entrusted the true riches. A man who writes verses is not necessarily a model of virtue, even if he has more in him than a mere knack of writing them for effect, or for pay. But Byron **was constant** in *friendship;* he felt that with *passion* entered fickleness and change ; so he says in his diary. Shelley deifies a new acquaintance to-day, and is for damning her to-morrow. But no doubt some poets may have more imagination and fancy than heart. In this light Byron represented himself to Lady Blessington.

At any rate, there is in Byron's poetry, as in Shelley's, a burning and inspired indignation with all shameful acquiescence in dead idols, and conventional standards, involving, as these may, the dwarfing and stunting of our human nature, the abasement and degradation of our myriad-fold, so-called "common," populations. This Samson cannot deliver himself, is himself a captive in the idol temple of our conventions ; can only grasp the huge pillars of our vaunted social fabric in mighty arms, and, bowing, drag chaos and ruin down upon himself, as upon the self-complacent, cynical society of Philistines, who have enthralled him. No gospel of organization, and edification has he to preach—he is the hurricane that overthrows, yet at the same time purifies. But one admits that a hurricane, or a whirlwind must be "gae ill to live with !" Saluting Lady Byron, therefore, and congratulating her on her escape from home-duties too hard for her, one passes on. Both husband and wife had much to learn ; but, perhaps, if they loved, they understand each other better now.

In October Byron set out with Hobhouse for Italy. They crossed the Simplon, and went to Milan by the Lago Maggiore. Through Verona they proceeded to Venice, where, partly from sheer recklessness and despair, Byron led a very dissipated life. Claire had made him promise

that Allegra should be brought up by either her or himself, by one of the parents, and had protested (I know
not why) against Mrs. Leigh's taking charge of the child
in England, as Byron wished. The mother came out
again with Shelley and Mary Godwin to Venice, but
previously Allegra had been sent to her father at his
Venetian place of residence. By August, 1818, when
Claire came to Venice with her friends, Byron seems
to have become utterly tired of her, and had taken
up with other mistresses. He believed that she and
Mary Godwin were living in promiscuous intercourse
with Shelley, and worse, that she and Shelley had placed
their own new-born child in a foundling hospital. That
story was spread by the malice of a female servant and
her husband, who had been in the employment of
Shelley and Mary, and who considered themselves
aggrieved by Shelley's dismissal of the husband. These
people told it to Consul-General Hoppner and his wife,
who again, believing it, told it to Byron. Byron, in
turn, very unwarrantably took it for gospel, and actually
informed his friend of the accusation when Shelley came
to Venice. Shelley was indignant, and wrote to Mary,
who was then away from him, asking her to write a disclaimer to Mrs. Hoppner, formerly a friend of the
Shelleys'. Mary sent this disclaimer to Shelley, and
the latter took it to Byron, asking him to forward it.
Shelley understood that Byron consented to do so ; yet
this very letter was found among Byron's papers after his
death, which fact has given rise to considerable comment
and controversy, and to savage abuse of Byron by the
devotees of Shelley. Why did not Byron forward that

letter? It was wrong. Yet we must remember Byron
had promised Hoppner not to tell Shelley what
Hoppner had told him. And it is by no means
clear to me that Byron himself believed the disclaimer.
I fear that he had conceived an aversion to poor
Claire, and was ready to credit any scandal about
her. Claire had unquestionably very free notions
about the intercourse of the sexes. And we know by
a letter Byron wrote *after* this date, that he did at any
rate still think that to Claire *had* been born another
child, which *she* had placed in a foundling hospital,
whether Shelley were the father of it or not. Moreover,
Shelley had not quite correctly represented to Mary what
Byron had said as to the details of the accusation, so
that Mary's disclaimer was not completely to the point.
He may only have promised to transmit the *substance* of
this letter to Hoppner, and may have done so—as Mr.
Jeaffreson has very plausibly argued—though I am bound
to add that Professor Dowden tells me he has in his
possession a letter from Lady Shelley, by which it would
appear that Mrs. Hoppner, in later years, when Lady
Shelley met her, did not know of any such disclaimer on
the part of Mary. Yet surely too much has been made
of this whole business of the letter![1] It was wrong no

---

[1] From Mrs. Julian Marshall's "Letters Mary Shelley," lately
published, as well as from other sources, it certainly appears that
Shelley and Claire were very intimate indeed. Only this conviction
on Byron's part about Claire's free way of life can at all palliate
his not contributing to her immediate necessities after their separation. Fletcher thought his master was trying to give some directions
about her when his speech became unintelligible at the last. (See
this same book.)

doubt on Byron's part if he did not send it, *or* impart the disclaimer to the Hoppners. But we now learn, by a recently published letter of Harriet Shelley, that *she* believed her husband to be living with "Godwin's two daughters" (see *Academy*, October 26, 1889, report of Shelley Society meeting)—and if Byron was not so certain that Mary's denial, though sincere, could be substantiated by the facts, as to the true nature of which she may, indeed, well have been ignorant, was the omission so *very* unpardonable in him? I know, on the best authority, that there exists a letter from Hoppner showing that, at all events, *he* was so absolutely convinced of the accuracy of the information he had received that he may well have imparted this strong conviction to Byron, with whom he was on very intimate terms at Venice, Byron no doubt being only too ready to believe anything against poor Claire. *Neither* poet, we must remember, held *very* "correct," and normal views about the exact and absolute demarcations of right and wrong in matters of sexual relation. To me, what does seem *more* wrong and pitiful is that Byron should so lightly have conceived an aversion to the mother of his child. Such inconstancy does appear inhuman—though it is common.

Byron would not listen to the mother's protest when she wrote remonstrating against his intention of sending Allegra to a Catholic convent at Bagni Cavallo, and proposed that the girl should be placed in a good English school, she herself paying all the charges. She accused Byron of breaking his word to her that one of the parents should keep the child, and urged that it was in convents

Italian women learned so much evil. She may have been mistaken ; but it was indeed hard that the mother was not allowed a voice in the disposal of her child, if Byron could not keep her under his own care. Yet, considering his way of life, *he* was hardly the person to take charge of Allegra; nor indeed was Theresa; and we have seen what he thought (truly or not) about her mother's lightness of character. Besides, he did not wish the child brought up by Claire, and the Shelleys, as a freethinker, but rather as a Catholic. As for his making no provision in his will for Claire, there is this to be said—he was Shelley's executor, and knew that Shelley himself had made a *very large* provision for her (might not this confirm him in the belief about Shelley, which Hoppner shared so strongly ?) Yet one would have thought that when Allegra died, some kind communication would have been made by the father to her (perhaps there was such a letter ?). Shelley gives a few interesting lines about the child in " Julian and Maddalo." Yet Byron seems to have consulted the best interests of Allegra in sending her to the convent, where Shelley went to see her, finding her happy and well treated—though she contracted an illness, and died there. Earlier, Byron had put her under the charge of Mrs. Hoppner. Her father was very fond of her, and of course provided for her in his will ; his letters clearly show he had done all he could for her welfare. When he first heard of her death he was almost speechless from emotion, and Theresa feared for his reason (April, 1822) ; but next day he said : "Allegra is dead ; she is more fortunate than we. It is God's will ; let us mention it no more." On her tablet in the church, near his favourite elm at Harrow, are the words : "*I shall go to her, but she shall not return to me.*" She seems to have had fine eyes, like her father, and to have been a playful, bright, vivacious child—in character, as in appearance, reminding people of the poet.

Byron formed, when he first went to Venice, an intimacy with Marianna Segati, the wife of a linendraper, in whose house he lodged. He describes her as a woman "like an antelope ; with Oriental eyes, wavy hair, a voice like the cooing of a dove, and the spirit of a Bacchante !" In December he took lessons in Armenian from the monks in the Armenian convent, glad to find, he says, " something craggy to break his mind upon." He got a bad attack of malarian fever, which was one of the causes which prevented him from returning to England in the spring of 1817, though he had entertained some intention of doing so. He now started on an expedition to Rome. At Ferrara he was inspired by the sight of the poet Tasso's prison to write his " Lament of Tasso," a fine, strongly realized work. Passing through Florence and Foligno, he met his old friends, Lord Lansdowne and Hobhouse, at Rome, in May. There he visited on horseback the celebrated historical sites, Albano, Tivoli, Frascati, the falls of Terni, and the Clitumnus ; recasting the first crude third act of " Manfred " into its actual form ; and sitting for his bust to Thorwaldsen. The sculptor told Hans Andersen that Byron, when he sat for it, put on an expression not usual to him. " ' Will you not sit still ?' said I, 'you need not assume that look.' 'That is my expression,' said Byron, 'In-

deed,' said I; and I then represented him as I wished.
When the bust was finished, he said: 'It is not at all
like me; my expression is more unhappy.'" And West,
the American, who painted the poet four years later, at
Leghorn, says he was a bad sitter; he assumed a countenance that did not belong to him, as though he were
thinking of a frontispiece for "Childe Harold." "The
dominant impression," says Prof. Brandes, of Copen-
hagen, "is that of some irresistible power."[1] Later,
the same sculptor executed the marble statue intended
for Westminster Abbey, and now in the library of
Trinity College, Cambridge. Byron gathered everywhere
also material for the fourth canto of "Childe Harold."
Toward the end of the month—after witnessing with horror
the guillotining of three bandits—we find him anxious to
get back to Marianna, and he soon established himself
with her at the Villa of La Mira, on the Brenta.

"Childe Harold," canto iv., was published early in
1818, with a dedication to Hobhouse, who supplied most
of the notes. Here came the terse, graphic descriptions
of the Falls of Velino, Clitumnus, the Coliseum, classic
in clear severity of outline, romantic in their feeling, and
rich imaginative detail; for this poet belonged half to
the old school, to the eighteenth century, whose chief
poet, Pope, he unduly exalted, although rightly admiring
him for sententious, epigrammatic expression of strong

---

[1] The original is in the possession of Lady Dorchester, the
daughter of Hobhouse, afterwards Lord Broughton. It is far less
pretty; a more rugged and powerful face than that of the Cambridge
statue, suggesting the very spirit of the storm. Passion, turbulence,
and pride are there.

thought, and the unerringly wounding power of his delicate satirical Toledo-blade. See his long letter to the Rev.
Lisle Bowles in defence of Pope. But his own verse has
a good deal of the rhetorical and didactic element which
he cared for in that master: it sparkles with epigram,
moreover. There is nothing allusive, prismatic, profound, or mystical in him ; no dream-like atmosphere, no
tender, blending haze—all is sharp, distinct, direct. The
ear-shattering trumpet arouses and quickens. There are
no low cadences to linger in the heart with pervading
sweetness. There is little of magic and mystery ; and he
is brilliant, rather than tender. He had affinities with
Dryden, and Pope—great poets of the town, of good
society, and satirical. Moreover, he observed the "unities" in drama, like the classical school. Nor, indeed,
were his sympathies with unity of subject matter, and
classical treatment in art, altogether misplaced. His own
desultory genius felt the need of dykes and barriers—of a
kind of blow-pipe, as it were, for concentration's sake.
Yet "Don Juan" is one great revolt in matter and form.
Byron's is a poetry of transition; and Byron was the
great popular champion of the Romantic movement, and
return to *Nature*, inaugurated by Chatterton, Cowper,
Blake, and Burns—though we perhaps have hardly given
Goldsmith, Gray, and Thomson enough credit for their
very charming and *affectionate* pictures of Nature, painted
as they are with classical decision of outline, lucidity,
and repose. In this respect Byron partly follows
them. "The Dying Gladiator" is unsurpassed for
accurately penetrated truth, as well as for profound
human pathos, the more poignant for its severely Dan-

tesque breadth and brevity of treatment. While Shelley
places an exquisite iridescent halo of words *about* his
subject matter, Byron transfixes the heart of it with a
line. Let it, after this, be fully granted to Mr. Swinburne, and his fellow Shelleyans, that Byron said "lay"
when he should have said "lie" (though so did Shelley
in those splendid Apennine lines of his !), and perpetrated
bad blank verse in his dramas—got also into a muddle
with his metaphors anent the "young Earthquake," spoil-
ing some of his lyrics with prosaic epithets, and indifferent metre. What can be worse than "*whose actions I
ape*," for instance, in the "Deformed Transformed"?—(!)

His lyrics have not the rare ethereal and melodious
subtlety of Shelley's. Some are wooden, common—some
jar, and trail their wings in dust—yet who has written
finer lyrics than "Sennacherib," "Oh ! Snatched Away!"
"And thou art dead," "She walks in Beauty," "The
Isles of Greece," "Could Love for ever," "So we'll go
no more a-roving"? They are more germane to the
common loving human heart than Shelley's—firmer,
clearer, stronger. Is it criticism to rave against a poet's
faults, and ignore his beauties? If so, then every
reviewer would be a critic—which is absurd. As to
descriptive poetry, the lines commencing—

> "There is a pleasure in the pathless woods,
> There is a rapture on the lonely shore,"

and the Address to the Ocean, whatever their faults, can
perish only with the language ; the same is true of the
best things in "Don Juan," with their strange, fascinating,
abrupt, forked flashes of cynicism, shooting through the

vivid or tender colours and shapes presented. What can be nobler than the apostrophe to Rome, as " Niobe of Nations," in the first canto of " Childe Harold " ? Even the personal passages are full of force in their passionate invective, wrung from his great agony, like the agony of waters in that boiling cauldron or Phlegethon of Terni.

The summer and early autumn of 1817 were spent at La Mira, where he used to ride along the banks of the Brenta with the few Englishmen of his acquaintance. The temper of Marianna did not improve, and her lover discovered that she had sold the diamonds he gave her. Her pretty sister-in-law one day sought an interview with Byron, and Marianna, suddenly entering the room, seized her by the hair, and gave her sixteen slaps on the face, which caused her to fly in terror. He now sent the frail fair back to her husband, and established himself at the Palazzo Mocenigo on the Grand Canal, where his sensual excesses gave much occasion for scandal (especially during the Carnival), even in Venetian society. His debaucheries brought him to the verge of the grave, moreover—together with low diet and fasting, alternated with immoderate drinking.

To Marianna succeeded Margarita Cogni, the wife of a baker, who proved as accommodating as the draper, and as Count Guiccioli afterwards. Byron describes her as a handsome virago, with brown shoulders and black hair, with the strength of an Amazon, a face like Faustina's, and the figure of a Juno—tall and energetic as a Pythoness. She reduced the expenses of his household, kept everything in good order, was very violent, and also very devout, crossing herself three times at the *Angelus.*

This is the woman who has been called Byron's
Fornarina. He gives a graphic and amusing account
of a scene, in which she figured as heroine :—

"In the autumn one day, going to the Lido with my gondoliers,
we were overtaken by a heavy squall, and the gondola put in peril,
hats blown away, boat filling, oars lost, tumbling sea, thunder, rain
in torrents, and wind unceasing. On our return, after a tight
struggle, I found her on the open steps of the palace on the Grand
Canal, with her great black eyes flashing through her tears, and the
long dark hair which was streaming, drenched with rain, over her
brows. She was perfectly exposed to the storm, and the wind
blowing her dress about her thin figure, and the lightning flashing
round her, made her look like Medea alighted from her chariot, or
the sibyl of the tempest, that was rolling around her, the only living
thing within hail at that moment, except ourselves. On seeing me
safe, she did not greet me as might have been expected ; but calling
out to me '*Ah! can, della Madonna, xe esto il tempo per anda'r al'
Lido,*' ran into the house, and solaced herself with scolding the
boatmen for not foreseeing the '*temporale.*' Her joy at seeing me
again was moderately mixed with ferocity, and gave me the idea of
a tigress over her recovered cubs."

Some months later she became too violent, threw
plates and knives about, and snatched caps from the
heads of women if they only looked at her lover in
public places. On Byron telling her she must go, she
threatened him, and threw herself in the darkness of
night into the canal, though she was rescued by his
boatmen.

The boatmen said that Byron would have made a
first-rate gondolier, but was spoiled by being a poet and
a lord ; they called him the "English fish," from his
habit of frequent swimming, and used to say that he
"dived for his poetry !" He now wrote "Beppo,"

"Mazeppa," and the early books of "Don Juan."
"Mazeppa" is full of spirit and "go"—strongly out-
lined, and graphic in delineation. "Beppo" is a slight,
but very charmingly written, Venetian sketch; and herein
the poet first struck upon the vein that was to prove so
full of rich poetic ore in "Don Juan." The measure of
both poems was suggested by Frere's "Whistlecraft";
but the poetry, measure and all, was indeed the out-
come of his readings in Italian poetry, passed through
his own powerful and original idiosyncrasy—of Pulci,
Casti, Berni, Ariosto, Baffo, but especially of Buratti, a
living poet, whose satires were lent to him in MS., being
too bold and free for publication. Silvio Pellico had
told him of them. These poems were a fascinating
hodge-podge of grave and gay. Everything that Byron
thought and felt could go into those wonderful verses
with little or no plan—exquisite description, tenderness,
pathos, sly humour, rollicking adventure, scathing satire.
How accurate the knowledge of woman, and of the
world, in Donna Julia's letter, and in the sketch of
Lady Adelaide Amundeville! The episode of Don Juan
and Donna Julia is, however, borrowed from "Faublas";
the cynically told story of the shipwreck, with the
touching incident of the two fathers, being likewise taken
almost *verbatim* from prose narratives, as we have seen.
But the idyl of Haidee and Juan in the Cycladean island,
contains some of the most exquisite love-poetry in the
world, flushed with the freshness of early morning,
played over by, and lustrous in the well-spring of young
passion, for background the calm Ionian Sea of that
fair island, margined by flowery hills, and hollowed into

solitary sea-grottoes, all in warm vernal sunshine or
starry twilight. The voluptuous beauty of the harem
scenes is Ovidian in luscious warmth, and, where
" boyish blood is mantling," may assuredly be fraught
with danger. But " Don Juan " is not always *poetry*
proper. The trivial, semi-satirical banter, and indiscriminate chatter about everything or nothing are occasionally tedious, yet generally clever and amusing, flashing
ever and anon with diamond-like couplets, or lines
facet-cut into epigram. Playful it is, with the playfulness
of a tiger. The English cantos toward the end gave
much offence in England, yet abound with merited
invective and sarcasm—verbal thongs now and again
steeped in vitriol, laid upon the stolidly self-complacent
shoulders of a hard and cruel respectability, often idle,
unproductive, loafing on the starved labour of nobler
men and women.

I admit, of course, that Byron, who lashed " cant,"
canted himself now and again. But he felt, and could
tell of, its hatefulness. Carlyle, the querulous, preached
stoicism with profound conviction, and burning words.
How Byron scorns the bloody pastime of war, all the
baubles and gewgaws of our vain-glory, even fame, less
innocent toys of man's maturer years! And what
mastery here over rhythm and rhyme, over grave and
gay moods, rapidly passing into one another! Of
course the poem aroused much good and sterling
moral indignation; for it was anti-domestic, and made
little of the homely virtues, fidelity, and constancy,
foundations of social happiness. It was undoubtedly
too cynical, too much of a mere man of the world's

poem, a result of his depravation; it was in parts too
sensuous, and bitter with disbelief in men and women.
Still, as Mr. Morley says, even the misanthropy is a sort
of inverted social solicitude.   But—

> " Let us have wine and women, wine and laughter ;
>   Sermons and soda-water the day after ! "

does not indeed express an ideal view of women !   The
best and cleverest women of the present day, in which
we have developed the idea of their rights, and of their
equality with men, are not generally found in the ranks
of his defenders; he sneered at "the Blues"; he had
quarrelled with a learned woman in the person of his
wife; and assuredly Madame de Staël was not a *physically*
favourable specimen of a clever woman, though he liked
and respected her.   The women he had met in the
society he frequented were not as a rule of the highest
type.   Nor had he been educated to respect them.   Yet
the very affection and sympathy he felt, inconstant
though he was, for even the lowest of those poor
creatures with whom he formed connections, which
Mr. Jeaffreson imputes as a fault to him, is, I fancy, just
the one redeeming point about his sexual immorality.
His sister, however, might have given him pause in
his unfavourable estimate of the sex.   But he has
drawn in the person of Adah, Cain's sister, one of the
most exquisite sketches of a good and self-sacrificing
woman ever drawn by any writer.   And the lines about
Aurora Raby, in " Don Juan," are of ideal loveliness.
Clever, cultivated, beautiful women were not very common then ; there were no " girl graduates in their golden

hair." Still, "Don Juan" was so very much alive,
not in the least the work of an enervated debauchee!
for all its cynicism and despair it was a young poem,
full of fun, salt and fresh, and vigorous. Wherefore it is
not uninvigorating; while the measure of it rushes and
bounds like sea waves. "Don Juan," "Beppo," and the
"Vision of Judgment," are written in ottava rima,
of which measure the poet is absolute master. "If
things are farcical," he said to Trelawny, during
their voyage to Greece, "they will do for 'Don Juan';
if heroical, you shall have another canto of 'Childe
Harold.'" There was no plan in either poem, and
either might have gone on for ever. Still, the range of
flight, and sweep of pinion, in "Don Juan" are immense.
It is certainly not true that Byron could only paint one
man, and one woman, as Macaulay alleges. He had not,
indeed, as yet displayed much dramatic power; he could
not get out of himself. But, then, he had more than
one personality *in* himself, and could represent each
and either of these: Conrad, Lara, Cain, Manfred, were
made out of one mood of himself; Don Juan and
Sardanapalus, out of another. Again, Gulnare is the
fierce, passionate woman; Haidee, the young, innocent,
loving girl; Donna Julia, Lady Adelaide, are women of
the world; Aholibamah is hot and haughty; Zarina and
Angiolina are kindly, virtuous, dignified; while Adah
stands apart, a high and holy figure of ideal loveliness.
Of "Don Juan" Shelley writes: "It sets him not only
above, but far above, all the poets of the day. Every word
has the stamp of immortality." If an epic can be without plan, then "Don Juan" may be regarded as the epic

of that unsettled period of turbulence, passion, war,
adventure, unrest, universal question. Yet would not
the poet have concluded it, had he survived the liberation
of Greece, with the hero's devotion of himself to the
cause of human emancipation, after having exhausted
self-seeking experience, and found the mere pursuit of
personal pleasure unsatisfying to the truer self? That,
at least, was the history of his own career, and he is
reflected faithfully in his work. He told Medwin Juan
should die on the guillotine. His descriptive powers
here attain their apotheosis—in the pictures of "Newstead," "The Siege," "The Shipwreck," "The Island";
and what tender pathos in such passages as the "Ave
Maria," and "Oh! Hesperus!" as in the lines about
Nero! The magnificent "Isles of Greece," too, are
here, with their comical birth out of, and relapse into,
buffoonery. But he says :—

> " If I laugh at any mortal thing,
> 'Tis that I may not weep."

And that he has

> " Nothing planned,
> Except to be a moment merry."

Life, after all, is half comic, half tragic; tears and
smiles succeed one another very rapidly over that
mystical face of Nature. This poet throws all remorselessly into his crucible or melting pot, the common
polished metal of decorous convention, and political
tradition, ay, even the fine gold of fair, time-honoured
domesticities and moralities : he is Siva the destroyer

in this "Epic of Nihilism," and "omnivorous appetite"; all is in flux and passes; yet out of the seething mass shall not even nobler and more vital forms be moulded ?

I believe that Byron did once, and only once, love utterly and perfectly, and that this love was for his sister. What are all the prurient scandals of conventional propriety in the face of this certainty ? He loved, and was beloved—"the most angelic being that ever trod God's earth," he calls her; and she, while regretting his faults, ay, blaming them candidly to his face, was always tender and loving to him. She is indignant at Lady Byron's harsh portraiture of him, drawn after his death. *She* was his good angel, and he knew it. For the rest, Augusta was a good mother and wife. It was she who put up the humble marble tablet in the little church of Hucknall, near their beloved Newstead, where their ancestors lie buried (and now herself, with his dear child). Her sweet, simple, warmly affectionate words in her letters to Hodgson, after Byron's death, make one reverence and love her. In one of these she mentions looking at the embalmed remains when they arrived in England: "It was awful to behold what I parted with convulsed, absolutely convulsed with grief, now cold and inanimate, and so altered—not a vestige of what he was." (Lady Byron had declined to have anything to say to the disposal of the body, when applied to.)

When Shelley visited Venice, he lived in a villa near Este, which Lord Byron lent him, having hired it from the Hoppners. He describes the poet as looking the

worse for his sexual excesses. He had become very
fat, and wore his hair, which was beginning to get thin
and turn grey, quite long. So also Leigh Hunt says,
rather later. But the description in "Julian and Maddalo," and in Shelley's letters, shows that his great
intellectual powers had not degenerated. Of Count
Maddalo Shelley says :—

> "He is a person of the most consummate genius, and capable, if he
> would direct his energies to such an end, of becoming the redeemer
> of his degraded country. I say that Maddalo is proud, because I
> can find no other word to express the concentred. and impatient
> feelings which consume him ; but it is on his own hopes and affec-
> tions only that he seems to trample, for in social life no human
> being can be more gentle, patient, and unassuming than Maddalo.
> He is cheerful, frank, and witty. His more serious conversation is
> a kind of intoxication ; men are held by it as by a spell. He has
> travelled much, and there is an inexpressible charm in his relations
> of his adventures in different countries."

Against the ill-conditioned, spiteful narrative of Leigh
Hunt, we are to set this testimony of Shelley; Leigh
Hunt so exaggerated Byron's canker of worldliness as to
represent it as if this were the whole man ; being under
many obligations to him, and heartily hating a lord. But
Hobhouse, and the Guiccioli, Moore, Hodgson, Harness,
and his later friends in Greece, are to be heard on the
other side.

Byron and Shelley rode together on the Lido, and practised with pistols, both being good shots. The inquisi-
tive English tourist used to go and see them alighting
from their gondola. Byron kept his horses in a stable
on this narrow strip of land. That is also the place

where he wished to be buried had he died at Venice; for he writes :—

"Some of the epitaphs at Ferrara pleased me more than the more splendid monuments at Bologna ; for instance :—

> ' Martini Luigi
> Implora pace . . .
> Lucrezia Picini
> Implora eterna quieta.'

Can anything be more full of pathos? These few words say all that can be said or sought. The dead have had enough of life ; all they wanted was rest, and this they implore. There is all the helplessness, and humble hope, and death-like prayer, that can arise from the grave—*implora pace.* I hope whoever may survive me, and shall see me put into the foreigner's burying-ground at the Lido, within the fortress of the Adriatic, will see these two words and no more put over me. I trust they won't think of pickling me, and bringing me home to Clod, or Blunderbuss Hall ! "

But it was in connection with Shelley that the worldly taint in Byron most remarkably appeared. For Shelley he expresses the greatest admiration and respect in his private letters, for his intense, earnest, benevolent character, as for his intellect and conversation, and even for some of his poetry. Yet when Trelawny, riding one day with Byron, asked him why he did not do Shelley, who remained absolutely unknown and unappreciated, public justice, the former shrugged his shoulders, and said it would never do to " praise the Snake " (so the friends jokingly called him). " If we puffed the Snake, it might not turn out a profitable investment. All trades have their mysteries. If we crack up a popular author, he repays us in the same coin, principal and interest—if we introduce Shelley to our readers, they might draw comparisons, and they are odious !" This is disgusting. But then remember three things : First, what instance does one know of a popular praising an unpopular author of high merit, and bringing him forward? That is rare indeed : the virtue involved is well-nigh super-human ; quite a counsel of perfection for the literary character, which is usually obliged, from a professional point of view, to reserve its slender stock of virtue for words, a very little bit remaining over for life. And, therefore, is double honour due to those noble excep-tions we are sometimes privileged to witness; as when Coleridge preached his friend Wordsworth. Secondly, Byron did praise Coleridge's " Christabel " warmly, getting well abused in the *Edinburgh* (the great *arbiter literarum* of that day) for his pains,—"Christabel" appear-ing to this "Sir Oracle " a ridiculous poem, very inferior to the " Pleasures of Memory." Thirdly, it seems doubtful how far Byron admired Shelley's poetry—though Shelley says, " I despair of rivalling Lord Byron, as well I may ; the sun has extinguished the glow-worm." But Shelley was more catholic than Byron, and had a sweeter, gentler, humbler spirit.

In August, when Hobhouse came to see him, at La Mira, a very remarkable document concerning the separation was drawn up, *in Hobhouse's presence,* including the declaration that Hobhouse had proposed, at the time on his friend's behalf, to go into court. The persons understood to be the legal advisers of Lady Byron had declared their lips to be sealed upon the cause of the separation. "They are not sealed up by me, and the greatest favour they can confer upon me will be to open them."

In October, 1819, Tom Moore visited Byron at La Mira, and went to Venice with him.   Moore records that his person and face had grown fatter, and the latter had suffered mostly by the change, " having lost through enlargement of the features some of that refined and spiritualized look that had in other times distinguished it; but although less romantic, he appeared more humorous."   One gets the impression of quite uproarious spirits from this account; the friends are full of old London adventures and jokes, very like a couple of schoolboys out for a holiday.   He insisted on Moore taking up his quarters in his Palazzo; and, as they were groping their way through dark halls, the host called out, " Keep clear of the dog !   Take care of the monkey, or he will fly at you ! "

At this time he sat up very late at night writing his poetry, and got up very late in the morning.   But the most hideous lies were invented here, as usual, about his misconduct, being malignant distortions of real facts, or else pure inventions.   " Of this I am certain," says Hoppner, " that I never witnessed greater kindness than in Lord Byron."   He was provoked to cynicism (and this was partly affected) by the lies in question, and the implacability with which he was treated ; though his countrymen and countrywomen avoided him, many of them would force their way into his rooms on the sly (having bribed his servants to admit them), that they might catch a glimpse of the monster.   Such are the penalties of popularity; though it certainly *heartens* a man for work, and to revise his work. But nothing could be more conducive to the self-conscious attitudinizing with which Byron is reproached than the knowledge that he was the cynosure, or target for all eyes, malicious, admiring, or only curious.

Hoppner says his servants were devoted to him, and even when they misbehaved he would banter rather than seriously reprove them; while hardly ever could he be induced to discharge one of them. He was always ready to assist the distressed, and was most unostentatious in his charities; he contributed largely by weekly and monthly allowances to persons whom he had never seen, and who, as the money reached them by other hands, did not even know who was their benefactor. Shelley says that his income at this time amounting to about £4,000 a year, he gave away £1,000 in charity.

As to his financial position, he was now better off by the sale of · Newstead to Colonel Wildman, in 1818; and later, on Lady Noel's death in 1822, when he was living at Pisa, he came into his share of the Wentworth property, which was to be divided between him and his wife, on his taking the name of Noel. Arbitrators were appointed to arrange their respective shares. He has been blamed for touching Lady Byron's money, but her fortune of £10,000 he could not touch, because it was settled upon her. And it is hardly obvious why he should be blamed, since *she* had not forborne to avail herself of the settlement he had made upon her, which was a particularly large one, and of which she took the full benefit up to the time of her death. Among his restless romantic projects was the purchase of a Greek island, where he wanted to establish a kind of Pachalik. But, in fact, a large part of this money was devoted to the popular cause of liberty in Italy, and finally to the liberation of Greece.

It was at this juncture that the celebrated autobiography first appeared on the scene. "A short time after dinner," says Moore, "Byron left the room, and returned, carrying in his hand a white leather bag. 'Look here,' he said, holding it up, 'this would be worth something to Murray, though you, I dare say, would not give sixpence for it.' 'What is it?' I asked. 'My life and adventures,' he answered. 'It is not a thing that can be published during my lifetime, but you may have it if you like. There, do whatever you please with it.'" In December, 1820, Byron sent several more sheets of memoranda from Ravenna ; and in the following year suggested an agreement by which Murray paid over to Moore, who was then in difficulties, £2,000 for the right of publishing the whole, under the condition, among others, that Lady Byron should see the "Memoirs," and have the right of reply to anything that might seem to her objectionable. But she declined to have anything to do with them. With her consent and Augusta's, Hobhouse's desire that they should be burned was carried out by Murray, Moore then refunding the £2,000 to Murray ; the latter, however, paid him 4,000 guineas for editing "Byron's Life and Correspondence," which, if only because it contains the poet's own delightful letters, must always remain invaluable. Moore has, perhaps, embodied in the "Life". what is most important and reliable in the "Memoirs ;"

yet, as they were Byron's own version of the separation, one regrets their complete destruction.

While in Venice, he suffered from a sharp attack of malarial fever, to which he was very much predisposed, both from constitution and habit of life.

CHAPTER V.

WE now come to the Countess Guiccioli, who swayed the poet's affections until his death in Greece. She was the daughter of Count Gamba, a poor Romagnese noble, brought up in a convent, and married by her parents at sixteen to a rich widower of sixty, Count Guiccioli, who had been a friend of Alfieri. She had some reading and taste for literature; was a pretty blonde, with very fair skin, and a profusion of fine yellow hair.

Byron first saw her at a reception of Madame Albrizzi, but was not introduced to her till April, 1819, at a party of Countess Benzoni. "Suddenly," says Moore, "the young Italian found herself inspired with a passion, of which till that moment her mind could not have formed the least idea. She had thought of love as an amusement, and now became its slave." Till the middle of the month they met daily, and, when the Count left with her for Ravenna, she wrote Byron a series of impassioned letters, entreating him to follow her, for they had become lovers before she started; an irrepressible yearning for her lover made her ill on the road—ill also when she arrived at Ravenna.

Accordingly he set out on the 2nd of June, travelling by Padua, Ferrara, and Bologna, and on the banks of the Po, wrote the verses commencing:

> " River that rollest by the ancient walls,"

among which are the now familiar words—

> "A stranger loves the lady of the land,"

and—

> "My blood is all meridian."

He arrived at Ravenna ostensibly as a poet attracted thither by poetic interest in Dante. At his hotel he soon received a visit from the Count, who begged him to come to the bedside of his dying wife. Byron, assuring the Count how much he looked forward to the pleasure of *his*, the Count's, society, naturally lost no time in acceding to this request, and his visits appeared to do the young bride much good. The scenes that took place daily between this curious trio, at the lady's bedside, certainly partook of the nature of comedy! While the husband was present all was very grave and solemn, but the notes of the tune seem to have become gayer when the trio had dwindled to a duet! The elderly husband's complaisance puzzled the lover, and he writes to Murray: "I can't make him out at all; he visits me frequently, and takes me out (like Whittington the Lord Mayor) in a coach and *six* horses." It would seem, from what happened later, that the Count wanted to get money out of Byron; but the latter had become rather fond of it, having announced in " Don

Juan" that he meant to take up with "Avarice, that good old gentlemanly vice." *A cavalier servente* (a lover) for a married woman was indeed a sort of recognized institution in Italy. But then it was necessary that the lady should not leave the protection of her husband's roof. Now, however, as the hour approached for the married pair to migrate to Bologna, Byron entreated his mistress to fly with him. Theresa would do anything for him but this; had she done this, her people would have counted her so entirely among the fallen; but she actually proposed in desperation the expedient resorted to by Juliet, of feigning death and being buried; however, this proved unnecessary, and Byron was allowed to join the Guicciolis at Bologna.

His munificence to the poor of Ravenna was great, and they sorrowfully mourned his departure, covering him with blessings. Here he rode in the pine-forest, alluded to in the lines commencing "Sweet hour of Twilight," in "Don Juan;" and wrote the "Prophecy of Dante," on the whole the finest of his reflective, semi-dramatic compositions. We feel that the mantle of the grand, severe, lonely exile, whose spirit had brooded sorrowful amid these scenes, and whose tomb is here, had indeed descended upon him now. What scorn of all that is low and little, what awful inward loneliness, and proud self-infolding of solitary genius, rejected by the world—vengeance invoked on his enemies, tempered anon by Christian submission to God, and self-scorn for the too frequent pettiness of his own feeling! What love of country, and ardour of prophetic faith in her dear future! How beautiful the passage, where the exile's heart yearns to his native Florence, though she has cast him from her, in the first canto, commencing—

"To envy every dove his nest and wings ! "

Some of Byron's grandest imagery, loftiest aspiration, most majestic rhetoric are here, though indeed the terza rima cannot always be pronounced successful. But this is a noble definition of true poetry—

"Many are poets, but without the name ;
For what is poesy but to create,
From overfeeling good or ill?—— "

reminding one of a later writer, Ibsen—"To write poetry is to hold a doomsday over oneself."

At Bologna he experienced a kind of hysterical seizure from violent emotion, while sitting with Theresa at the theatre, witnessing a performance of Alfieri's " Mirrha "—like that former one which led his charitable *sposa* to fancy him mad, on a similar occasion in London. Here he wrote his amusing letter to the Editor of " My grandmother's review, the *British*," and had a violent quarrel with an officer about an unsound horse the latter had sold him, after warranting it sound. He proposed pistols, and, as the man objected, swords, which he had by him, on the spot; but the lieutenant seems to have "funked," and rushed out of the house, crying "Murder!" However, Byron says, "I have been in a rage these two days, and am still bilious therefrom," (see the description of Lara's rages). And he writes to

Murray (as also in his own private journal) that he often feared he should go mad—referring to Swift's strange pause, in one of his daily walks, before a fine tree that was dead at the top, uttering the prediction that he too should "die from the top." Spirits, he said, made him sullen and ferocious, which explains, together with deranged liver, a great deal of his bad conduct to his wife.

When Theresa and the Count left Bologna to visit some of their other property, Byron used to go daily to her rooms, and sit there at the hour of his usual visit to her, reading and writing in her books; in one, a "Corinne," he wrote a very charming little love-note; indeed, most of his letters to her are full of passionate affection. "You will recognize the handwriting of him who passionately loved you, and you will divine that over a book which was yours he could only think of love. In that word, beautiful in all languages, but most so in yours, *Amor mio*, is compressed my existence here and hereafter." "I love you, and cannot cease to love you." But dreamfully gazing into the waters of a fountain in her beautiful garden, he bursts into tears when he thinks of what unhappiness his love may bring on her, since his love has always been fatal to its object. He sent for Allegra to be with him here—an English lady having meanwhile offered to adopt her, if Byron would renounce all parental authority over her; but he would not. Soon after the return of the Guicciolis, Theresa left Bologna for Venice with her lover—strangely enough, with her husband's consent—and he settled her at La Mira, living under the same roof with her; she had thus taken the step which proclaimed to the world that she was the poet's mistress. There can be not the smallest doubt of her passionate devotion to him, and she had been offered up as a sacrifice by her friends to the rich, elderly widower. Here she received a letter from her husband, begging her to get Byron to lend him £1,000! But Byron "did not see it." He was still most generous, and gave his money liberally in great causes, yet he always showed a commendable objection to being swindled. Then the Count came and insisted on her going back to Ravenna with him. Venetian society being scandalized at Theresa's conduct, and showing it, Byron himself, feeling strongly that he was compromising and injuring the lady whom he loved, persuaded her to go. But soon after her arrival she became so very seriously ill that not only the husband, but her father and uncle, invited Byron to join them all at Ravenna! He had been on the very point of returning to England. Many things, however, besides his passion for Theresa, made him hesitate. And Trelawny insists that irresolution was a marked trait in his character. That would be likely in so many-mooded a man. Theresa had just nursed him through another attack of malarial fever (in the delirium of which he had written verses). He was, Moore tells us, quoting from a lady's account, ready dressed for the journey to England, his boxes on board the gondola, his gloves and cap on, and even his little cane in his hand, "when my lord declares that, if it should strike one—which it did—before everything was in order, he would not go that day." "It is evident that he had not the heart to go." So, instead, he returned to

Ravenna and his mistress, where her family actually
organized a great gathering of three hundred of the best
people in Romagna, with music and dancing, to do him
honour! "The Guicciolis' object seemed to be," he
writes, "to parade her foreign friend as much as possible;
and, faith! if she seemed to glory in so doing, it was not
for me to be ashamed of it. Nobody seemed surprised.
The Vice-Legate, and all the other vices, were as polite
as could be." Moreover, the lover, at the husband's
own invitation, took possession of a suite of rooms in
the Palazzo Guiccioli—for which he paid a good rent!
What La Guiccioli said to her *cicisbeo* one day (in
Italian), on seeing him pensive, is, however, worth trans-
lating: "You are thinking of your wife; your wife is
the woman you love, and have always loved."

Count Guiccioli now endeavoured to obtain a divorce,
but it was not easy; public opinion was against him,
since he declared he had not hitherto known that Byron
was his wife's lover, whereas it was very clear that he had
connived at the *liaison*. Byron was warned that, though
the husband was not a fighting man, he was suspected
of two assassinations by deputy, and therefore the poet
was advised always to go out armed: henceforth he rode
with his pistols ready. A Papal decree of separation,
at the instance of Theresa herself, was obtained in July,
on condition that the lady should reside in her father's
house, or return to a convent; but this engagement was
afterwards violated. Byron made the Palazzo Guiccioli
itself a storehouse for arms, and a centre for the Car-
bonaro conspiracies against Austrian rule. The Carbonari
met together there to plot, and he offered to defend the

house as a fortress against the enemy, if necessary—
(whether Count Guiccioli approved is doubtful). In
April he wrote, "We are on the verge of a row here.
Last night they have placarded all the city walls with
'*Up with the Republic!*' and '*Death to the Pope!*'"
"*Down with the Nobility!*" also was scrawled on their
houses. The Commandant of the Austrian troops, a
man obnoxious to the people, was found riddled with
slugs close to Byron's door, who had him carried into
the house to be nursed, and he died there. Theresa
herself and her family, the Counts Gamba, father and
son, favoured the national movement. Count Pietro
Gamba, her brother, a young soldier, naturally prejudiced
against his sister's foreign lover, on making his acquaintance about this time, conceived so enthusiastic an affection and veneration for him that he accompanied him to
Greece, and wrote in the most ardent terms of the poet's
greatness and nobility of character after his death. The
malicious Hunt hints that his nerves were shaky; doubtless he had "accesses of nerves," whose firmness he had
recklessly impaired, as he confessed to Trelawny; but the
latter, no less than the whole of Byron's own life, bears
witness to his courage. The man of imaginative sensibility
who conquers his fears is far more to be honoured than
the mere callous savage, or the bulldog whose blind
ferocity cannot even conjure up the idea of danger or
suffering. The poet was appointed *capo*, or chief, of the
"Mericani," who were the fighting section of the Carbonari.

But spies came to the secret councils at the palace, as
well as conspirators, and, deceived by one of these, Byron

confided to him a letter offering a thousand louis to the insurrectionary party at Naples, and service even as humblest volunteer. "We are going to fight next month," he writes, "if the Huns don't cross the Po." His diary has an interesting passage, in which he chronicles sitting up replenishing the fire one night, reading, and feeding his many pet animals, but expecting to be called out to fight at any moment. "I always loved a row from a boy," he says. But this movement of 1820-1 came to nothing, and the Gambas were banished from the Romagna, Theresa, according to the articles of her separation, having to follow them to Florence. Byron, however, lingered some months, with his friends of the national party, and the poor who loved him; since, as an Englishman of rank, *he* had not been banished, though the Government was making it very hot for him.

It has been objected that he admired Napoleon, and that his Liberalism was not genuine. But he admired Napoleon for his genius, and demonic force of character; lamenting that he was beaten "by three stupid legitimate old dynasty boobies of regular sovereigns." "What right have we to prescribe laws to France?—poising straws on kings' noses, instead of wringing them off." "The king-times are fast finishing! there will be blood shed like water, and tears like mist, but the peoples will conquer in the end. I shall not live to see it, but I foresee it." "Give me a republic. Look in the history of the earth—Rome, Greece, Holland, Venice, France, America, our too short Commonwealth—and compare it with what they did under masters." To Wellington he says—

" You might have freed fallen Europe from the unity
   Of tyrants, and been blessed from shore to shore."

His enthusiasm for Italy inspired much of "Harold,"
"The Lament of Tasso," the "Ode on Venice,"
and "The Prophecy of Dante," in which he urged
Italians to seek that national unity which is now
achieved. He admired Washington also, but was not
bigoted in favour of any one form of government as adapted
to all possible conditions. It is very odd how few people
seem able to comprehend mixed motives. A man must
be either all angel or all devil to force himself into
their understandings ; yet surely even the majority act
from mixed motives, and are not always self-consistent.
That Byron cared for personal display, as for power and
fame, to be *aut Cæsar, aut nullus*—also loving excitement
and a row—is true ; that he even childishly delighted in
baubles, may be granted to those bitten with some insane
desire to "judge all nature from her feet of clay." The
individuality of the man was pronounced and aggressive;
he was no saint, no Gordon, no Damien ; but, as Col.
John Hay says, in his noble ballad about Jim Bludsoe,
"Christ ain't a-going to be too hard on a man that died
for men." Cannot we honour also a Cromwell, a
Nelson, a Mirabeau ? Is not much good and great work
done in the world by men who, in the Pantheon of their
divided worship, build one altar to the ideal, another to
human welfare, and a third to personal aggrandizement ?
There is just as little doubt that Byron cared for human
welfare, and for the ideal, as that he cared for personal
honour. His poetry, his life, his conversations, his
letters prove it. Like Alfieri, and Rousseau, he had

taken for his motto, "I am of the opposition." Partly like his more firm and consistent, though less amiable and humane heroes, he "raised the humble but to bend the proud." That he became, however, more and more capable of merging himself in human and unselfish causes is fully shown by his wise, devoted, and humane conduct in Greece, as by the testimony of all those who surrounded him toward the end.

Byron, requesting Shelley's aid and counsel, by his assistance and Theresa's, induced the Gambas to take up their residence in Pisa, rather than at Geneva, and to Pisa the poet followed them. Shelley, writing in August from Ravenna, says :—

"I arrived last night at ten o'clock, and sat up talking with Lord B. till five this morning. . . . He was delighted to see me. He has completely recovered his health, and lives a life totally the reverse of that which he led in Venice. . . . Poor fellow, he is now immersed in politics and literature. We talked a great deal of poetry and such matters, and, as usual, differed, I think, more than ever. He affects to patronize a system of criticism fit only for the production of mediocrity ; and although all his finer poems and passages have been produced in defiance of this system, yet I recognize the pernicious effects of it in the 'Doge of Venice.' . . . Lord B. is greatly improved in every respect, in genius, in temper, in moral views, in health, and happiness. His connection with La Guiccioli has been an inestimable benefit to him. . . . Lord B. and I are excellent friends ; and were I reduced to poverty, or were I a writer who had no claim to a higher position than I possess, I would freely ask him any favour. Such is not now the case" (this in reference to Hunt).

Shelley secured for Byron the Palazzo Lanfranchi at Pisa, an old building on the Lung' Arno, once the family palace of the destroyers of Ugolino, and said to be haunted by their ghosts. On the road thither, between Imola and Bologna, occurred the meeting with Lord Clare, which has been mentioned; and Clare tells Moore of his old schoolfellow's affectionate warmth. At Bologna he met Rogers, who records the event in some of the most interesting lines of his "Italy." Together they re-visited Florence and its galleries. Byron arrived at Pisa in November, 1821.

At Ravenna the poet wrote a great deal. Here he produced his dramas. The historical ones are, for the most part, his least successful works—though "Cain" is one of his best. "The Two Foscari" contains indeed a fine passage about swimming, and Marina is inte-resting. But this, and "Werner" are, on the whole, poor, the latter being a mere plagiarism. The blank verse in all is very bad. Yet I think "Sardanapalus," and perhaps "Marino Faliero," have been under-rated. Goethe does not seem to have thought meanly of the dramas. Still Byron had little dramatic faculty, for what is good in those two is chiefly derived from introspection. The old Doge Marino's struggle between his native predisposition in favour of his own patrician order, and his desire to revenge an unendurable insult to his young wife, as well as to help in establishing a more popular form of government, would be a motive very familiar to Byron's own conflicting nature. These are good lines :—

> "They never fail who die
> In a great cause; the block may soak their gore;
> Their heads may sodden in the sun; their limbs
> Be strung to city gates and castle walls:
> But still their spirit walks abroad."

"Sardanapalus," however, seems to me one of our really excellent plays. The hero, like Don Juan, is the pleasant, Epicurean, sensual, indolent, irresolute Byron, raised into the hero, who is latent in him, at the call of a momentous crisis, and the elevating influence of a noble woman who loves him.   Salemenes, the stern, honest warrior, is the poet's best realization of a character other than his own, though but a sketch.   The play has defects ; yet the scene is admirable where the beautiful, effeminate king, surprised feasting with women and parasites in his summer pavilion by the rebels, whom his lazy good nature has pardoned, starts up, brave and reckless, but too late to save his kingdom, calling in his vanity for a mirror while arming.   Full of lusty onset are the fighting scenes.   Zarina is also an effective sketch of a self-possessed, yet good and affectionate woman, probably suggested by Lady Byron—an amiable likeness.   The poet, however, remained in bondage to the so-called "unities" (time and place) of classical art, quite unadapted to the spirit and circumstances of modern drama.   But Byron's great dramatic poem is "Cain."   The scene between Cain and Abel, prior to the murder, before the two altars, and those that follow, are tremendous, equal to anything in our literature. The terrible situation is wonderfully realized, and the protagonists start out before us, revealed as by a lightning flash, lurid and awful, in the supreme moment of their career, into which moment their whole life and character are, as it were, fused and concentrated—of colossal stature; so to speak, cast in bronze.   From the third act onward to the end the work is grand.   Cain embodies the spirit of revolt and denial, Abel that of tranquil, reverent faith; Cain is the outcast, the Denier, the Rebel, and Abel is as fine as Cain when he confronts the blasphemer, who would overthrow the chosen altar of Jehovah, his offering left unaccepted, his altar smitten to the dust. Then, having slain his brother with a burning brand, Cain bows in horrified remorse over the corpse, knowing himself fated—even he—to bring that heretofore unknown, dread doom of death into the world! Eve curses her firstborn, but Adah, his wife-sister, when the stricken murderer bids her leave him, only answers in troubled wonder: " *Why, all have left thee !* " So Cain wanders forth into the wilderness with her, she leading their little Enoch, kissing Abel's cold clay, and praying: " *Peace be with him !* " to which Cain, in the last words of this great poem, responds with so much weight of meaning: " *But with me !* "

But this work raised such a storm of reprobation in England, that Murray was threatened with prosecution, and so Byron offered to come over and stand his trial as the author. It was thought very blasphemous; at which continental critics are surprised; but free thought had not then made much progress in this country. This is Byron's most important contribution to the discussion of religious problems, so far as they bear upon life and conduct; yet it is of small value in that respect. Byron had no metaphysical or speculative faculty. Still his powerful intellect brooded over these questions, but he remained always more or less of a sceptic. His was not a constructive period in speculative, or political questions, so far as England was concerned. And few poets are in advance of their age. If they are, they have no audience. Byron's curious conversations with Dr. Kennedy in Cephalonia are sometimes very *naïfs* in their unfamiliarity with the deeper problems of thought, and helpless flounderings in quest of some solution. He even sometimes appears disposed to take the whole orthodox position for granted in sheer despair of finding anything better; and many observers judged him to be a Christian. In his vehement negative dogmatism, Shelley, throwing his arms about, shrilly shrieked one day to Mary that he feared "Byron was no better than a Christian after all" (see Trelawny). Shelley in speculative questions was of little help to him, because Byron's deep ethical instinct, and vigorous common sense did indeed cling to that which is eternally true in Christian teaching; while Shelley, in his somewhat puerile and unballasted *fougue*, was for throwing the whole away as "superstition"—although his earnestness and thoroughness of temper, as well as subtlety, must have been of the highest service to his less serious, and more popularly (*i.e.*, more coarsely) moulded brother; whose love of a joke, *à la* Don Juan, was even more imperious than his zeal for knowledge. "Cain," therefore, so far as its contribution to thought is concerned, is chiefly important for its negation, and revolt against unworthy conceptions of religious truth. The inward disharmony and discontent of a nature not reconciled with itself is the psychological condition most powerfully depicted in the character of "Cain." He is one who overclouds all past, present, and future good with the shadow of his own sullen frown, out of which must inevitably spring the lightning of his crime. But there is no alchemy in "Cain" potent for the transmutation of suffering and endurance into richer life or deeper vision. Even honest labour seems to him a mere curse, unfruitful in blessing. All that happens is unjust, and evokes defiance; disappointment is never borne with the heroic fortitude that converts it into priceless self-education. How have we retrograded here from the serene and brave philosophy of Epictetus, and Marcus Aurelius! Yet there are such elements, it must be admitted, in the lovely patience and devotion of Adah, as also in the gentle and religious submission of Abel.

Cain, whatever the author might pretend, is felt to be a main channel for what is most characteristically personal in Byron. And the poem was an undoubtedly powerful protest against certain officially orthodox representations of the Divine Character, upon which so much that was immoral and unlovely in some of our most cherished institutions had long rested. Hence a great part of the loud horror, and shocked protest of our official and privileged classes against it. There are, indeed, two great ideas in Byron, though both Goethe and Matthew Arnold are disposed to deny him any; these are *Individuality*, and *Popular Freedom*—no patient fortitude does he teach; but aggressive energy, defiance, daring. Manfred "meets the devil and bullies him "— asserts the eternal dignity, and permanent importance of the human spirit *quâ* human spirit, though chiefly, no doubt, of the *elect* individual. Therefore, both Lucifer and Cain (Lucifer is only a shadowy Cain) declaim passion-

ately against a God who forbids a man to use his own in-
alienable spiritual inheritance, his reason and conscience,
to develop his personality in his own way. Lucifer and
Cain, like Prometheus, while rebelling against the established order, personified whether in Zeus, or Jehovah,
even as Byron against the "Holy Alliance" of states and
hierarchies for the benefit of usurping privilege, and for
the oppression of peoples—are indeed champions of the
true hidden God, of the Ideal, who manifests Himself pro-
gressively, who ever breaks up, and recasts, even the best
customs, habits, and institutions which have served their
purpose and become tyrannical, no longer protective
of that expanding life within, but, on the contrary, im-
prisoning and fatal. Yet the earlier portions of this
poem, imaginatively considered, where Byron competes
with Milton, seem to me poor ; while the verse often
halts.   With   occasional   hesitations,   Byron   did believe in God, and in the immortality of the soul.
Pantheism he had not speculative subtlety to grasp.
Latterly, he inclined to Catholicism.   But the poem is
full of superficial objections, like the following :

> " *Cain.* Then my Father's God did well
> When he prohibited the fatal tree.
>   *Lucifer.* But had done better in not planting it ! "

The idea that from Discord may grow a higher Harmony was beyond its scope.   It is a pity that Byron had
recourse to evasions in defending his work against the
almost universal chorus of objectors ; but then he
wavered in his own mind as to his own beliefs.   Scott,
to whom he dedicated it, called "Cain" "a grand, tremendous poem ;" and Shelley said, " in my opinion it

contains finer poetry than has appeared in England since 'Paradise Lost.' 'Cain' is apocalyptic."

Of the "Deformed Transformed" little need be said, except that it is interesting as showing the bitterness of the poet's personal feeling concerning his deformity. But "Heaven and Earth," written October, 1821, and the "Vision of Judgment," begun at Pisa, and published in the pages of *The Liberal*, Hunt's and Byron's joint venture in journalism, may be noticed before we proceed with our narrative. "Heaven and Earth: a Dramatic Mystery," founded on the Biblical story of the Deluge, is a very beautiful and unique composition, more in the spiritual and ideal region than anything else of Byron's. Here the gloom of coming Deluge and its deepening terrors are palpably, yet with appropriate indistinctness of visionary imagery, rolled around mystic loves of "woman wailing for her demon lover." There is a harmonious lyrical atmosphere pervading this fine, shadowy creation. Then the "Vision of Judgment" is a stupendous satirical work in the style of "Don Juan." In 1821, Southey, the Poet Laureate, who wrote some really good poetry, and excellent prose, produced a very preposterous panegyric in verse on the late king, which he termed a "Vision of Judgment" — purporting to describe the apotheosis of George III., with a note prefixed, characterizing "Don Juan" as "a monstrous combination of horror and mockery, lewdness and impiety," regretting that it had not been prosecuted, and saluting the writer as the "chief of the Satanic school, inspired by the spirit of Moloch and Belial." Byron had brought accusations of apostasy

and slander against the Laureate before this, and he now
replies with much ferocity and fury.   Southey rejoins in
similar strong language, whereupon Byron despatches a
challenge to him, through the Hon. Douglas Kinnaird.
But as Hodgson had suppressed Moore's challenge to
Byron, so Kinnaird now suppresses Byron's to Southey.
Byron, meanwhile, had written his own " Vision of Judgment," which was refused both by Murray and Longman.
When it appeared in *The Liberal*, the British public was
indignant at this assault on the memory of their sainted
sovereign ; so the publisher, John Hunt, was prosecuted
and fined.   Why, this was even worse than the poet's
recent assault upon yet more august Powers in "Cain."
He was getting a little *too* bad !   The point of the great
burlesque, which describes the obstacles encountered by
the late king in obtaining admission to heaven, is that
private domestic virtues in a sovereign scarcely atone for
his disastrous, self-willed, and stupidly obstinate errors,
amounting to crime, as head of the State, entailing, as
they did in the present instance, upon the mother-
country, no less a loss than that of her American
Colonies !   The attack upon Southey himself is a perpetual source of inextinguishable laughter to gods and men.
The whole vision is a burlesque indeed, but rendered with
a few broad, absolutely effective strokes, as by the chisel
of a Michael Angelo—not a stroke too much, nor too
little.   It is full of wit, and of a giant's large humour.

At Ravenna Byron also translated Pulci's " Morgante,"
and the episode of Francesca di Rimini, from Dante.
There also Augusta, and La Guiccioli induced him to lay
aside "Don Juan" for a time, the latter saying, " I would

rather have the fame of 'Childe Harold' for three years than an immortality of 'Don Juan.'" In September he writes to Murray about "the drivelling idiotism of the manikin Keats"; but after the death of Keats he retracts, and calls "Hyperion" "sublime as Æschylus." Only the fantastic fopperies of Keats's early "cockney" style were repulsive to him. But Walter Scott, Moore, Campbell, Crabbe, and Rogers are the only contemporaries he seems to have *unreservedly* admired. He was allowed to resume "the Don" on promising to make him behave better.

Byron lived in the Palazzo Lanfranchi at Pisa for ten months, with an interval of six weeks passed near Leghorn. He rose late, and rode in the pine-forest, or practised with pistols, together with Shelley, both being good shots. The early evenings he passed with Theresa, established under the same roof with him, and wrote far into the night. His intimates, besides Shelley, were Trelawny, who joined him here, Captain Williams and his wife, Captain Medwin, Shelley's cousin, and an Irishman named Taafe. In March, as the party were out riding, a corporal of dragoons rode roughly through them, nearly unseating this Mr. Taafe, who urged pursuit. Byron, in a rage, dashed after the soldier and threw his glove at him, taking him for an officer—then his fellow-soldiers at the city gate turned out, and gave Shelley a sabre cut on the head, while the dragoon was wounded by one of Byron's servants in passing the Lanfranchi palace. Later, at Montenero, near Leghorn, young Count Gamba was stabbed, and threatened by another of Byron's turbulent menials; this second affray made the Tuscan authorities banish the Gambas, they knowing that Theresa, by the terms of separation, to avoid a convent, would soon be compelled to follow her father, and that Byron would probably accompany her, his presence being equally unwelcome to them.

At Pisa the poet received a letter from a Mr. Sheppard, a clergyman, communicating to him the record which he had found of an affectionate and touching prayer his lately deceased wife had offered for the poet's conversion,—who replied expressing his utmost interest and gratitude, as well as heartfelt sympathy with Mr. Sheppard in his loss of one so evidently good and estimable. " I would not exchange the prayer of this pure and virtuous being in my behalf for the united glory of Homer, Cæsar, and Napoleon," he answered. Lady Blessington, whom he met at Genoa, and who has recorded her impressions, advised him, while he was praising his wife to her, to seek a reconciliation; and he wrote a letter with this object, but it was never sent. Obviously the malice of Lady Byron's (or Mrs. Stowe's) explanation of this fact is at fault—it was a very natural letter for him to write, but sent it would only have made the lady more implacably angry. Upon his daughter Ada, now in her sixth year, were his fondest thoughts fixed, and he requested Murray to procure him a miniature of her. In the withheld letter, he acknowledges receipt of the child's hair, sent by Lady Byron through Augusta, with name and date written in his wife's own hand; and he thanks her for writing them, since they are the only words he possesses in her handwriting, except the one word " Household " in an old account - book—which shows that he still felt affection for her. He asked Lady Blessington, moreover, if she could get him the miniature of his wife, which had been in the possession of Lady Noel, who had recently died—but gave vent at the same time to natural indignation at the clause in Lady Noel's will, which expressed her wish that his daughter should not be allowed even to see her father's portrait. And, in fact, Ada was brought up in complete ignorance of everything connected with her father. But only about a year before her death, Colonel Wildman asked her to Newstead, and one day read her a poem there, which she greatly admired. On her inquiring whose it was, Colonel Wildman pointed to the portrait of her father by Philips. She, greatly moved, shut herself up in her father's apartments, and, studying his works, now first learned how he had loved her. Shortly after, she was taken ill, and, finding her end near, she wrote to ask that she might be buried by her father at Hucknall, where now she rests. " Though the grave closed between us—'twere the same "—" I know that thou wilt love me," Byron had written.

It is strange, if the poet were still so attached to La Guiccioli, that he should seek this reconciliation with his wife now. Many thought that he was becoming less fond of the former. His not providing for her in his will, indeed, signifies little, for she had *entreated* him not to do so, lest her motives in sacrificing so much for him should be misconstrued. He had intended to leave her £10,000.

We now come to Byron's ill-starred literary partnership with Hunt. He had wished Moore to join him in founding a journal, but Moore was too cautious and prudent. Then, by Shelley's advice, he proposed the venture to Leigh Hunt, who fell in with the idea. Hunt was to be editor, and his brother publisher, while Byron, giving his own contributions gratis, undertook to leave the profits of the proprietorship to the Hunts. There is no reason to doubt that Byron, believing the journal would succeed, wished to do Hunt a good turn when he asked him to come to Italy with his family, and lodge in his Palazzo, furnishing him with the means of living there—though some of the money came from Shelley, who pressed Hunt to come. The latter had defended Byron in England, when so many attacked him, and Byron had dined with Hunt when he was in gaol. On the other hand, Byron wished to be able to publish whatever he chose to write in this journal, without demur, for Murray was beginning to be afraid of his unconventional, unorthodox patron's MSS. But Leigh Hunt was a thorough Radical, and Byron personally, in spite of his strong Liberal convictions, an aristocrat, who liked and expected deference, so that the pair stood often on each other's toes. Byron is said by Trelawny to have received Mrs. Hunt, who was an invalid, with scant courtesy. This would have been so ungentlemanlike that one is glad to know he was in a bad humour at the moment of their arrival—settling that quarrel between Gamba and the servant who had stabbed him. Mrs. Hunt was even with Byron, for she told him, when he was speaking of his " morals," that it was the first time she had ever heard of them. She and Madame Guiccioli do not seem to have got on well together, and they could not speak each other's language. Hunt appears to have received Byron's money ungraciously, and Byron may possibly have been rather "caddish" in his way of giving it; though he certainly was not so on other occasions.[1] But Hunt expected too much. Moreover, the connection began with a fundamental misconception, for which Hunt himself seems to have been (not very creditably) responsible. Shelley and Byron had both believed that Hunt would continue editor of *The Examiner*, and his brother the proprietor. Before Hunt came out, Byron wrote that. he ought to make certain of an independent position from it, whereas Hunt had given it up, and proved to be entirely dependent on his host, and on Shelley, or else on the problematical success of the new journal,—*The Liberal*, which, in fact, proved quite unsuccessful. Byron, however, maintained the family till they left Genoa for Florence in 1823, and paid their expenses when they moved from Pisa to Genoa at the same time with himself. The unexpected death of Shelley by drowning, soon after Hunt came to Pisa, was another serious blow

---

[1] "I have always treated Hunt, in our personal intercourse," declares Byron, in a letter, "with such scrupulous delicacy that I have forborne intruding advice which I thought might be disagreeable, lest he should impute it to what is called taking advantage of a man's situation." That statement is to be set against Hunt's ill-tempered picture of his host. But Tom Moore, and other friends of Byron were always entreating him to decline, or renounce all literary partnership with a plebeian radical like Hunt, and an unpopular atheist like Shelley; they feared for his own fame. This was characteristic of them. Byron soon gave up all connection with *The Liberal*, which had a short life. Still he had contributed the best things to it.

to the undertaking. But *The Liberal* contained some
good things—"The Vision of Judgment," "Heaven
and Earth," Byron's translation from Pulci, besides the
"Blues," a rather silly satire on learned women—some
beautiful lyrics of Shelley, his translation from Faust,
and a few of Hazlitt's essays. Hunt being out of health
and spirits, his own many contributions were feeble.

The Guiccioli and Byron sat to the American painter
West for their pictures, and the latter to Bertolini, a
Florentine sculptor, for his bust. They took up their
quarters for five or six weeks at Monte Nero, near Leghorn ; but Byron returned to Pisa with the Hunts after
they arrived at that port, to establish them on the ground
floor of the Lanfranchi Palace. Shelley took up his
quarters at the Villa Magni, in the Gulf of Spezzia, near
Lerici. It was on his return to Lerici from Leghorn
in his boat, the *Don Juan*, that the boat succumbed
either to a white squall, or foul play, and he was
drowned, with the latest volume of Keats in his pocket.
This boat had been built for him when the *Bolivar* was
built for Byron. The bodies of Shelley, Williams, his
friend, and Vivian, the sailor boy, having been cast
ashore, and Trelawny having ridden to Pisa to inform
Byron of the tragedy, the surviving friends determined to
burn the remains on a funeral pile erected by the sea-
side. Each of them has graphically described the weird,
beautiful, but ghastly ceremony. Byron, Hunt, and
Trelawny were all present, but the latter assumed the
active direction ; his nerves alone permitting him to do
personally what was necessary, without shrinking. All
were afterwards seized with a kind of hilarious delirium,

which, as Nichol says, is "one of the phases of the
tension of grief." Byron's laughter was rather often of
that kind, I fancy ! Some of us may remember laughing
at the most awful, and horrible moments of our lives.
"Thus," writes Byron, "there is another man gone,
about whom the world was ill-naturedly, and ignorantly,
and brutally mistaken. It will perhaps do him justice
now, when he can be no better for it."

In July the Gambas received notice from the police to
leave Tuscany, and in September Byron left Pisa with
Theresa for Genoa, passing by Lerici, where he visited
Shelley's house, Villa Magni. He took up his quarters
at Albaro, about a mile from Genoa, in the Villa Saluzzo,
which Mrs. Shelley found for him. Cantos vi. to xi. of
"Don Juan" were written at Pisa ; Cantos xii. to xvi. at
Genoa. There seems to be no good authority for the
Guicciolis' statement that many other cantos of "Don
Juan" were found after his death among his papers and
destroyed, or that Mavrocordatos destroyed a journal
Byron kept up to the last. But I am informed that
there are some unpublished stanzas of one unfinished
canto of "Don Juan," and Trelawny does say he found
some stanzas for "Childe Harold," and a journal. [1]
"The Age of Bronze," and "The Island," an idyllic tale
of the South Seas, belong to this period. The latter
poem has been, I think, underrated. There is considerable idyllic beauty of a tranquil, marine kind about it ;
all is in keeping, and the tender, gentle loves depicted

---

[1] None of these verses are in the possession of Lady Dorchester.
I believe them to be in Mr. Murray's. About the journal I know
nothing.

are in harmony with the sunny seas and caves of the tropical island that witness them. There are notable lines about the animation of Nature, and a charming description of a freshwater rill near the sea—

> "While far below the vast and sullen swell
> Of ocean's Alpine azure rose and fell."

Lady Blessington made some acute feminine observations about the poet. She says he talked a good deal for effect, and that the opinions he expressed depended much on the mood of the moment. She noted also his " flippancy and want of self-possession," the minutiæ of his dress, and his riding with all sorts of trappings about the horse, and with holsters for pistols. Both she and Trelawny aver he was nervous on horseback. Of his appearance this lady remarks : " One of Byron's eyes was larger than the other ; his nose was rather thick, so he was best seen in profile ; his mouth was splendid, and his scornful expression was real, not affected, but a sweet smile often broke through his melancholy. He was at this time very pale and thin (which indicates the success of his *régime* of reduction since leaving Venice). His hair was dark brown, here and there turning grey. His voice was harmonious, clear, and low." He told Lady Blessington that he felt prematurely old, and expected to die young, which he wished. In conversation she thought he claimed a sort of literary dictatorship, like Johnson. Autocracy, and world-admitted supremacy are not good for any man.

CHAPTER VI.

HOBHOUSE, early in the spring of 1823, mentioned to Byron the war of Greek independence, already proceeding, as a cause worthy of his personal assistance, if he wanted a field for active service. Begun in 1821, the struggle had been carried on for two years with remarkable success, but early in 1823 the tide seemed to be turning. Dissensions broke out among the patriots, and funds for carrying on the enterprise were wanting. A committee was formed in London, which endeavoured to procure money from foreign sympathizers, and they thought it would be advisable to interest some notorious Englishman in the undertaking; hence the propositions made by them to Byron; the Honourable Douglas Kinnaird, the poet's friend, was one of their number, and Byron, who had become restless again, began, though with considerable hesitation, to entertain the idea. But his hesitation was only natural. It was not quite obvious to him what he could do to help the cause, if he went to Greece in person—his vacillations are recorded in Lady Blessington's "Conversations";—he was not a soldier by profession, and was, moreover, in extremely bad health. It is not clear that Theresa encouraged him to pursue this enterprise, although she *had* warmly encouraged him in the assistance he gave to Italian popular movements; for one thing, he would have to leave her in Italy; he could hardly take her to the Ionian Islands, where she would not be received into society, nor to a disturbed country like Greece. But in June, Byron consented to meet Captain Blaquière at Zante, and, on hearing the results of his expedition to the Morea, decide finally on what he would do. He had a presentiment that he should die in Greece; yet in his uncertainty and irresolution he spoke of returning to Italy in a few months. He mentioned his approaching departure, at a farewell call he made on the Blessingtons, with despondency, even leaning his head on the sofa, and bursting into a fit of hysterical tears. So had he dreaded leaving Ravenna; his letters to Theresa were then full of foreboding. But how things are over-ruled! Had he gone to England, and been reconciled to Lady Byron, he would not have died for Greece. And, while her original obduracy was responsible for many of his irregularities of conduct, these in their turn made reconciliation with her less and less possible. Then perhaps the ears of Europe would never have been so concentrated on his poetry that his following in literature should be the leading poets of Europe—Espronceda in Spain; Berchet in Italy; Heine in Germany; Hugo, De Musset, Lamartine, Delavigne in France; Puschkin in Russia. Gervinus and Karl Elze have shown how the Slavonic youth of Poland and Russia, no less than the Teutonic and French races, received from him

ineffaceable influence, and responded in their great
political movements, as also in their literature. His
discontent, his "world-sorrow," impressed them equally
with his love of revolution and freedom. Italy, Spain,
and Greece also responded in their spirit of progress
and emancipation, even as Alp answers Jura during
a thunderstorm. Had a domestic reconciliation been
effected, and he remained in England, he might have
been a better and happier man; but probably his poetry
would never have been so great and so individual, nor
its *rôle* European. Nature in her grand march to far
goals remorselessly sacrifices persons; though in the end
doubtless they shall triumph with Her—She and they
being indeed one.

There is no sufficient evidence that Byron was tired
of Theresa, as some have alleged; for his casual random
remarks as to his being determined to go somewhere
away with Captain Roberts in the *Bolivar*, whether to
Greece or elsewhere (he had thought of America),
and being "sick of Italy and all the people in it," were
mere splenetic ebullitions of a sick man's ill-humour.
She, at any rate, was not dissatisfied with the lover of
her youth. I have said that Byron was himself a captive
to the conventions of the corrupt society against which
he fought. And one of the most salient instances
of it was his snobbish, immoral remark, that he owed
Theresa all affectionate duty because she had made
great sacrifices for him, belonging, as she did, to his
own caste. The poor man was still bound hand and
foot in the grave-clothes of polite society—though
beginning to revive after his sepulture. The most un-

consciously comical thing he ever said was his observation, that, of course, he and Moore wrote better poetry
than the Lakers, because they had both enjoyed the
advantage of living among fashionable people—that
being exactly what prevented Byron writing it *very* well,
—till these same people shut their drawing-room doors
against him in a fit of quasi-virtuous spleen.

He told Lady Blessington that he had no character
at all. Certainly it was not always amiable. He wrote
epigrams on his friends when he was out of humour
with them; and on one occasion, in Italy, when Rogers
came to visit him, having a grievance against Rogers,
he made the latter *sit upon* an epigram about himself.
At least so Trelawny declares. But, in spite of his mobility
and his affectations, there was a strong backbone of
practical reasonableness and common sense, of strong
will, and sincere, definite purpose. On the whole,
looking back along his career, the great course and
current of it seem consistent and harmonious—save
indeed that he was "light o' love"; but, responsive as
he was in so many directions, there were dallyings, and
side-eddies of the main stream. He vacillated, yet once
embarked upon his enterprise, he held on like grim
death; luxurious Epicurean, he could control and
dominate his love of pleasure for a purpose. His
cynicism was partly real, but partly affected, to veil
the tenderness of his heart from cold people. His
political panaceas were not up in the clouds, like
Shelley's; but he could see what was good and practic-
able for the present hour. If his eye was fixed on the
pole-star, his foot was firmly planted on the ground;

he did not devise constitutions for cloud-cuckoo-land—
and so common men and women welcomed him as
their brother. How reverent and measured was he in
toning down the puerile and superficial contempt for
religion of Gamba, learned from shallow sciolists, as
they rode together in the pine-forest of Ravenna, or sat
out on the balcony at Albaro, with "Genova la Superba"
in all her beauty before them !

On the 14th of July, Byron embarked on board the
English brig *Hercules*, which he had hired, accompanied
by Trelawny, Pietro Gamba, Bruno a young Italian
physician, Scott the captain, Fletcher, Tita his favourite
Venetian gondolier, and other servants. They took
two guns, with other arms, five horses, an ample supply
of medicines, and fifty thousand Spanish dollars in
coin and bills. He had been visited by Captain
Blaquière at Albaro in April—and on the 7th of July
he wrote to Mr. Bowring: "We sail on the 12th for
Greece." He urges a loan, "for which there will be
offered a sufficient security by deputies now on their
way to England. . . . I mean to carry up, in cash
or credit, above £8,000 or nearly £9,000 sterling,"
(and apply it in the manner most likely to be useful
to the cause),—"having of course some guarantee that
it will not be misapplied to any individual speculation."
He also promises to use other considerable portions of
his income for the same purpose. The *Hercules*, a
rolling old tub, having been towed out of Genoa harbour
by American boats, sent out of compliment to the
poet from the American squadron, was so punished by
the squall that the horse-boxes got broken, and the

horses were in danger; so Trelawny, who secured them, advised putting back—Byron acquiescing. They put to sea again on a Friday. At first, "the Pilgrim" sat apart, solemn and sad, but once well out his spirits rose. In five days they were at Leghorn, where Byron received some cordial verses from Goethe, to whom, as to his "liege lord and master," he had dedicated "Sardanapalus," and the English poet returned a suitable acknowledgment. Here Mr. Hamilton Brown, and two Greeks (suspected of being spies), joined the party. They passed by Stromboli, but the volcano emitted no fire; yet Byron said, "You will see this scene in a fifth canto of 'Childe Harold.'" His companions suggesting that he should write something on the spot, he tried; but threw the verses away, observing, "I cannot write poetry at will, as you smoke tobacco." Trelawny confesses he never was on shipboard with a better companion, and that a severer test of good fellowship it is impossible to apply. Coming in sight of the Morea, the poet remarked to Trelawny, "I feel as if the eleven long years of bitterness I have passed through since I was here were taken from my shoulders, and I was scudding through the Greek Archipelago with old Bathurst in his frigate." They passed Elba, Soracte, the Straits of Messina, Etna, and determined to land at Cephalonia, in order to seek the advice and assistance of Colonel (afterwards General) Sir C. Napier, an ardent Philhellene; there also Byron hoped to meet Blaquière on his return from the Morea, but this gentleman had left for England, without even leaving so much as a message or a letter for the poet. This annoyed him much, and Colonel Napier being away, his deputy, though he received Byron with much courtesy, could give him little information about the state of affairs. He was obliged, therefore, to wait at Cephalonia till he obtained it, for he was unwilling to put himself at the disposal of a faction, and become its tool, but wished to obtain clear evidence that the Greeks really wanted him, and that he could be of substantial use to the cause of national independence. The long delay in the Ionian island, Cephalonia, was undoubtedly deliberate, and probably wise. Much was already achieved by the Greeks. The third campaign had commenced with success. Odysseus had dispersed two Turkish armies. Corinth, though still held by the Turks, was in great extremities—the Morea was almost free from their yoke. But the dissensions of the chiefs threatened to cancel all the advantages gained, and the funds were at a low ebb. Colocotronis and Mavrocordatos were at daggers drawn; it had almost come to civil war. Byron received emissaries, who tried in turn to persuade him to go to Athens, to the Morea, to Acarnania; but choosing a place of residence at once would have been virtually to cast in his lot with a faction. He preached union to the parties perpetually. The Exarch of Mesolonghi, and the illustrious Marco Bozzaris, besought him to come at once to Mesolonghi, the key of Western Greece, which was blockaded by the Turkish fleet, and to the investment of which the Pasha of Scutari was advancing. Having arrived, and provisioned forty Suliotes, he sent them to join in the defence of that town, and after the battle, in which

Bozzaris, while checking the Turkish advance, was killed, sent bandages, medicines, and pecuniary relief; but he resolved to communicate only with the regular government; and though at first wishing to retain Trelawny, who grew weary of inaction, Byron subsequently employed him, and Mr. Hamilton Brown, to negotiate with the legislature at Salamis, and procure information for him. " He by no means over-estimated the Greeks, but, aware of their faults, judged them fairly," said Colonel Napier, "knowing that allowance must be made for emancipated slaves."

For six weeks he remained on board the *Hercules*, taking his swim overboard daily; and afterwards fixed his quarters at Metaxata, a small village within five miles of Argostoli, the capital of Cephalonia. From thence he made an excursion to Ithaca, one of the loveliest of the islands, with Trelawny and Gamba. He rejected irritably an offer to show him the antiquities, the Castle of Ulysses, &c. "Do I look like one of those emasculated fogies?" he said to Trelawny. "Do people think I have no lucid intervals, that I came to Greece to scribble more nonsense? I will show them that I can do something better. I wish I had never written a line, to have it cast in my teeth at every turn. Let's have a swim." After it, he went to sleep in the cave of Ulysses, and Gamba woke him, for which he got some curses. He was received with all honour at Vathi, the chief town, by our resident, Colonel Knox, but probably partook too freely of the good things provided, and a terrible fit of stomachic cramp came on, in consequence of which he seems to have become really mad for awhile. He behaved like a maniac after ascending on muleback to a monastery, whose Abbot had been apprised of his arrival; for while he was being received with all ceremony in the illuminated hall, and boys were swinging incense under his nose, the Abbot, followed by all his monks in full canonicals, reading a long address to the "*Lordo Inglese,*" deliverer of his country, the lordo himself burst into a torrent of Italian execrations, seized a torch, and rushed out of the hall; so that the Abbot stood stupefied, and presently touching his forehead observed, "Eccolo, è matto, poveretto !" Later, he barricaded himself into his room, and when his fellow-tourists went to try and relieve him, drove them from him with frantic fury, hurling the furniture after them. Brown at last induced him to take the necessary medicines, and he slept. Next morning no allusions were made to these incidents, but with a concerned and courteous expression of face the poet put a handsome donation into the alms-box, and left with the blessing of the holy men. On returning along the flowery and vine-clad ravine, he exclaimed, "If this isle were mine, I would break my staff, and bury my book !" He left a sum of money for the Greek refugees, with the Resident.

In Cephalonia occurred those "Conversations on religion" with Dr. Kennedy, the good and earnest, but narrow and rather prosy, Calvinistic Scotch doctor, which the latter has recorded in a book. They do not give a high idea of Byron's speculative ability. The doctor found it difficult to keep the poet serious—indeed, the

doctor was himself so funny—wanting his auditors to
listen twelve hours on end! but, on the whole, Byron
was reverential, and well disposed to pay attention to
a man for whose character he felt sincere respect.
The most interesting part of Kennedy's book relates to
what Byron said about his wife, and her religious
opinions, with which he seemed now disposed very much
to concur, though he was still in doubt. But latterly
Augusta's Bible was always by his bed. One day, while
he was at dinner, he heard that some workmen had been
buried by the fall of a large mass of earth, and started
up from table, accompanied by Bruno, to render assistance. Those who were digging soon became alarmed
for themselves, and saying they believed all had been
dug out, refused to proceed, until Byron seized a spade,
and shaming the people into joining him, two more
persons were rescued alive.   Many and various were his
benefactions in Cephalonia. He despatched a very able
State paper to the Government, on the importance of
immediately merging all differences in the common
cause, since otherwise the loan so much needed would
certainly not be forthcoming from England, and the
Great Powers might interfere in a manner not favourable
to independence, regarding the people as unfit to govern
themselves. "I desire the well-being of Greece, and
nothing else. I will do all I can to secure it, but I
will never consent that the English public be deceived
as to the real state of affairs ; you have fought gloriously ;
act honourably towards your fellow-citizens and the world,
and it will then no longer be said, as has been repeated
for two thousand years with the Roman historians, that

Philopœmen was the last of the Grecians." Prince
Mavrocordatos, having been deposed from the Presi-
dency, was now commissioned to collect a fleet for the
relief of Mesolonghi ; he again entreated Byron to hasten
thither, and, if possible, to help with money for the fleet;
for, he urged, " the heart of the people is not divided, and
when once the money for paying the fleet and army
is found, dissensions will cease." Byron accordingly
advanced £4,000 for this purpose. He had been
assured that the majority wished for a foreign king, who
would compose the feuds of rival chieftains and rival
tribes, and unite all into a nation. " If they make me
the offer," the poet said to Trelawny, " I may not refuse
it. I shall take care of my own 'sma' peculiar ; ' for if it
don't suit my humour, I shall, like Sancho, resign." In
electing to ally himself finally with Mavrocordatos, he
certainly chose an aristocrat, known to favour a foreign
monarchy for Greece. And in fact that was the form of
Government the people actually chose. " Had he lived to
reach the Congress of Salona," said Trelawny, "as Commissioner of the loan, the dispenser of a million
silver crowns would have been offered a golden one."
Trelawny, after quitting head-quarters at Salamis, joined
the Chief Odysseus as his aide-de-camp ; and now Byron,
whose great present difficulty was in negotiating his
Italian bills, and whose correspondence at this date
relates almost entirely to procuring from England every
penny of his income that could be made available for
the cause he had at heart, made serious preparations for
departure, the long-looked-for fleet having arrived with
Mavrocordatos at Mesolonghi, and the Turkish squadron,

with the loss of a treasureship, having retired up the
Gulf of Lepanto. Col. the Hon. L. Stanhope also
arrived to join him, sent from England by the Greek
Committee. On the 28th of December he embarked on
a small swift sailing-ship, called a mistico, while the
servants and baggage with Count Gamba sailed in a
heavier one. Byron was almost captured by a Turkish
vessel, but, taking refuge inside the Scrophes rocks,[1] was
safe there for awhile; Gamba, however, was actually
taken by Yussuf Pacha; only through his own address,
and a fortunate circumstance did he escape, arriving at
Mesolonghi before Byron; for the latter had afterwards
been nearly wrecked on a shoal near Dragomestri, dis-
playing much coolness and courage on the occasion.
Byron was in his wet clothes day and night, and
had to rough it considerably. On the 4th of January,
moreover, he made an imprudent plunge in the sea
when violently heated, and he fancied he was never
after free from a pain in his bones. On the 5th he
arrived at Mesolonghi, and, habited in a scarlet uniform,
was greeted like a prince, with salvos of artillery, with
music, and tempestuous acclamations from the multitude,
Mavrocordatos and his officers standing to receive him
before the entrance of the residence which had been
prepared for him and Colonel Stanhope. Next day the
western chiefs, rejoicing that he had cast in his lot with

---

[1] "I am uneasy at being here," writes Byron, from his insecure
refuge near the Scrophes rocks, ". : . on account of the Greek
boy with me—for you know what his fate would be—and I would
sooner cut him in pieces myself than have him taken out by those
barbarians."

them, attended what may be termed his *levée.* He now surrounded himself with a body-guard of five hundred Suliotes—rude warriors, who had fought under Bozzaris —and did all he could for their discipline, gaining their respect through his dexterity with the pistol. All the Suliotes were, moreover, placed under Byron's command, and he received the title of *Archistrategos*, commander-in-chief. It was determined that an expedition against Lepanto should be undertaken, and that Byron should lead it. "Lord Byron," wrote Stanhope, "burns with military ardour and chivalry, and will accompany the expedition to Lepanto." On the morning of his thirty-sixth birthday he came to Stanhope's room, saying "You were complaining that I never write any poetry now," and read the stanzas beginning

> "'Tis time this heart should be unmoved;"

and ending

> "Seek out—less often sought than found—
> A soldier's grave, for thee the best,
> Then look around, and choose thy ground,
> And take thy rest."

It is impossible to read the accounts left of these his last days, by Stanhope, Mr. Finlay the historian, Dr. Bruno, and Count Gamba, without feeling how surely good was gaining the difficult victory over evil in this man of commanding genius, and dazzling, heterogeneously-compounded, character. His generosity, his heroic self-devotion to the one cause, and scorn of selfish indulgence, his merciful and active regard for the weak and suffering, at this later period, appear in every line they wrote, no less than his practical sagacity in counsel, and statesmanlike moderation, which made all feel that they had a strong and capable man to deal with. With such a record before him it is difficult to pardon the quasi-stoical "strong man," and dyspeptic Jeremiah of Chelsea, for his coarse, unveracious caricature of Byron's character. I solemnly believe that we are individually responsible for our conduct; but modern science has taught us two things—the solidarity of mankind, and the law of heredity—that a man is *very much* the creature of his age and circumstances, as well as the resultant of ancestral influences. Now if a man of infinitely varied sympathies, as also of exceptional genius, possesses in one aspect a very distinctive individuality, and a corresponding initiative, in the other he is peculiarly the channel and focus of such alien influences as belong to his period, the temper and bent of his contemporaries, the modifying lives of his progenitors, the external circumstances of his own career. One, like Byron, who did not live apart, as did Shelley and Wordsworth, but in the very centre and turmoil of human society, whose aggregate life and daily affairs interested and impressed him even more deeply than did the mountains and the sea, who was the very elect representative, and vocal expression of the tumultuously-conflicting, shattered, and fragmentary ideas, agitating the men and women of his own day—the political poet, the poet of revolution, and rehabilitation of the flesh—*how could he* have been, one is tempted to ask, other in character than in fact he was? He believed in Destiny, or Divine Predestination, because

he felt it; felt the immense and infinite life-currents surging
impetuously, uncontrollably through one quivering heart,
and through one large intelligence—" Pleasure," as
Rogers sings,

> " While yet the down was on thy cheek,
> Uplifting, pressing, and to lips like thine,
> Her charmèd cup."

But hard men, comparative strangers, do not weep
around the death-bed either of a "fiend," or of a
merely cold, selfish, indifferent man, a "poser," or
even a mere artist, as the companions of Byron wept
around his death-bed at Mesolonghi. The Italians,
Bruno and Gamba, as well as his servants, lamented in
him the father, the friend, the brother; and Mavrocordatos, the Greek, now made Governor-General by the
Government, is at first dazed, utterly at a loss how to act
without his assistance.

A main part of his attention was devoted to mitigating
the necessary horrors of war, and introducing more
humanity into the conduct of it. He dealt firmly with
the foreign officers when they were for inflicting severer
punishment on some refractory Greeks than he approved,
and he saved the life of a poor Turk who had sought
refuge in his house from the fury of two Greek soldiers,—
they, pursuing him sword in hand, still insisted on their
right to kill him, even when Byron told them they must
strike through his own body to do so. For this man he
provided fully, concealing him in the house, doctoring,
and finally sending him back to his friends. So also he
provided for a Turkish lady and her daughter, who had

been well off, the mother wishing to send the child to be educated in Italy; but after his death they said that, having lost "their father, Byron," they preferred returning to their native country. The unfinished letter to Augusta, which Trelawny found after his death, contained a proposal that this little girl (Hatagee) should be educated in England with Ada, if Lady Byron approved. Besides, he procured the release of nine and twenty Turkish prisoners, men, women, and children, sending them to Yussuf Pacha, commander at Patras, and to Prevesa, at his own expense. He wrote also a letter to the Pacha, thanking him for his courtesy toward Count Gamba when in his power, and expressing a hope that he would exercise the same humanity toward any Greek prisoners who might fall into his hands. Quite endless were Byron's acts of kindness, often done secretly, in Italy, Cephalonia, and Greece, which came to the knowledge of Gamba, who says the record would fill a volume; not pecuniary kindnesses only, but likewise acts of personal service.

When he could not ride on account of the rain, he practised with the foils and the broadsword, or assisted at the drill exercise of his Suliotes. The Albanian garrison of Lepanto had promised to deliver up the place if Byron should appear before it with their arrears of pay. He was daily expecting Parry with the military stores needed for the siege. On the 5th of February Parry came with artillery and gunpowder, and a laboratory was established in the old Seraglio under his direction. This William Parry, a ship's carpenter, had served in Woolwich Arsenal.

But now began a series of vexations and disappointments. The German Philhellenes in Greece who had
served under General Normann, and had been invited
to give their help at Mesolonghi, refused to serve
under Parry, since he was a man of low origin, and
a very "rough diamond." He was indeed "a fellow of
infinite jest," and greatly amused Byron by his racy
anecdotes, later on furnishing materials for the book
entitled "Parry's Last Days of Lord Byron." But he
drank like a fish. This Parry was mortally afraid of earth-
quakes—there had been one already,—and even in these
last days Byron's love of fun and mischief found food
for gratification in this circumstance. He made some
Suliotes roll barrels full of cannon balls about on the upper
floor of the house, and jump on it, to make Parry think
there was an earthquake. When all was ready for the
siege, the Suliotes suddenly struck for better terms—
a month's payment in advance,—and this being granted,
they put forward such extravagant demands as could
only be met by flat refusal; so Byron told them through
Gamba that, though he would continue to support their
families, he could no longer be their chief. This brought
about their submission, and he forgave them; yet a few
days later they declared they would not march against
stone walls. It was proved afterwards that they had
been tampered with by Colocotronis. Then, again, Byron
and Colonel Stanhope, a disciple of Bentham, differed
entirely about the measures that ought to be adopted
in Greece, and this was the cause of frequent disputes
between them, during which Byron seems to have kept
his temper well under control. Stanhope wished to

establish hospitals, schools, post-offices, and to set up
a printing-press for the publication of Greek newspapers.
Byron thought this premature, especially the printing-
press, since the people could not read.   He held that
all present efforts should be concentrated on getting
them to organize, and fight the common enemy.   As to
the tracts, and testaments in modern Greek, sent by Dr.
Kennedy and the Committee, he deemed it doubtful
policy to alienate the Greek priests, who were very
influential.   "It is odd," he said to Gamba, "that
Stanhope, the soldier, is all for writing down the Turks;
I, the writer, for fighting them down."   "Despot!" cried
Stanhope, "after professing liberal principles from boyhood, you, when called upon to act, prove yourself a
Turk!"   "Radical!" retorted Byron, "if I had held up
one of my fingers I could have crushed your press."   But
Stanhope being very determined, Byron yielded his
point, so far as to take part in the distribution of the
tracts and Bibles (see Bruno, and Gamba to Kennedy),
even to subsidise a newspaper, help the school, and assist
in the building of a hospital, out of his own limited
means.   Stanhope, however, set up another journal, and
this (the "Telegrapho") took a very radical line, of
which, under the circumstances, Byron disapproved, as
calculated to alienate the Great Powers, which were
attacked in it, from the national cause; thus it called on
the Hungarians to rise against Austria.   Yet after one
of the discussions between them, which had grown
warm, Byron went up to Stanhope with "Give me
that honest right hand!"   At last Stanhope left for
Athens, where he joined the republican party.   "Byron

disliked drudgery," the latter says, and put it on *him*.
He was, however, now a practical politician, having
been witness to the miserable failure of Carbonarism in
Italy. What he had set his heart upon in this last
venture was the national independence of the Greek
race, which could only be achieved by the countenance
and favour of the great European powers. *This* was
not a struggle of Democracy against the Holy Alliance,
but of Christian civilization against Moslem oppression
and misgovernment, of the descendants of a race, to
whom all Europe is indebted, for an independent
position among nations. He therefore disapproved
Stanhope's perpetual denunciation of the Government
of the Ionian islands, bad as that might be, for it
was essential not to alienate England; and free intercourse with the islands was necessary to the young and
struggling nationality. According to Parry, Byron considered a federation the best form of government for
Greece, and would have had a president elected by the
inhabitants of the Morea, the Islands, and the Western
provinces. He would have wished to be sent as
Ambassador of the New State to America, believing
that recognition by the United States would be followed
by that of Europe. He had provisionally rejected an
offer from the authorities to make him Governor-General
over a large portion of the enfranchised country. But
he might not eventually have rejected this, or a still
more dignified offer, had it been made at the projected
Congress of Salona, to which Odysseus, Trelawny, and
Stanhope invited him and Mavrocordatos, so giving
proof that the internal dissensions were mitigated already.

13

One day, when, in Stanhope's room, he was declaring
playfully that, after all, the author's brigade would be
ready before the soldier's printing-press, he was seized
with a fit which seemed to have the nature of epilepsy
(February 15th); next day leeches were applied to his
temples, and the bleeding was with difficulty stopped.
His lowering irrational diet, together with harassing
vexations and disappointments, were predisposing causes.
He was living mainly on toast, vegetables, and cheese,
and was still more frugal in his diet after this fit,
thinking it was from a full habit, not weakness—
and then upon this to bleed him copiously! Rightly
did his instinct lead him to deprecate that then much-
accredited remedy! "Soon after his dreadful paroxysm,"
Colonel Stanhope writes, "when he was lying on his
sick-bed, with his whole nervous system completely
shaken, the mutinous Suliotes, covered with dirt and
splendid attires, broke into his apartment, brandishing
their costly arms, and loudly demanding their rights.
Lord Byron, electrified by this unexpected act, seemed
to recover from his sickness, and the more the Suliotes
raged the more his calm courage triumphed. The scene
was truly sublime." "It is impossible," writes Count
Gamba, "to do justice to the coolness and magnanimity
which he displayed upon every trying occasion. Upon
trifling occasions he was certainly irritable" (absurdly so
with Gamba himself about some red cloth he had bought,
worrying him incessantly about it), "but the aspect
of danger calmed him in an instant, and restored him
the free exercise of all the powers of his noble nature.
A more undaunted man in the hour of peril never

breathed." And this was Carlyle's "sham strong man "!
These favourite Suliotes of Byron's had already killed
a burgher of the town while forcing their way into his
house when he had refused to quarter some of their
number; were turbulent, lawless, and kept the whole
town in terror; they were even said to meditate actual
treason. On recovering his power of speech after the
fit, Byron said, "Let me know. Do not think I am
afraid to die. I am not." . But pain his sensitive
organization found it very difficult to bear patiently, and
he described the pain in this attack as terrible. He
experienced several other slighter seizures before his
death. With his irritable temperament and delicate
health, he had undertaken a task physically too arduous
for him. At one time the town, after the departure of
the Greek flotilla, was again blockaded by Turks; then
there was a threatening of plague; a real shock of earthquake; and besides the brawls of the Suliotes there
were tribal brawls; a body of armed men, in canoes,
under one Cariascachi penetrated into the place from
Anatolico, and to avenge some tribal affront, carried off
two of the Primates with them. Some of the Suliotes
swaggering insolently into the laboratory, and refusing
to retire, one of them was struck by the officer on
guard, a Swede, Captain Sass, with the flat of his sword,
and upon this he shot that officer dead; nor would his
comrades deliver the murderer up, because a blow with
them justified any retaliation. Moreover, the English
mechanics, under Parry, now objected to stay any
longer, alleging that they had been told they were
coming to a safe place, which Mesolonghi certainly was

not. But as there was nobody there who could fill their place, the chance of procuring the munitions of war necessary for the siege of Lepanto became more remote, and the military undertaking on which the poet had set his heart was of necessity abandoned.

"I am not in love with what I possess, but with that which I do not possess, and which is difficult to obtain." So Byron avowed to Stanhope. And he owned that he was ambitious of taking a leading part in the civil and military government of Greece—an intention deprecated by Stanhope. The latter writes :—

"The mind of Lord Byron was like a volcano, full of fire and wealth, sometimes calm, often dazzling and playful, but ever threatening. It ran swift as the lightning from one subject to another, and occasionally burst forth in passionate throes of intellect, nearly allied to madness. A striking instance of this sort of eruption I shall mention. Lord Byron's apartments were immediately over mine at Mesolonghi. In the dead of the night, I was frequently startled from my sleep by the thunders of his lordship's voice, either raging with anger, or roaring with laughter. He was, however, superstitious, and dreadfully alarmed at the idea of going mad, which he predicted would be his sad destiny. As a companion no one could be more amusing ; he had neither pedantry nor affectation about him, but was natural and playful as a boy. His conversation was a mixture of philosophy and slang, of everything, like his ' Don Juan.' He was a patient and, in general, very attentive listener. He professed a deep-rooted antipathy to the English, though he was always surrounded by Englishmen, and in reality preferred them to all others. . . . He was chivalrous even to Quixotism. . . . He said Lady Byron had committed no fault but that of having married him. The truth is he was not formed for marriage. His riotous genius could not bear restraint. His character was indeed poetic like his works. He was original and eccentric in all things. . . . If anything like justice be done to him, his character will appear far more extraordinary than any his imagination has produced."

But he absurdly depreciated Shakespeare, and Stanhope believed was jealous of him. Yet there could be no comparison between them. Byron was a subjective, narrative, reflective, and satirical poet. His model in drama was Alfieri. We know how foolishly he depreciated Wordsworth also, and his subtlety may be gauged by the astounding criticism he made on a tenderly true passage in Coleridge, asking " *Who ever saw a green sky ?* "

Mesolonghi was a fever-bed, situated on a muddy malarial swamp, and Byron's house was in the unhealthiest spot, standing on the margin of a shallow, marshy creek. Moreover, he was predisposed to fever. But for awhile he rallied after his seizures, and when the weather permitted made excursions on horseback through the neighbouring country. Although the Suliotes had now been removed from the town on account of their insubordination, Byron still retained a bodyguard of fifty, who accompanied him when he rode out, running beside him when he galloped ; he was also attended by Tita, his handsome gondolier, and a negro, made over to him by Trelawny, a black servant being regarded in Greece, and in the East, as a note of dignity, both attired *en chasseur.*

Things were looking up for Greece. The loan was being successfully negotiated in London through the influence of the poet's name, and volunteers, following his example, were flocking to the country from all parts.

Byron was strongly recommended by his medical advisers, and by his friends, to quit the pestilential neighbourhood of Mesolonghi for the restoration of his health; indeed the gravest apprehensions prevailed amongst them as to the consequences should he remain. But while some weight may be attached to Trelawny's representation of his " indolent and dawdling habits" as *one* cause of his lingering at Cephalonia, yet his main motive in not quitting Mesolonghi was that he considered it would be a desertion of his post to do so, and would set a bad example. But to be cooped up in this "fever trap," and condemned to inactivity, must have been almost unendurable to so impetuous and restless a spirit, disgusted as he was with the cruelty, and insatiable greed which characterized the Greeks—though the moderns, he thought, were not very different from the ancients! Colonel Stanhope, who had gone to Salona, wrote entreating him to leave, "not to sacrifice your health, and perhaps your life, in that bog." But, " while I can stand at all, I must stand by the cause," he said in reply to a kind offer from Zante; "there is a stake worth millions such as I am." The Congress at Salona, however, would unite the eastern and western chiefs, and enable them to devise measures for co-operating with all their forces in the ensuing campaign. Odysseus sent Mr. Finlay, and Colonel Stanhope Mr. Humphries, to persuade Byron and Mavrocordatos to attend the council. The latter was very unwilling, not caring to meet Odysseus, whom he distrusted; they were men of very different character. Byron was quite ready to go; he did not wish to appear to favour only the western chiefs, or to be the tool of Mavrocordatos, much as he liked the prince ; this indeed had been his original diffi- culty in fixing on a place of residence. However, he was too diplomatic and courteous at this juncture not to yield a little to the prince's preference, and so there occurred a delay, for which also the state of the roads, rendered impassable by heavy rains, was in part re- sponsible. They were to have left on the 27th March, but did not; and on the 30th the freedom of the city was conferred on the poet. On April 9th he received a letter from Augusta, giving good accounts of her own and of Ada's health, and enclosing a letter from Lady Byron to herself, in answer to some inquiries he had made about Ada, through Augusta. This letter, con- taining many interesting details about the child's cha- racter and habits, is certainly written in a friendly and kindly spirit, which must have gratified the father—and even the husband—for, after all, he cared about his wife. When Trelawny arrived at Mesolonghi, he found the dead poet's unfinished reply to Augusta lying on the writing-table of the room where the body lay; while a profile of Ada, which the mother had enclosed, and a cambric handkerchief, having a woman's name marked in it with hair, and stained with his own blood, with other valued treasures, strewed the floor. In this letter he expressed gratitude for the report, together with his strong interest in the fact that the child's disposition in some respects resembled his own; and this induced him to mention his recent seizure, supposed to be epileptic, so that precautions might be taken in the case of Ada, the rumour of whose ill-health had recently caused him much anxiety.

But the fierce splendour of this hot heart was burning itself away, like a great fire. The English loan had been already secured, and the poet appointed Commissioner of it. But the Congress was not held till the 16th of April; and then Byron was on his death-bed. He rode with Gamba on the 10th, and got wet to the skin with rain, insisting on getting into a boat at the city gate, as was his custom, saying playfully to Gamba, who remonstrated, "I should make a pretty soldier if I cared for such a trifle." Next day he again rode in the olive woods, though suffering from chill and rheumatic pains; but complained that the saddle had been damp, and in the evening rheumatic fever set in. Bruno, and another young physician, Millingen, urged bleeding, but he had promised his mother never to be bled, and resisted this proposal; when Millingen, however, on the 16th, hinted that insanity might develop if he were not bled, with the angriest look he held out his arm, exclaiming, "There! you are, I see, a damned set of butchers—take away as much blood as you like, and have done with it." On the 17th the bleeding was repeated twice, and blisters were put on his legs, above the knees, for he objected to their being put on his feet. All this was probably a simply murderous treatment for one like Byron, and he was worse on the 18th, though able to move for a few minutes, leaning on Tita's arm, to the adjoining room. After each of the bleedings he fainted; and he now remarked to Fletcher that he had not slept for a week, but that a man must go mad without a certain amount of sleep, adding, "I would ten times rather shoot myself than be mad, for I am not afraid of dying—I am more fit to die than people think." So Tita, when he was delirious, removed the pistols and stiletto from his bed-side. He said again to Fletcher, "I fear that you and Tita will be ill by sitting up constantly night and day ;" but they did all they could for a master they loved so dearly.

He was with difficulty persuaded to see two other doctors — but this was not till two hours before he died. He had no woman to nurse him, and the rest seem to have been very incapable of doing so. They scarcely understood one another's language ; but the tears they could not restrain probably showed him that they thought him dying. He now wished to give certain directions to Fletcher, attaching evidently much importance to them. But his powers of utterance were failing him, and then occurred the painful last scene, in which the valet played the leading part. On Fletcher asking whether he should bring pen and paper, he replied that there was no time to lose. Fletcher's own account is that his master began by saying, "You will be pro-vided for," and that he continued, "Oh ! my poor child —my dear Ada—my God ! Could I but have seen her ! Give her my blessing—and my dear sister Augusta, and her children. And you will go to Lady Byron, and say— tell her everything—you are friends with her." "His lordship," adds Fletcher, "appeared to be greatly affected at this moment. Here my master's voice failed him, so that I could only catch a word at intervals ; but he kept muttering something very seriously for some time, and would often raise his voice and say, 'Fletcher, now if you do not execute every order I have given you, I will torment you hereafter, if possible.' Here I told his lordship that I could not understand a word of what he said, to which he replied, 'O my God! then all is lost, for it is now too late. Can it be possible you have not understood me?' 'No, my lord, but I pray you to try and inform me once more.' 'How can I,' rejoined my master; 'it is now too late, and all is over!' I said, 'Not our will, but God's be done;' and he answered, 'Yes, not mine be done—but I will try.' His lordship did indeed make several efforts to speak, but could only repeat two or three words at a time—such as 'my wife! my child! my sister!—you know all—you must say all —you know my wishes,'[1] the rest was quite unintelligible." Gamba adds that in his dying hours the poet spoke concerning Greece: "I have given her my time, my means, my health—and now I give her my life! What could I do more? Poor Greece, poor town, my poor servants! Why was I not aware of this sooner? I do not care for death, but why did I not go home before I came here? *Io lascio qualche cosa di caro nel mondo.* For the rest I am content to die." When he was delirious, he appeared to fancy he was leading the assault on Lepanto, and called out, "Forwards, forwards —courage—follow my example — don't be afraid!" Before this he kept hold of Tita's hand, who averted his face, weeping, and Byron exclaimed, "*O! questa è una bella scena!*" In his delirium he quoted verses from the

---

[1] The widow showed deep and genuine distress when Fletcher visited her on his return, and told her of that last unintelligible message, she pacing the room with tears and sobs. (See Miss Martineau's "Sketches.")

Bible, and sometimes swore at the terrible pain. He seems also to have named Hobhouse and Kinnaird. It was about six o'clock in the evening of the 18th of April when he said, " *Now I shall go to sleep*," and these were his last words. Appropriate surely for such as he!—" the dead but seek rest, they have had enough of life, and this they implore," he had observed, on reading the epitaphs at Ferrara, " *Implora pace*." After lying another four and twenty hours in a state of unconsciousness, partly under the influence of narcotic drinks, he opened his eyes at a quarter past six in the evening of April 19th, and then immediately, during a terrible thunderstorm, the storm-loving spirit took flight. Byron was dead.

By order of Mavrocordatos, thirty-seven shots, one for each year of the poet's life, were fired from the battery, being answered by the Turks from Patras with exultant volleys. The poet received princely honours at the funeral service, soldiers lining the streets, and a procession of ecclesiastics chanting psalms, as they preceded the rude coffin, on which were placed a sword, helmet, and laurel crown—the warrior-bard's horse also following. Gamba and Mavrocordatos attended the funeral, and a company of Byron's brigade. Tricoupi delivered a funeral oration in Greek.

A post-mortem examination having been made, and the remains embalmed, the bier was left open till the following evening, and multitudes came to take a last look at their great friend and Liberator. It was ordered that all shops and public offices should be closed for three days, the Easter festivities suspended, a general mourning observed, and in all churches prayers for the dead offered up. The Greeks desired that the poet might be buried in the Temple of Theseus at Athens: But it was decided that the body should be conveyed to England for sepulture in Westminster Abbey. Stanhope therefore accompanied it in the *Florida.* Permission, however, was refused by the Dean. So, after lying in state for some days in London, Byron was buried with his mother and his ancestors in the little church at Hucknall, such being the desire of the woman who loved him, his sister Augusta.[1] His ashes do not rest in the great English Abbey; but "*si monumentum quæris, circumspice !*"

> " This should have been a noble creature—he
> Hath all the energy, which would have made
> A goodly frame of glorious elements,
> Had they been wisely mingled."

---

[1] By the recently published "Autobiography of Mary Howitt," it appears that not one of the "respectable," and conservative little gentry about Nottingham responded to the invitation to attend the funeral procession at Hucknall, so strong was their instinctive feeling that he was the enemy of their pretentions ; but the great-hearted common people attended in masses the burial of their illustrious friend. The faithful and excellent Hobhouse, pale and careworn, alone represented the intimates of the poet.

APPENDIX.

BYRON'S GRAVE.[1]

(In Hucknall Church, the sexton had said to me, "You are now standing just over where the head lies.")

NAY, Byron, nay ! not under where we tread,
Dumb weight of stone, lies thine imperial head !
Into no vault lethargic, dark, and dank
The splendid strength of thy swift spirit sank :
No narrow church in precincts cold and grey
Confines the plume that loved to breast the day ;
Thy self-consuming, scathing heart of flame
Was quenched to feed no silent coffin's shame !
A fierce, glad fire in buoyant hearts art thou,
A radiance in auroral spirits now ;
A stormy wind, an ever-sounding ocean,
A life, a power, a never-wearying motion !
Or deadly gloom, or terrible despair,
An earthquake-mockery of strong creeds that were
Assured possession of calm earth and sky,
Where doom-distraught pale souls took sanctuary,
As in strong temples.   The same blocks shall build,
Iconoclast, the edifice you spilled,

---

[1] From "Songs of the Heights and Deeps" by Honble. Roden Noel (Kegan Paul and Co.).

More durable, more fair : O Scourge of God,
It was Himself who urged thee on thy road ;
And thou, Don Juan, Harold, Manfred, Cain,
Song-crowned within the world's young heart shalt reign !
Whene'er we hear embroiled lashed ocean roar,
Or thunder echoing among heights all hoar,
Brother ! thy mighty measure heightens theirs,
While Freedom on his rent red banner bears
The deathless names of many a victory won,
Inspired by thy death-shattering clarion !
In Love's immortal firmament are set
Twin stars of Romeo and Juliet,
And their companions young eyes discover
In Cycladean Haidee with her lover.

May all the devastating force be spent ?
Or all thy godlike energies lie shent ?
Nay, thou art founded in the strength Divine ;
The Soul's immense eternity is thine.
Profound Beneficence absorbs thy power,
While Ages tend the long-maturing flower :
Our Sun himself, one tempest of wild flame,
For source of joy, and very life men claim
In mellowing corn, in bird and bloom of spring,
In leaping lambs, and lovers dallying.
Byron ! the whirlwinds rended not in vain ;
Aloof behold they nourish and sustain !
In the far end we shall account them gain.

R. N.

FRAGMENT FROM THE " MONK OF ATHOS," BY LORD BYRON.

BESIDE the confines of the Ægean main,
Where northward Macedonia bounds the flood,
And views opposed the Asiatic plain,
Where once the pride of lofty Ilion stood,

Like the great Father of the giant brood,
With lowering port majestic Athos stands,
Crowned with the verdure of eternal wood,
As yet unspoil'd by sacrilegious hands,
And throws his mighty shade o'er seas and distant lands.

And deep embosomed in his shady groves
Full many a convent rears its glitt'ring spire,
Mid scenes where Heavenly contemplation loves
To kindle in the soul her hallowed fire,
Where air and sea with rocks and woods conspire
To breathe a sweet religious calm around,
Weaning the thoughts from every low desire,
And the wild waves that break with murm'ring sound
Along the rocky shore proclaim it holy ground.

Sequestered shades where Piety has given
A quiet refuge from each earthly care,
Whence the rapt spirit may ascend to Heaven!
Oh, ye condemned the ills of life to bear!
As with advancing age your woes increase,
What bliss amidst these solitudes to share
The happy foretaste of eternal Peace,
Till Heav'n in mercy bids your pains and sorrows cease.

ERRATUM.

Page 77, 4th line from bottom,

For "if only" *read* "only if."

14

INDEX.

BIBLIOGRAPHY.

BY

JOHN P. ANDERSON

(British Museum).

I. WORKS.

The Poetical Works of Lord Byron. From the last London edition. 2 vols. Boston, 1814, 12mo.

The Works of Lord Byron. Vol. i. (-viii.). London, 1815, 17-20, 12mo.

The Works of Lord Byron. 5 vols. London, 1817, 16mo.

The Works of the Right Honourable Lord Byron. 8 vols. London, 1818-20, 16mo.

The Works of Lord Byron. Vols. i.-iii. London, 1819, 8vo.

The Works of Lord Byron, comprehending all his suppressed poems. Embellished with a portrait and a sketch of his lordship's life. Second edition. Paris, 1819, 12mo.

The Works of Lord Byron. 12 vols. Paris, 1822-24, 12mo.

The Works of Lord Byron. 16 vols. *Galignani:* Paris, 1822-24, 12mo.

The Works of Lord Byron. Vols. v., vi., vii. London, 1824-25, 8vo.

Vol. v. published by Knight and Lacey; vols. vi. and vii. by John and Henry Leigh Hunt. Vol. viii. is advertised, but was not published. A supplementary edition, comprising Hours of Idleness, English Bards and Scotch Reviewers, Werner, Heaven and Earth, The Island, The Vision of Judgment, The Deformed Transformed, and some miscellaneous poems.

The Works of Lord Byron. Another edition. The Complete Works of Lord Byron, with a biographical and critical notice by J. W. Lake. 7 vols. Paris, 1825, 8vo.

The Works of Lord Byron, including the suppressed poems. [The Life of Lord Byron, by J. W. Lake.) *Galignani*: Paris, 1826, 8vo.

——Another edition. 13 vols. Paris, 1826, 32mo.

——Another edition. Paris, 1827, 8vo.

The Works of Lord Byron. 4 vols. London, 1828, 12mo.

The Works of Lord Byron, including the suppressed poems. (The Life of Lord Byron, by J. W. Lake.] Paris, 1828, 8vo.

The Works of Lord Byron. 4 vols. London, 1829, 12mo.

The Complete Works of Lord Byron, including his suppressed poems, with others never before published. Paris, 1831, 8vo.

The Works of Lord Byron. 6 vols. London, 1831, 16mo.

The Complete Works of Lord Byron, reprinted from the last London edition, with considerable additions, now first published; containing notes and illustrations by Moore, Walter Scott, Campbell, Jeffrey, E. Brydges, Wilson, Hobhouse, Dallas, Hunt, Milman, Lockhart, Bowles, Heber, Medwin, Gamba, Croly, Ugo Foscolo, Ellis, Kennedy, Parry, Stanhope, Galt, Nathan, Lady Blessington, Mrs. Shelley, etc., and a complete index; to which is prefixed a Life, by H. L. Bulwer. Paris, 1835, 8vo.

The Works of Lord Byron, with his letters and journals, and his life, by Thomas Moore. 17 vols. London, 1835, 32, 33, 8vo.

The Complete Works of Lord Byron, from the last London edition, now first collected and arranged, and illustrated with notes. To which is prefixed the life of the author, by J. Galt, etc. Paris, 1837, 8vo.

Byron's Complete Works, etc. 8 vols. London, 1839, 8vo.

The Poetical Works, Letters, and Journals of Lord Byron, with notices of his life, by Thomas Moore. [This collection was formed by Wm. Watts, Esq., and consists of "The Poetical Works of Lord Byron, in eight volumes," published by Murray in 1839; and the "Letters and Journals of Lord Byron, with notices of his life, by Thomas Moore. In two volumes," published by Murray in 1830; to which have been added Byron's "Letter to * * * * * * * * * *", on the Rev. W. L. Bowles' strictures on the life and writings of Pope. Second edition," and a few other printed papers; also numerous views, portraits, autograph letters, and signatures of distinguished persons, etc.] 44 vols. London, 1844, 4to.

This collection is in the British Museum Library. The above general title, printed expressly for it, is prefixed to each volume. There is a full MS. Index in folio. "Many of the portraits are from private plates, many of the autographs are historically and otherwise interesting. The views, many of them, are proof impressions of rare quality."

The Poetical Works of Lord Byron. Collected and arranged, with illustrative notes, by Thomas Moore, Lord Jeffrey, Sir Walter Scott. With a portrait, etc. (Fac-similes of Lord Byron's handwriting at various periods of his life.) London, 1845, 8vo.

The Works of Lord Byron, in verse and prose. Including his letters, journals, etc. With a sketch of his life. [Edited by Fitz-Greene Halleck.] Hartford, 1847, 8vo.

The Poetical Works of Lord Byron (complete in one volume). Collected and arranged, with notes and illustrations of Thomas Moore, Lord Jeffrey, Sir Walter Scott, Bishop Heber, Samuel Rogers, etc. London 1850, 8vo.

The Works of Lord Byron, with a life and illustrative notes. By W. Anderson. 2 vols. Edinburgh [1850], 8vo.

The Poetical Works of Lord Byron. Containing several attributed and suppressed poems. With a memoir by H. L. Bulwer. London, 1851, 12mo.

The Illustrated Byron, with upwards of two hundred engravings from original drawings, by K. Meadows, B. Foster, H. K. Browne, G. Janet, and E. Morin. London [1854, 55], 8vo.

The Poetical Works of Lord Byron. A new edition. 6 vols. London, 1855, 56, 8vo.

——New edition. London, 1857, 8vo.
Re-issued in 1867, with a new title-page, and without the line border.

The Poetical Works of Lord Byron. Collected and arranged, with notes, by Sir Walter Scott, Lord Jeffrey, Professor Wilson, Esq. New and complete edition. With portrait and illustrative engravings. London, 1859, 8vo.

In this edition objectionable pieces have been excluded. The Poetical Works of Lord Byron. With life. Edinburgh [1859], 8vo.

The Poetical Works of Lord Byron. With illustrations, by K. Halswelle. (The life of Lord Byron, by A. Leighton.) Edinburgh, 1861, 8vo.

The Poetical Works of Lord Byron. 10 vols. Boston, 1861, 8vo.

The Works of Lord Byron, complete in five volumes. Second edition. Leipzig, 1866, 12mo.
Vols. 8-12 of the "Tauchnitz Collection of British Authors."

The Poetical Works of Lord Byron. With illustrations [and life of the author, by A. Leighton]. New edition. Edinburgh [1868], 8vo.

The Poetical Works of Lord Byron. Reprinted from the original editions, with explanatory notes, etc. London [1869], 8vo.
Part of the "Chandos Classics."

The Poetical Works of Lord Byron, with life and portrait, and sixteen illustrations, by F. Gilbert. London [1869], 8vo.

The Poetical Works of Lord Byron. With illustrative notes, by Moore, Lord Jeffrey, Sir Walter Scott, etc. New York, 1869, 8vo.

The Poetical Works of Lord Byron. Edited, with a critical memoir, by W. M. Rossetti. Illustrated by Ford Madox Brown. London, 1870, 8vo.

The Complete Works of Lord Byron. With an introductory memoir by W. B. Scott. With illustrations. London [1874], 8vo.

The Poetical Works of Lord Byron. Illustrated edition. London [1874], 8vo.

The Poetical Works of Lord Byron. Illustrated edition. London [1878, etc.], 8vo.

The Poetical Works of Lord Byron. London [1878], 8vo.

The Poetical Works of Lord Byron. Edited, with a critical memoir, by William Michael Rossetti. Illustrated by Thomas Seccombe. London [1880], 8vo.
    Part of "Moxon's Popular Poets."

Poems by Lord Byron. London, [1880], 8vo.
    Part of the "Excelsior Series."

The Poetical Works of Lord Byron. Reprinted from the original editions, with life, explanatory notes, etc. The "Albion" edition. London [1881], 8vo.

The Poetical Works of Lord Byron. With life, etc. Edinburgh [1881], 8vo.
    Part of the "Landscape Series of Poets."

The Poetical Works of Lord Byron. Edited with a critical memoir, by W. M. Rossetti. Illustrated by T. Seccombe. London [1882], 8vo.

The Complete Poetical Works of Lord Byron, with an introductory memoir by William B. Scott. London, 1883, 8vo.

The Poetical Works of Lord Byron. With original and additional notes. 12 vols. London, 1885, 8vo.

The Complete Poetical Works of Lord Byron, with memoir by W. B. Scott. 3 vols. London, 1886, 8vo.

The Complete Poetical Works of Lord Byron. With an introductory memoir by W. B. Scott. London, 1887, 8vo.

II. — MISCELLANEOUS COLLECTIONS, ETC.

Review of Wordsworth's "Poems," 1807. (*Monthly Literary Recreations*, vol. 3, 1807, pp. 65, 66.)

Review of Gell's "Geography of Ithaca and Itinerary of Greece." (*Monthly Review*, vol. 65 N.S., 1811, pp. 371-385.)

Imitations and Translations, etc. Collected by J. C. Hobhouse. London, 1809, 8vo.
    Contains nine poems by Byron.

An Ode [on Waterloo]. On the Star of the Legion of Honour. Napoleon's Farewell. Fare Thee Well. And a Sketch, etc. New York, 1816, 8vo.

Three poems, not included in the Works of Lord Byron. Lines to Lady J—— [Jersey]. The Ænigma. The Curse of Minerva. London, 1818, 8vo.

English Bards and Scotch Reviewers; Ode to the Land of the Gaul. Sketch from private life. Windsor Poetics, etc. Second edition. Paris, 1818, 12mo.

The Works of Lord Byron; containing English Bards and Scotch Reviewers; the Curse of Minerva, and the Waltz, an apostrophic hymn. Philadelphia, 1820, 8vo.

Beppo; Mazeppa; Ode to Venice, a Fragment; a Spanish Romance; and Sonnet translated from Vittorelli. London, 1820, 12mo.

The Liberal: Verse and Prose from the South. [By Leigh Hunt, Lord Byron, and others.] 2 vols. London, 1822-23, 8vo.

Byron's contributions were:—Vol. 1—The Vision of Judgment; A Letter to the Editor of "My Grandmother's Review"; Heaven and Earth, A Mystery. Vol. 2—The Blues, a Literary Eclogue; Il Morgante Maggiore (translation from Pulci).

The Blues, a Literary Eclogue. (*The Liberal*, vol. 2, pp. 1-21.) London, 1823, 8vo.

Il Morgante Maggiore. (Translation from Pulci. *The Liberal*, vol. 2, pp. 193-249.)

Miscellaneous poems, including those on his domestic circumstances. To which are prefixed Memoirs of the author, and a tribute to his memory by Sir Walter Scott. London, 1824, 12mo.

Don Juan, complete: English Bards and Scotch Reviewers; Hours of Idleness; the Waltz; and all the other minor poems. London, 1827, 12mo.

Don Juan; Hours of Idleness; English Bards and Scotch Reviewers; the Waltz; and other poems. 2 vols. London, 1828, 12mo.

Fugitive pieces and reminiscences of Lord Byron; containing an entire new edition of the Hebrew Melodies, with the addition of several never before published. Also some original poetry, letters, and recollections of Lady Caroline Lamb, by I. Nathan. London, 1829, 8vo.

The Miscellaneous Works of Lord Byron. Containing Werner, a tragedy; Heaven and Earth; Morgante Maggiore; Age of Bronze; the Island; Vision of Judgment; and the Deformed Transformed. London, 1830, 8vo.

Lord Byron's Tales : consisting of the Giaour, the Bride of Abydos, the Corsair, Lara, Hebrew Melodies, and other poems. Halifax, 1845, 16mo.

The Giaour, and the Bride of Abydos. London, 1848, 16mo.

Tales and Poems. London, 1848, 8vo.

——Another edition. London, 1853, 16mo.

Hours of Idleness. English Bards and Scotch Reviewers. Poems on domestic circumstances, etc. London, 1851, 8vo.
    In vol. ii. of the "Cabinet Edition of the British Poets."

Miscellanies. 2 vols. London, 1853, 16mo.

Dramas. 2 vols. London, 1853, 16mo.

Beppo and Don Juan. 2 vols. London, 1853, 16mo.

Poems. With his memoirs. London, 1855, 32mo.

——Another edition. London, 1859, 8vo.

Eastern Tales ; comprising the Corsair, Lara, the Giaour, the Bride of Abydos, and the Siege of Corinth. With the author's original introductions and notes. Illustrated. London [1859], 8vo.

Byron's Siege of Corinth and Ode to Napoleon Buonaparte, etc. Madras, 1876, 12mo.

III. SEPARATE WORKS.

The Age of Bronze : or, Carmen seculare et annus haud mirabilis, etc. London, 1823, 8vo.

Beppo, a Venetian story. London, 1818, 8vo.

——Seventh edition. London, 1818, 8vo.

The Bride of Abydos. A Turkish Tale. London, 1813, 8vo.

This work ran into ten editions during 1813, 1814. The eleventh edition appeared the following year.

——Another edition. London, 1825, 12mo.

——Another edition. [London, 1844], 12mo.

Cain, a Mystery. London, 1822, 12mo.

First published with "Sardanapalus" in 1821.

——Second edition. To which is added a letter from the author to Mr. Murray. London, 1822, 8vo.

——Another edition. London, 1824, 12mo.

——Lord Byron's Cain, a Mystery: with notes; wherein the religion of the Bible is considered, in reference to acknowledged philosophy and reason. By Harding Grant. London, 1830, 8vo.

——Cain; a Mystery, etc. London, 1832, 8vo.

Childe Harold's Pilgrimage. [Cantos I. and II.] A Romaunt. London, 1812, 4to.

Five editions appeared the same year.

——Sixth edition. London, 1813, 8vo.

——Seventh edition. London, 1814, 8vo.

——Tenth edition. London, 1815, 8vo.

——Eleventh edition. London, 1819, 8vo.

——Childe Harold's Pilgrimage. Canto the third. London, 1816, 8vo.

——Childe Harold's Pilgrimage. Canto the fourth. London, 1818, 8vo.

——Childe Harold's Pilgrimage. A romaunt in four cantos. 2 vols. London, 1819, 8vo.

——Another edition. London, 1825, 12mo.

——Another edition. London, 1826, 12mo.

——Another edition. London, 1827, 24mo.

——Another edition. London [1830], 12mo.

——Campe's edition. Nuremberg and New York [1831], 12mo.

——Another edition. London, 1841, 8vo.

——Another edition. London, 1853, 16mo.

——Another edition. Illustrated from original sketches. London, 1859, 8vo.

——New edition. London, 1860, 8vo.

——Another edition. With a memoir by Spalding. Illustrated. London [1866], 8vo.

——Illustrated edition. London, 1869 [1868], 4to.

——Another edition. London, 1877, 12mo.

——Another edition. With explanatory notes. Edited by W. Hiley. London, 1877, 8vo.

——Another edition. Edited, with introduction and notes, by H. F. Tozer. Oxford, 1885, 8vo.

Part of the "Clarendon Press Series."

——Another edition. Illustrated. Boston, 1886, 8vo.

——Another edition. London, 1888, 16mo.

Part of "Routledge's Pocket Library."

—— —— Venice from Lord Byron's Childe Harold. With original drawings made in Venice by L. Sambourne. London, 1878, fol.

Conversations of Lord Byron with the Countess of Blessington. London, 1834, 8vo.

Conversations of Lord Byron with Thomas Medwin, Esq. 2 vols. London, 1832, 8vo.
No. 14 of Gleig's "National Library."

The Corsair, a tale. London, 1814, 8vo.
Seven editions appeared the same year.

——Tenth edition. London, 1818, 8vo.

——Another edition. London, 1825, 12mo.

——Another edition. [London, 1844], 8vo.

——Another edition. London, 1867, 16mo.
Part of "Murray's Standard Poets."

The Curse of Minerva, a poem. London, 1812, 4to.

——Another edition. Philadelphia, 1815, 8vo.

——Third edition. Paris, 1818, 12mo.

——Fourth edition. Paris, 1820, 12mo.

The Deformed Transformed ; a drama [in two parts with the opening chorus of a third part, and in verse]. London, 1824, 8vo.

——Second edition. London, 1824, 8vo.

Don Juan. [Cantos I. and II.] London, 1819, 4to.

——New edition. London, 1819, 8vo.

——Don Juan. [Cantos I.-II.] An exact copy from the quarto edition. London, 1819, 8vo.

——Another edition. An exact copy from the quarto edition. London, 1820, 4to.

——New edition. London, 1820, 8vo

Don Joan. Another edition. London, 1820, 8vo.

——Don Juan. Cantos III., IV., and V. London, 1821, 8vo.

——Another edition. London, 1821, 8vo.

——Another edition. London, 1821, 4to.

——Don Juan. Cantos VI., VII., and VIII. London, 1823, 8vo.

——Don Juan. Cantos IX., X., and XI. London, 1823, 8vo.

——Don Juan. Cantos XII., XIII., and XIV. London, 1823, 12mo.

——Another edition. London, 1823, 12mo.

——Don Juan. Cantos XV. and XVI. London, 1824, 12mo.

——Don Juan. 4 pts. London, 1822, 12mo.

——Don Juan. [Cantos I. and II.] A new edition. (Cantos III., IV., and V. Fifth edition, revised and corrected.) 2 vols. London, 1822, 8vo.

——New edition. (Cantos I.-V.) with notes, and three engravings after Corbould. London [1825], 12mo.

——A correct copy from the original edition. [Cantos I.-V. only. With coloured illustrations.] London [1826], 8vo.

——Don Juan. 6 pts. London, 1820-24, 12mo.

——Don Juan. (Cantos I.-V.) With a preface by a Clergyman. London, 1822, 12mo.

——Another edition. London, 1823, 12mo.

——Another edition. 2 vols. London, 1826, 8vo.

——Another edition. London, 1826, 8vo.

——Another edition. With a short biographical memoir of

the author (signed Z). London, 1827, 12mo.

——Another edition. 2 vols. London, 1828, 8vo.

——Another edition. London, 1833, 12mo.

——Another edition. London, 1835, 12mo.

——Another edition. London, 1849, 12mo.

——Another edition. London, [1874], 16mo.

——Another edition. London, 1875, 16mo.

Part of "The Golden Library."

——Complete edition. With notes. London, 1886, 8vo.

——Another edition. With notes. London, 1886, 8vo.

Part of the "Excelsior Series."

——Don Juan. Cantos XII.-XVI. 2 vols. Paris, 1824, 12mo.

Byron's Dream, illustrated by Mrs. Lees. [London] 1849, fol.

Gothic letters printed in gold on cardboard. Appeared originally in 1816 with the "Prisoner of Chillon, and other poems."

English Bards and Scotch Reviewers. A satire. London [1809], 12mo.

——Another edition. London [1809], 8vo.

The copy in the British Museum has the variations of other editions in MS.

——Second edition, with considerable additions and alterations. London, 1809, 8vo.

——Third edition. London, 1810, 8vo.

Re-issued the same year with a new title-page and new preface.

——Fourth edition. London, 1810, 8vo.

——Fourth edition. London, 1811, 8vo.

——Fourth [or rather fifth] edition. London, 1811, 8vo.

"This is one of the few copies preserved of the suppressed edition,

which would have been the fifth. No title-page was printed, the one prefixed was taken from the fourth edition."

——Fourth edition. London, 1811, 8vo.

This and the preceding, though each purporting to be of the "fourth edition," are in reality different editions. This copy, moreover, contains on supplemented leaves, revisions of its text, and also of that of the first edition, two prefaces, two postscripts, and pp. 1 to 6, 29 to 32, 49 to 52, 59, 60, and 79 to 82 of the text of the first edition.

——Another edition. English Bards, etc. Ode to the Land of the Gaul, etc. Third edition. Paris, 1819, 12mo.

——Another edition. With notes and preface. Brussels, 1819, 8vo.

——Another edition. Geneva, 1820, 12mo.

——Another edition. Leicester, 1823, 12mo.

——New edition, with a life of the author. To which is added "Fare thee Well," a poem. Glasgow, 1824, 12mo.

——Another edition. (*The British Satirist*, pp. 1-43.) Glasgow, 1826, 12mo.

——Another edition. (*Gifford's Baviad and Maviad*, pp. 143-176.) London, 1827, 12mo.

——Another edition. Glasgow, 1825, 12mo.

——Another edition. London, 1825, 12mo.

——New edition. London, 1827, 8vo.

Fare thee Well. [London?] 1816, 4to.

Privately printed.

——Fare thee Well, a poem. A sketch from private life, a poem. Bristol, 1816, 8vo.

——Fare thee Well! and other poems. Edinburgh, 1816, 8vo.

Fugitive pieces. A fac-simile reprint of the suppressed edition of 1806. London, 1886, 8vo.
Printed for private circulation.

Poems on various occasions. Newark, 1807, 8vo.
There were one hundred copies only, privately printed. This is the second edition of a collection, of which the first edition, in 4to, was suppressed. The preface is dated December 23, 1806. Most of the poems in this collection were subsequently published under the title, "Hours of Idleness." The copy in the British Museum contains a few MS. notes by the author and another.

——Poems original and translated. Second edition. Newark, 1808, 8vo.

Hours of Idleness, a series of poems, original and translated. Newark, 1807, 8vo.
There is a copy on *large paper* in the British Museum Library.

——Second edition. Paris, 1819, 8vo.

——Another edition. London, 1820, 8vo.

——Third edition. Paris, 1820, 8vo.

——Another edition. London, 1822, 12mo.

——New edition. Glasgow, 1825, 8vo.

The Giaour, a fragment of a Turkish tale. London, 1813, 8vo.

——New edition, with some additions. London, 1813, 8vo.

——Third edition, with additions. London, 1813, 8vo.

——Fifth edition, with considerable additions. London, 1813, 8vo.

——Sixth edition. London, 1813, 8vo.

——Seventh edition, with some additions. London, 1813, 8vo.

The Giaour. Ninth edition. London, 1814, 8vo.
Three other editions were published the same year.

——Fourteenth edition. London, 1815, 8vo.

——Another edition. London, 1825, 12mo.

——Another edition. London, 1842, 12mo.

——Another edition. [London, 1844], 8vo.

Heaven and Earth ; a Mystery. London, 1824, 12mo.
Appeared originally in Part II. of *The Liberal.*

——Another edition. [London, 1825 ?], 12mo.

Hebrew Melodies. London, 1815, 8vo.

——Another edition. London, 1823, 12mo.

——Another edition. London, 1825, 12mo.

The Island, or Christian and his Comrades. London, 1823, 8vo.

——Second edition. London, 1823, 8vo.

——Another edition. Paris, 1823, 8vo.

——Third edition. London, 1823, 8vo.

The Lament of Tasso. London, 1817, 8vo.
Five editions appeared the same year and a sixth in 1818.

Lara, a Tale [by Lord Byron]. Jacqueline, a Tale [by Samuel Rogers]. London, 1814, 8vo.

——Fourth edition. London, 1814, 8vo.

——Fifth edition. London, 1817, 8vo.

Manfred, a dramatic poem. London, 1817, 8vo.

——Second edition. London, 1817, 8vo.

——Another edition. Brussels, n. d. 8vo.

Manfred. Another edition. London, 1824, 12mo.
——Another edition. London [1864], 12mo.
    Part of vol. 60 of "Lacy's Acting edition of Plays."
Marino Faliero, Doge of Venice; an historical tragedy, in five acts. With notes. The Prophecy of Dante; a poem. London, 1821, 8vo.
——Second edition. London, 1821, 8vo.
——Another edition. London, 1823, 8vo.
——Another edition. London, 1842, 12mo.
Mazeppa, a poem. (Ode [to Venice]. A fragment.) London, 1819, 8vo.
——Second edition. Paris, 1819, 8vo.
——Another edition. London, 1824, 12mo.
——Another edition. London [1854], 32mo.
Monody on the death of the Right Hon. R. B. Sheridan. Written at the request of a friend, to be spoken at Drury Lane Theatre. London, 1816, 8vo.
——New edition. London, 1817, 8vo.
——New edition. London, 1818, 8vo.
Ode to Napoleon Buonaparte. London, 1814, 8vo.
——Second edition. London, 1814, 8vo.
——Twelfth edition. London, 1816, 8vo.
——Thirteenth edition. London, 1818, 8vo.
The Parliamentary Speeches of Lord Byron. Printed from the copies prepared by his Lordship for publication. London, 1824, 8vo.

Poems on his Domestic Circumstances. I. Fare thee well! II. A Sketch from Private Life. With the Star of the Legion of Honour, and other poems. London, 1816, 8vo.
——Second edition. London, 1816, 8vo.
——Second edition. Bristol, 1816, 12mo.
——Another edition. Dublin, 1816, 8vo.
——Sixth edition, containing eight poems. London, 1816, 8vo.
——Eighth edition. With his memoirs and portrait. Containing nine poems. London, 1816, 8vo.
——Fifteenth edition. London, 1816, 8vo.
——Twenty-third edition, etc. London, 1817, 8vo.
——Another edition. To which are added several choice pieces from his works. London, 1823, 12mo.
——Another edition. The Miscellaneous Poems of Lord Byron [on his domestic circumstances]. London, 1825, 12mo.
——Another edition. London, 1825, 12mo.
Poems. Second edition. London, 1816, 8vo.
The Prisoner of Chillon, and other poems. London, 1816, 8vo.
——Another edition. Lausanne, 1818, 8vo.
——Another edition. London, 1824, 12mo.
——Another edition. Geneva, 1830, 16mo.
——Another edition. [London, 1825?], 12mo.
——Another edition, illuminated by W. and G. Audsley—Chromo-

lithographed by R. W. Tymms. London [1865], 4to.

The Prophecy of Dante: A poem. London, 1825, 12mo.
  Originally appeared with "Marino Faliero" in 1821.

The Genuine Rejected Addresses, presented to the Committee of Management for Drury Lane Theatre; preceded by that written by Lord Byron, and adopted by the Committee. London, 1812, 8vo.

Sardanapalus, a tragedy [in five acts and in verse]. The Two Foscari [in five acts and in verse]. Cain, a Mystery [in three acts and in verse]. London, 1821, 8vo.

——Sardanapalus; a tragedy. London, 1829, 8vo.

——Arranged for representation in four acts by C. Calvert. Manchester [1855?], 8vo.

——Another edition. London [1853], 12mo.
  Forms part of vol. xi. of "Lacy's Acting Edition of Plays."

The Siege of Corinth, a poem. Parisina, a poem. London, 1816, 8vo.

——Second edition. London, 1816, 8vo.

——Third edition. London, 1816, 8vo.

——Another edition. London, 1824, 12mo.

The Two Visions; or Byron v. Southey. Containing the Vision of Judgment by Dr. Southey, also another Vision of Judgment by Lord Byron. London, 1822, 1mo.
  The Vision of Judgment appeared originally in Part 1 of the *Liberal,* 1822, pp. 15-39.

——The Vision of Judgment, by Quevedo Redivivus. Suggested by the composition so entitled by the author of "Wat Tyler" [R. Southey]. London, 1824, 8vo.

Waltz; an Apostrophic Hymn. By H. Hornem, Esq. [London, 1813] 8vo.

——Another edition, followed by some fugitive pieces. London, 1821, 8vo.

Werner; a tragedy. London, 1823, 8vo.
  Published in December 1822.

——Another edition. London, 1887, 16mo.
  Part of "Routledge's Pocket Library."

IV. SELECTIONS.

Life and Select Poems of Lord Byron, arranged, etc., by C. Hulbert. London [1828], 12mo.

The Beauties of Byron, consisting of selections from his works. By J. W. Lake. Paris, 1829, 16mo.

The Beauties of Byron, consisting of selections from his works; by A. Howard. London [1835], 12mo.

——New edition. London, 1837, 12mo.

The Beauties of Byron and Burns, being a collection of poems by the above authors. Hull, 1837, 32mo.

Beauties of English Poets. [Containing poems by Lord Byron and others, in English and translated into Armenian; together with several pieces of Armenian prose, with an English translation by Lord Byron.] Venice, 1852, 12mo.

Selections from the Writings of Lord Byron. By a Clergyman. 2 vols. London, 1854, 8vo.
  One of a series called "Murray's Railway Reading."

A Selection from the Works of Lord Byron. Edited and prefaced by Algernon Charles Swinburne. London, 1866, 8vo.
    Part of "Moxon's Miniature Poets."
——Another edition. London [1885], 12mo.

Rough hewing of Lord Byron in French, with the English text. By F. D'Autrey. London, 1869, 8vo.

Songs by Lord Byron. London, 1872, 16mo.

Lord Byron's Armenian Exercises and Poetry. [Consisting of English translations by him from Armenian literature and Armenian translations from his poetry, etc.] Venice, 1876, 12mo.

Favourite Poems. Illustrated. Boston, 1877, 16mo.

The Byron Birthday Book; compiled and edited by J. Burrows. London, 1879 [1878], 16mo.
——Second thousand. London [1880], 16mo.

Poetry of Byron; chosen and arranged [with a preface] by Matthew Arnold. London, 1881, 8vo.

Gems from Byron. With an introduction by the Rev. Hugh R. Haweis. London, 1886, 16mo.
    No. 33 of "Routledge's World Library."

Poems of Lord Byron. Carefully selected. London [1886], 32mo.
    Part of "Cassell's Miniature Library of the Poets."

V. LETTERS.

Correspondence of Lord Byron with a friend, including his letters to his mother, written from Portugal, Spain, Greece, and the shores of the Mediterranean, in 1809, 1810, and 1811. Also recollections of the Poet, by the late R. C. Dallas, and a continuation and preliminary statement of the proceedings by which the letters were suppressed in England, at the suit of Lord Byron's executors. By the Rev. A. R. C. Dallas. 3 vols. Paris, 1825, 12mo.

Letters and Journals of Lord Byron, with notices of his life by T. Moore. 2 vols. London, 1830, 4to.
——Another edition. Paris, 1831, 8vo.
——Third edition, with engravings. 3 vols. London, 1833, 8vo.
——New edition, complete in one volume. The Life of Lord Byron, with his letters, etc. London, 1847, 8vo.
——New edition, with portraits and illustrations. London [1859]-60, 8vo.
——New and revised edition, with twelve illustrations, etc. London, 1875, 8vo.

The Letters and Journals of Lord Byron. Selected. With introduction by Mathilde Blind. London, 1886, 8vo.
    Part of the "Camelot Series."

Letter to * * * * * * * * * * [John Murray] on the Rev. W. L. Bowles' strictures on the life and writings of Pope, etc. London, 1821, 8vo.
——Second edition. London, 1821, 8vo.
——Another edition. Paris, 1821, 8vo.

Letter to the Editor of "My Grandmother's Review," signed

"Wortley Clutterbuck." To the Editor of the British Review. (*The Liberal*, vol. i., pp. 41-50.)

Lord Byron. A fac-simile of an interesting letter written by Lord Byron, dated 15th January 1809. An Essay affording a curious insight into his character and early views of leading men, etc. London, 1876, 4to.

VI. APPENDIX.

BIOGRAPHY, CRITICISM, ETC.

Anton, H. S.—Byron's Manfred, [A lecture.] Naumberg, 1875, 8vo.

Arnold, Matthew. — Essays in Criticism. Second series. London, 1888, 8vo.
    Byron, pp. 163-204.

Aston, James and Edward.— Pompeii, and other poems. To which is added a dissertation on Lord Byron. London, 1828, 16mo.

Austin, Alfred.—A Vindication of Lord Byron [occasioned by Mrs. Stowe's article, "The true story of Lord Byron's Life"]. London, 1869, 8vo.

Axon, William E. A. — Stray Chapters in Literature, Folk-Lore and Archæology. Manchester, 1888, 8vo.
    Byron's Influence on European Literature, pp. 47-56. Published originally in the "Papers of the Manchester Literary Club," vol. x. 1884, pp. 323-329

B., F. H.—An Address to Lord Byron, with an opinion on some of his writings. By F. H. B. London, 1817, 8vo.

Bagnall, Edward.—Lord Byron [a poem], with remarks on his genius and character. Oxford, 1831, 8vo.

Belfast, Earl of. — Poets and Poetry of the Nineteenth Century. A course of lectures. London, 1852, 8vo.
    Byron, pp. 140-165.

Belloc, Louise Swanton.— Lord Byron. 2 tom. Paris, 1824, 8vo.

Benbow, William.—A Scourge for the Laureate [R. Southey], in reply to his infamous letter [to the "Courier"] of the 13th of December 1824, abusive of Lord Byron, etc. London [1825?], 12mo.

Bennett, D. M.—The World's Sages, Infidels, and Thinkers. New York, 1876, 8vo.
    Byron, pp. 706-710.

Bernard, Edward.—Pedigree of George Gordon, sixth Lord Byron of the family of Burun or Buron, or Byron. London, 1870, s. sh. fol.

Bernardi, Jacopo.—Lord Byron e il Generale A. Mengaldo. Pinerolo [1866?], 16mo

Best, John R.—Infidelity and Catholicism of Lord Byron. (*Satires, etc.*, by *J. R. Best*, pp. 159-171.) London, 1831, 8vo.

Blaquiere, Edward.—Narrative of a second visit to Greece, including facts connected with the last days of Lord Byron, extracts from correspondence, etc. London, 185, 8vo.

Bleibtreu, Karl.—Geschichte der Englischen Litteratur im neunzehnten Jahrhundert. Leipzig, 1887, 8vo.
    Byron, pp. 151-321.

Born, Dr. Stephen.—Lord Byron. Basel, 1883, 8vo.
    Part of Bd. 7 of "Oeffentliche Vorträge gehalten in der Schweiz."

Bowles, William Lisle. — Two letters to the Rt. Hon. Lord Byron, in answer to his lordship's letter to * * * * * * * * * * [John Murray], on the Rev. W. L. Bowles's Strictures on the life and writings of Pope, etc. London, 1821, 8vo.

——Letters to Lord Byron on a question of poetical criticism, etc. London, 1822, 8vo.

——A final Appeal to the literary public relative to Pope, etc. To which are added some remarks on Lord Byron's Conversations, etc. London, 1825, 8vo.

Brandes, Georg. — Die Hauptströmungen der Literatur des neunzehnten Jahrhunderts. Uebersetzt vou Adolf Strodtmann. 4 Bde. Berlin, 1872, 8vo.
Byron, Bde. iv., pp. 382-563.

——Hovedstromninger i det 19de Aarhundredes Litteratur, etc. Naturalismen i England. Byron og hans Gruppe. Kjobenhavn, 1875, 8vo.

Britannicus.—Revolutionary Causes; with a brief notice of some late publications; and Postscript, containing Strictures on Cain, etc. London, 1822, 8vo.

Brockedon, William. — Finden's Illustrations of the life and works of Lord Byron, with original and selected information on the subjects of the engravings, etc. 3 vols. London, 1833, 34, 4to.

Brougham, Lord.—Critique [by Lord Brougham], from the Edinburgh Review, on Lord Byron's poems, which occasioned "English Bards and Scotch Reviewers." London, 1820, 8vo.

Brydges, Sir Samuel E.—Letters on the character and poetical genius of Lord Byron. London, 1824, 8vo.

——An impartial portrait of Lord Byron, as a poet and a man, etc. Paris, 1825, 12mo.

Byron, Lord.—Anecdotes of Lord Byron from authentic sources; with remarks illustrative of his connection with the principal literary characters of the present day. London, 1825, 12mo.

——The Byron Gallery, a series of historical embellishments illustrating the poetical works of Lord Byron. A new and enlarged edition, with descriptive letterpress. London, 1838, 8vo.

——Biographical Notices. The late Lord Byron. London, 1824, fol.
A fragment comprising pp. 397-98 of some periodical.

——Byroniana. Bozzies and Piozzies. London, 1825, 8vo.

——Byroniana. With the Parish Clerk's Album kept at his burial-place, Hucknall Torkard. [Edited by J. M L.] London, 1834, 16mo.

——Byron painted by his Compeers; or, all about Lord Byron, from his marriage to his death, as given in the various newspapers of his day; showing wherein the American novelist [Mrs. H. B. Stowe] gives a truthful account, and wherein she draws on her own morbid imagination. (With two original poems by Lady Byron.) London, 1869, 8vo.
The poems attributed to Lady Byron are reprinted from Madame L. S. Belloc's biography of Lord Byron.

——Childe Harold's Monitor; or,

Lines occasioned by the last canto of Childe Harold, including hints to other contemporaries. London, 1818, 8vo.

——A Critique on the Address written by Lord Byron, which was spoken at the opening of the New Theatre Royal, Drury Lane, October 10, 1812. By Lord —— ——. London [1812 ?], 8vo.

——Despair: a Vision. Derry Down and John Bull: a Simile. Being two political parodies on "Darkness," and a scene from "The Giaour" by Lord Byron, etc. [London], 1820, 8vo.

——Don Juan, or Don Juan unmasked; being a Key to the mystery attending that publication. London, 1819, 8vo.

——An Apology for "Don Juan," Cantos I., II. London, 1824, 8vo.

——Juan Secundus. [A poem in imitation of Lord Byron's Don Juan.] Canto the first. London, 1825, 8vo.
No more published.

——The Footprints of Albé [*i.e.*, Lord Byron. A poem. By E. Brennan]. Part I. Milan, 1874, 8vo.
No more published.

——Gordon, a tale. A poetical review of Don Juan. London, 1821, 8vo.

——Historical Illustrations of Lord Byron's works in a series of etchings, by Reveil, from original paintings, by A. Colin. [With accompanying text.] London [1833], 8vo.

——The Home and Grave of Byron; an account of Newstead Abbey, Annesley Hall, and Hucknall-Torkard. London [1852], 8vo.

——New edition, enlarged. Also remarks on the architecture of Newstead Abbey. By A. Ashpitel. London [1855 ?], 8vo.

——Illustrations to the works of Lord Byron. The drawings by Chalon, Leslie, Harding. Engraved under the superintendence of Mr. C. Heath. [With illustrative extracts from the works of Lord Byron.] London [1846 ?], 4to.

——A Letter of Expostulation to Lord Byron on his present pursuits; with animadversions on his writings and absence from his country in the hour of danger. (*The Pamphleteer*, vol. 19, pp. 347-362.) London, 1822, 8vo.

——The Life, Writings, Opinions, and Times of George Gordon Noel Byron, including anecdotes and memoirs of the most eminent public and noble characters and courtiers of the age and court of his Majesty, King George the Fourth. In the course of the Biography is also separately given copious recollections of the lately destroyed MS. originally intended for posthumous publication, and entitled "Memoirs of my own Life and Times, by the Right Hon. Lord Byron." By an English gentleman in the Greek Military Service, and comrade of his Lordship. 3 vols. London, 1825, 8vo.

——Light or Darkness? A poem. With remarks on Lord Byron's detractors. London, 1870, 8vo.

——Lines addressed to a noble Lord [Lord Byron]. By one of the Small Fry of the Lakes [Miss Barker]. London, 1815, 8vo.

——Lord Byron in the other world. [Lord Byron's Immortality, by

W. Davenport. Death of Lord Byron, by Mrs. H. Rolls.] [London, 1825], 8vo.

——Mazeppa travestied: a poem, etc. London, 1820, 8vo.

——A narrative of the circumstances which attended the separation of Lord and Lady Byron, remarks on his domestic conduct, and a complete refutation of the calumnies circulated by public writers. London, 1816, 8vo.

——Narrative of Lord Byron's Voyage to Corsica and Sardinia, during the year 1821. Compiled from minutes made during the voyage by the passengers, etc. [A fabrication.] London, 1824, 8vo.

——Another edition. Paris, 1825, 12mo.

——A poetical epistle from Alma Mater to Lord Byron, occasioned by the following lines in a tale called "Beppo":—
'But for those children of the
　'mighty mother's,'
'The would-be wits and can't-be
　gentlemen.'
Cambridge, 1819, 8vo.

——A Reply to Fare thee Well. Lines addressed to Lord Byron. London, 1816, 8vo.

——The Shade of Byron. A mock-heroic poem, containing strange revelations not hitherto disclosed, with copious notes; a preface, with the author's comments on the "Story," by Mrs. Stowe. And a repudiation of the charges hurled against the memory of Lord Byron and his beloved sister, Ada Augusta. Vol. 1. London [1871], 8vo.
　No more published.

——A Sketch from Public Life: a poem, founded upon recent domestic circumstances. [A

satire upon Lord Byron.] London, 1816, 8vo.

——To the Departed. Stanzas to the memory of Lord Byron. London, 1825, 8vo.

——Uriel, a poetical address to Lord Byron, written on the Continent; with notes, containing strictures on the spirit of infidelity maintained in his works and several other poems. London, 1822, 8vo.

Byron, Lord, *pseud.*—Arnaldo; Gaddo; and other unacknowledged poems by Byron and some of his contemporaries, collected by O. Volpi, etc. 2 pts. Dublin, 1836, 8vo.

——Childe Harold's Pilgrimage to the Dead Sea; Death on the Pale Horse; and other poems. London, 1818, 8vo.

——Don Juan. Canto the Third. London, 1821, 8vo.

——The Seventeenth Canto of Don Juan, in continuation of the unfinished poem by Lord Byron. London, 1829, 12mo.

——Don Juan. Cantos XVII. and XVIII. London [1825], 12mo.

——A sequel to Don Juan. Cantos I.-V. London [1825], 8vo.

——Lord Byron's Farewell to England; with three other poems, etc. Ode to St. Helena, To my Daughter on the morning of her birth, and To the Lily of France. London, 1816, 8vo.

——Second edition. London, 1816, 8vo.

——Some rejected stanzas of "Don Juan," with Byron's own curious Notes written in double rhymes, after Casti's manner, from an unpublished manuscript in the possession of Captain Medwin. A very limited number printed. Great Totham, Essex, 1845, 4to.

——Don Juan, Canto the third. [By W. Hone?] London, 1819, 8vo.

——Reflections on Shipboard. London, 1816, 8vo.

——The Vampyre; a tale by the Right Honourable Lord Byron [or rather by Dr. Polidori]. London, 1819, 8vo.

Byron, Lady Anne Isabella Noel. Remarks occasioned by Mr. Moore's notices of Lord Byron's life. [London, 1830], 8vo.

——Another edition. A letter to Thomas Moore, Esq., occasioned by his notices of the life of the late Lord Byron. London [1830], 8vo.

——Life of Lady Byron, compiled from the best authorities, etc. To which is appended a Vindication of Lord Byron. Police News edition. [London, 1870?], 8vo.

——Vindication of Lady Byron. London, 1871, 8vo.

Byron, Henry J.—The Bride of Abydos; or the prince, the pirate, and the pearl. An original oriental burlesque extravaganza. London [1858], 8vo. Part of vol. 36 of "Lacy's Acting Edition of Plays."

C., C. C.—Remarks, critical and moral, on the talents of Lord Byron, and the tendencies of Don Juan. By the author of Hypocrisy, a satire [C. C. C., *i.e.*, Colton], with notes and anecdotes, political and historical. London, 1819, 8vo.

——Another edition, with additions. [London, 1819], 8vo.

C., W.—Don Juan reclaimed; or, his Peregrination continued, from Lord Byron. By W[illiam C[owley?]. Sheffield, 1840, 8vo.

Caine, T. Hall.—Cobwebs of Criticism, etc. London, 1883, 8vo. Byron, pp. 91-119.

Cantù, Cesare. — Lord Byron; discorso di C. Cantù. Aggiuntevi alcune traduzioni ed un serie di lettere dello stesso Lord Byron, ove si narrano i suoi viaggi in Italia e nella Grecia. Milano, 1833, 12mo.

——Lord Byron and his works; a biography and essay [translated from the Italian]. Edited, with notes, by A. Kinloch. London [1883], 8vo.

Castelar, Emilio. Vida de Lord Byron, etc. Madrid, 1873, 4to.

——Life of Lord Byron and other sketches. Translated by Mrs. Arthur Arnold. London, 1875, 8vo.

Cato, *pseud.* [*i.e.*, George Burgess]. —Cato to Lord Byron on the immorality of his writings. London, 1824, 8vo.

——Third edition. London, 1824, 8vo.

Characteristics. — Characteristics of Men of Genius, etc. 2 vols. London, 1846, 8vo. Lord Byron, vol. I., pp. 245-273.

Chorley, Henry F.—The Authors of England, etc. London, 1838, 4to. Lord Byron, pp 17-26.

——New edition. London, 1841, 8vo. Lord Byron, pp. 14-21.

Clarke, H. S.—In the matter of the Stowe Scandal. Lord Byron's Defence. [In verse.] London, 1869, 4to.

Claus, Wilhelm.—Byron und Frauen. Vortrag, etc. Berlin, 1862, 8vo.

Clinton, George.—Memoirs of the life and writings of Lord Byron. London, 1825, 8vo.

Cogniard, H., and Burat de Gurgy, E.—Byron à l'École d'Harrow, épisode mêlé de couplets. Paris, 1834, 24mo.
    There is inserted in the Museum copy an autograph letter from Lord Mahon, afterwards 5th Earl Stanhope, to Mr. Granville, dated Dec. 8, 1844.

Cotterill, H. B.—An Introduction to the Study of Poetry. London, 1882, 8vo.
    Byron, pp. 269-297.

Courthope, William J. — The Liberal Movement in English Literature. London, 1885, 8vo.
    The Revival of Romance: Scott, Byron, Shelley, pp. 111-156.

Cunningham, George G.—Lives of eminent and illustrious Englishmen, etc. 8 vols. Glasgow, 1837, 8vo.
    Lord Byron, vol. viii, pp. 295-305.
——Another edition. 5 vols. Edinburgh [1863-68], 4to.
    Lord Byron, vol. v., pp. 569-579.

Dallas, Robert Charles. — Recollections of the Life of Lord Byron from the year 1808 to the end of 1814. To which is prefixed an account of the circumstances leading to the suppression of Lord Byron's correspondence with the author, and his letters to his mother, lately announced for publication. [Edited by A. R. C. Dallas.] London, 1824, 8vo.

Darmesteter, James. — Essais de Littérature Anglaise. Paris, 1883, 8vo.
    Lord Byron, pp. 161-197.

Dennis, John.—Heroes of English Literature. English Poets. London, 1883, 8vo.
    Lord Byron, pp 344-364.

Devey, J.—A comparative estimate of Modern English Poets. London, 1873, 8vo.
    Byron, pp. 184-211.

Dimond, William.—The Bride of

Abydos: a romantic drama, in three acts, from Lord Byron's celebrated poem. Arranged for representation by T. H. Lacy. London [1866], 12mo.
    Forming part of vol. lxx. of "Lacy's Acting Edition of Plays"

Düntzer, Heinrich. — Göthe's Faust in seiner Einheit und Ganzheit wider seine Gegner dargestellt. Nebst Andeutungen über Idee und Plan des Wilhelm Meister und zwei Anhängen: über Byron's Manfred und Lessing's Doktor Faust. Köln, 1836, 12mo.

Eberty, Felix.—Lord Byron. Eine Biographie. 2 Thle. Leipzig, 1862, 8vo.

Edgcumbe, Richard.—History of the Byron Memorial. London, 1883, 8vo.

Elze, Karl.—Lord Byron [a biography]. Berlin, 1870, 8vo.
——Zweite, vermehrte Ausgabe. Berlin, 1881, 8vo.
——Lord Byron; a biography. With a critical essay on his place in literature. Translated and edited with notes. London, 1872, 8vo.

Erasmus, *pseud.*—The Outlaw; a tale by Erasmus. [Parody on the Bride of Abydos.] Edinburgh, 1818, 12mo.

Finden, William and Edward.— Finden's Byron Beauties: or the principal female characters in Lord Byron's poems. Engraved from original paintings, under the superintendence of W. and E. Finden. London, 1836, 4to.

Fourès, Elie.—Le premier amour de Lord Byron, nouvelle inédite. Paris, 1885, 32mo.

Friswell, James Hain.—Essays on English Writers, by the author of the "Gentle Life" [J. H.

Friswell]. London, 1869, 8vo.
Lord Byron, pp. 317-327.

G. W., *i.e.,* W. F. Deacon.—Warreniana, with notes, critical and explanatory, by the Editor of a Quarterly Review. London, 1824, 8vo.
The Childe's Pilgrimage, pp. 81-92.

Galt, John.—The Life of Lord Byron. London, 1830, 8vo.
No. 1 of Gleig's "National Library."

—The Life of Lord Byron. Second edition. London, 1830, 8vo.

Gamba, Pietro.—A narrative of Lord Byron's last journey to Greece. Extracted from the journal of Count Pietro Gamba, who attended his Lordship on that expedition. London, 1825, 8vo.

—Another edition. Paris, 1825, 8vo.

Gerard, William. — Byron re-studied in his dramas. An Essay. London, 1886, 8vo.

Gilfillan, George.—A Second Gallery of Literary Portraits. London, 1850, 8vo.
Lord Byron, pp. 39-61.

—Lord Byron, a lecture . . . in Exeter Hall, Feb. 3, 1852. London, 1852, 8vo.

Gordon, Sir Cosmo. — Life and genius of Lord Byron. London, 1824, 8vo.

Gottshall, Rudolf.—Porträts und Studien. Leipzig, 1870, 8vo.
Byron und die Gegenwart, Bd. 1, pp. 3-57.

Griswold, Hattie Tyng.—Home Life of Great Authors. Chicago, 1887, 8vo.
Lord Byron, pp. 94-101.

Gronow, Captain.—Reminiscences of Captain Gronow, etc. London, 1862, 8vo.
Lord Byron, pp. 208-212.

Gronow, Captain.—Captain Gronow's Last Recollections ; being the fourth and final series of his Reminiscences, etc. London, 1866, 8vo.
Lord Byron and Dan Mackinnon, pp. 100-102.

Guiccioli, Countess.—Lord Byron jugé par les temoins de sa vie. 2 tom. Paris, 1868, 8vo.

—Lord Byron jugé par les temoins de sa vie. My Recollections of Lord Byron ; and those of eye-witnesses of his life. [By the Countess Guiccioli; translated by H. E. H. Jerningham.] 2 vols. London, 1869, 8vo.

—New edition. London, 1869, 8vo.

Hamilton, Walter.—Parodies of the Works of English and American Authors, etc. London, 1886, 4to.
Lord Byron, vol. iii., pp. 100-229.

Hannay, James.—Satire and Satirists. London, 1854, 8vo.
Byron, pp. 241-257.

Harold.—Lines to Harold [*i.e.,* to Lord Byron], 1812. [London] reprinted, 1841, 12mo.

Harrison, James A.—A Group of Poets and their Haunts. New York, 1875, 8vo.
Italian Haunts of Lord Byron, pp. 31-63.

Harroviensis.—A letter to Sir Walter Scott, Bart., in answer to the remonstrance of Oxoniensis on the publication of Cain, a Mystery, by Lord Byron. London, 1822, 8vo.

Haussonville, Countess de. — La Jeunesse de Lord Byron. Par l'auteur de Robert Emmet [*i.e.,* Countess d' Haussonville]. Paris, 1872, 12mo.

—Les Dernières Années de Lord Byron. Par l'auteur de Robert Emmet. Paris, 1874, 12mo.

Hayward, A.—Sketches of Eminent Statesmen and Writers, with other essays. 2 vols. London, 1880, 8vo.
    Byron and Tennyson, vol. ii., pp. 305-359.

Hillard, George Stillman.—Six Months in Italy. 2 vols. London, 1843, 8vo.
    Lord Byron, vol. ii., pp. 338-344.

Hobhouse, John Cam, *Baron Broughton.*—Historical illustrations of the fourth Canto of Childe Harold, containing dissertations on the ruins of Rome. London, 1818, 8vo.

Hodgson, James Thomas.—Memoir of Francis Hodgson. With letters from Lord Byron and others. 2 vols. London, 1878, 8vo.

Hoffmann, Frederick A.—Poetry, its origin, nature, and history, etc. 2 vols. London, 1884, 8vo.
    Byron, vol. i., pp. 441-465.

Hohenhausen, Elise von.—Rousseau, Göthe, Byron, ein kritisch-literarischer Umriss. Hassel, 1847, 8vo.

Howell, Owen.—Abel; written, but with great humility, in reply to Lord Byron's Cain. London, 1843, 8vo.

Howitt, William. — A Poet's Thoughts at the interment of Lord Byron. [In verse.] London, 1824, 8vo.

——Homes and Haunts of the most eminent British Poets. 2 vols. London, 1847, 8vo.
    Byron, vol. i., pp. 467-504.

——Third edition. London, 1857, 8vo.
    Byron, pp. 322-340.

Hunt, James Henry Leigh.—Lord Byron, and some of his Contemporaries; with recollections of the Author's life, and of his visit to Italy. London, 1828, 4to.

Hunt, James Henry Leigh.—Second edition. 2 vols. London, 1828, 8vo.

——Another edition. 3 vols. Paris, 1828, 8vo.

——The Autobiography of Leigh Hunt; with reminiscences of friends and contemporaries. 3 vols. London, 1850, 8vo.
    Numerous references to Byron.

Irving, Washington.—The Crayon Miscellany. Philadelphia, 1874, 8vo.
    Newstead Abbey, pp. 323-441.

Jeaffreson, John Cordy.—The Real Lord Byron. New views of the poet's life. 2 vols. London, 1883, 8vo.

——Another edition. London, 1884, 8vo.

Johnson, Samuel. — Johnson's Lives of the British Poets, completed by William Hazlitt. 4 vols. London, 1854, 8vo.
    Lord Byron, vol. iv., pp. 204-240.

Kennedy, James.—Conversations on religion, with Lord Byron and others, held in Cephalonia, a short time previous to his Lordship's death. London, 1830, 8vo.

Kingsley, Charles.—The Works of Charles Kingsley. London, 1880, 8vo.
    Thoughts on Shelley and Byron, vol. xx., pp. 35-58.

Lake, J. W.—The life of Lord Byron. Paris, 1826, 16mo.

——Another edition. Frankfort-on-Main, 1827, 16mo.

Lamartine, M. L. A. de.—The Last Canto of Childe Harold. [Translated from the French.] London, 1827, 8vo.

——Méditations Poétiques. Paris, 1820, 8vo.
    "L'Homme. À Lord Byron," pp. 5-18.

Lang, Andrew.—Letters to Dead Authors. London, 1886, 8vo.
    To Lord Byron, pp. 205-215.

Layman.—A Layman's Epistle [in verse] to a certain Nobleman [Lord Byron]. London, 1824, 8vo.

Le Bas, C. W.—Review of the life and character of Lord Byron. [By C. W. Le Bas.] Extracted from the British Critic for April 1831. London, 1833, 8vo.

Leigh, Elizabeth Medora.—Medora Leigh; a history and an autobiography. Edited by C. Mackay. With an introduction, and a commentary on the charges brought against Lord Byron by Mrs. B. Stowe. London, 1869, 8vo.

Lescure, Adolphe.—Lord Byron, histoire d' un homme (1788, 1824). Paris, 1866, 12mo.

L'Estrange, A. G.—The Literary Life of the Rev. William Harness. London, 1871, 8vo.
Numerous references to Byron.

——History of English Humour, etc. 2 vols. London, 1878, 8vo.
Byron, vol. ii., pp. 184-190.

L'Etoile, A. E. de.—Lord Byron, sa biographie et choix de ses poëmes. Paris, 1885, 8vo.

Lorenzo y d'Ayot, Manuel. — Shakespere, Lord Byron, y Chateaubriand, como modelos de la juventud literaria. Madrid, 1886, 8vo.

M., J.—The True Story of Lord and Lady Byron as told by Lord Macaulay, T. Moore, L. Hunt, T. Campbell, the Countess of Blessington, Lord Lindsay, the Countess of Guiccioli, by Lady Byron, and by the Poet himself, in answer to Mrs. Beecher Stowe. [Edited by J. M.] London [1869], 8vo.

Macaulay, Thomas Babington.— Critical and historical Essays, contributed to the Edinburgh Review. 3 vols. London, 1843, 8vo.
Moore's Life of Lord Byron, vol. i., pp. 311-352.

——Lord Byron. [A biographical sketch.] Boston, 1877, 16mo.
A reprint of the article in the *Edinburgh Review.*

McDermot, M.—A Letter to the Rev. W. L. Bowles, in reply to his letter to Thomas Campbell, Esq., and to his two letters to the Right Hon. Lord Byron; containing a vindication of their defence of the poetical character of Pope, etc. (*The Pamphleteer*, vol. xx., pp. 119-144, 385-410.) London, 1822, 8vo.

Mackay, George Eric. — Lord Byron at the Armenian Convent. Venice, 1876, 8vo.

Mackay, William. — The true story of Lady Byron's life. Christmas Comic Version. London, 1869, 8vo.

Maginn, William.—Miscellanies: prose and verse. 2 vols. London, 1885, 8vo.
John Gilpin and Mazeppa, vol. i., pp. 92-102; Lament for Lord Byron (Verses), vol. ii., pp. 259, 260; Critique on Lord Byron (Verses), vol. ii., pp. 827-334.

Mason, Edward T. — Personal Traits of British Authors. Byron, Shelley, Moore, etc. New York, 1885, 8vo.
Lord Byron, pp. 5-71.

Maude, Thomas.—Monody on the death of Lord Byron. London, 1824, 8vo.

Mazzini, Joseph.—Life and Writings. London, 1870, 8vo.
Byron and Goethe, vol. vi., pp. 61-97.

Medwin, Thomas.—Journal of the Conversations of Lord Byron: noted during a residence with his lordship at Pisa in the years 1821 and 1822, by T. Medwin. London, 1824, 4to.

Medwin, Thomas.—Second edition. London, 1824, 8vo.
——Another edition. New York, 1824, 12mo.
——Captain Medwin vindicated from the Calumnies of the Reviewers. London, 1825, 8vo.

Milliken, E. J.—"From Punch." Childe Chappie's Pilgrimage, etc. London, 1883, 8vo.

Millingen, Julius. — Memoirs of the Affairs of Greece, with anecdotes relating to Lord Byron, and an account of his last illness and death. London, 1831, 8vo.

Milner, Henry M.—Mazeppa, or the Wild Horse of Tartary. A romantic drama, in three acts. Dramatised from Lord Byron's poem. London [1828], 12mo.
    Part of vol. v. of "Cumberland's Minor Theatre."
——Another edition. London [1874], 12mo.
    Forms part of vol. 96 of "Lacy's Acting Edition of Plays."

Minto, William. — Lord Byron. (In vol. iv. of the Encyclopædia Britannica, pp. 604-612.) 9th edition. Edinburgh, 1876, 4to.

Moir, D. M.—Sketches of the poetical literature of the past half-century. Edinburgh, 1851, 8vo.
    Byron, pp. 160-176.

Mondot, Armand.—Histoire de la Vie et des Écrits de Lord Byron, etc. Paris, 1860, 12mo.

Mongrelites. — The Mongrelites; or, the Radicals so called. A satirical poem. By ——. (An imitation of "English Bards and Scotch Reviewers.") New York, 1866, 8vo.

Monti, G.—Studi Critici. Firenze, 1887, 8vo.
    Giacomo Leopardi e Giorgio Byron, pp. 41-127; Il "Prigionero di Chillon" e il "Conte Ugolino" di Dante, pp. 131-155.

Moore, Thomas.—Memoirs, journals, and correspondence of Thomas Moore, edited by the Right Honourable Lord J. Russell. 8 vols. London, 1853-56, 8vo.
    Numerous references to Byron.

Morley, John.—Critical Essays. London, 1886, 8vo.
    Byron, vol. i., pp. 203-251.

Mortemart, Baron.—Lord Byron, par Mme. la Marquise de Boissy. Annotations sur cet ouvrage. Paris, 1874, 8vo.

Murray, John.—Notes on Captain Medwin's Conversations of Lord Byron. [London, 1824], 8vo.

Newstead Abbey. — Newstead Abbey: its present owner [Colonel Thomas Wildman], with reminiscences of Lord Byron. London [1857], 8vo.

Nichol, John.—Byron. London, 1880, 8vo.
    Part of the "English Men of Letters" Series.

Nicolini, Giuseppe.—Vita di Giorgio, Lord Byron. 3 vols. Milano, 1835, 16mo.

Nisard, D.—Portraits et études d'histoire littéraire. Paris, 1874, 8vo.
    Lord Byron, pp. 319-306.

Noel, Hon. Roden.—Essays on Poetry and Poets. London, 1886, 8vo.
    Lord Byron and his Times, pp. 50-113.

Notes and Queries.—Notes and Queries. Series i.-vii. London, 1849, etc., 4to.
    Numerous references to Byron.

Oliphant, Margaret.—The Literary History of England, etc. 3 vols. London, 1882, 8vo.
    Byron-Shelley, pp. 44-94; Shelley-Byron, pp. 95-132.

Oxonian.—The Radical Triumvirate; or, Infidel Paine, Lord Byron, and Surgeon Lawrence colleaguing with the patriotic Radicals to emancipate mankind from all laws, human and divine. A letter to John Bull. London, 1820, 8vo.

Oxoniensis. — A Remonstrance [subscribed : O.], addressed to Mr. J. Murray, respecting a recent publication [viz., Lord Byron's "Cain"]. London, 1822, 8vo.

Paget, John. — Paradoxes and Puzzles, etc. Edinburgh, 1874, 8vo.
Recollections of Lord Byron, pp. 264-282; Lord Byron and his calumniators, pp. 283-314.

Parry, William.—The Last Days of Lord Byron : with his Lordship's opinions on various subjects, particularly on the state and prospects of Greece. London, 1825, 8vo.

——Another edition. Paris, 1826, 12mo.

Pebody, Charles. — Authors at Work. London, 1872, 8vo.
Byron, pp. 247-279.

Phillips, W.—A review of the character and writings of Lord Byron. [By W. Phillips; reprinted from "The North American Review."] London, 1826, 8vo.

Philo-Milton, *pseud.*—A vindication of the Paradise Lost from the charge of exculpating "Cain, a Mystery." London, 1822, 8vo.

Pichot, Amédée.—Essai sur la vie, le caractère, et le génie de Lord Byron. Paris, 1830, 12mo.

Prentis, Stephen. — An Apology for Lord Byron, etc. London, 1836, 8vo.

Raineri, Luigi.—Le Vite di Dante Alighieri, di G. Galilei, di N. Macchiavelli, di L. Ariosto, di

G. Lord Byron, etc. Oneglia, 1860, 8vo.

Reed, Henry.—Lectures on the British Poets. London, 1857, 8vo.
Byron, pp. 312-334.

Reinsberg-Dueringsfeld, Ida von.— Byron's Frauen. [On the female characters in Byron's poems.] Breslau, 1845, 8vo.

Reynolds, G. W. M.—Don Juan junior ; a poem, by Byron's Ghost. [By G. W. M. Reynolds.] Edited by G. K. W. Baxter. London, 1839, 8vo.

Richardson, D. L. — Literary Leaves, or prose and verse. Calcutta, 1836, 8vo.
Lord Byron's Opinion of Pope, pp. 389-398.

——Literary Chit-Chat, etc. Calcutta, 1848, 8vo.
Lord Byron and his Lady, pp. 118-125; Sir Walter Scott and Lord Byron, pp. 163-179.

Rossetti, William Michael.—Lives of Famous Poets. London, 1878, 8vo.
Lord Byron, pp 287-307.

Salvo, Carlo de.—Lord Byron en Italie et en Grèce; ou aperçu de sa vie et de ses ouvrages d'après des sources authentiques, etc. [Edited by F. J. M. Fayolle.] London, 1825, 8vo.

Sarbot, Old, *pseud.*—Brum : a parody. [A satire on local celebrities at Birmingham in the form of a parody on part of Byron's "Childe Harold."] By Old Sarbot. [Birmingham ? 1860 ?] 8vo.

Schaffner, Alfred.—Lord Byron's Cain und seine Quellen. Strassburg, 1880, 8vo.

Scherr, Johannes.—Geschichte der Englischen Literatur. Leipzig, 1854, 8vo.
Byron, pp. 223-244.

Scherr, Johannes.—A History of English Literature. Translated from the German. London, 1882, 8vo.
Byron, pp. 219-243.

Schmidt, Immanuel.—Byron im Lichte unserer Zeit, etc. Hamburg, 1888, 8vo.
Part of Series III. Neue Folge, of Virchow's "Sammlung gemeinverständlicher wissenschaftlicher Vorträge."

Schmidt, Julian.—Portraits aus dem neunzehnten Jahrhundert. Berlin, 1878, 8vo.
Lord Byron, pp. 1-49.

Scott, Sir Walter.—Miscellaneous Prose Works. 3 vols. Edinburgh, 1841-47, 8vo.
Death of Lord Byron, vol. i., pp. 422-424 ; appeared originally in the Edinburgh Weekly Journal, 1824 : Review of Childe Harold, pp. 424-201 ; appeared originally in the Quarterly Review, vol. xvi., 1816.

——A Discourse on the comparative merits of Scott and Byron, as writers of poetry. Delivered before a Literary Institution in 1820. [Glasgow] 1824, 8vo.

Simmons, J. W.—An Inquiry into the Moral Character of Lord Byron. London, 1826, 8vo.

Stanhope, Leicester.—Greece in 1823 and 1824, etc. London, 1824, 8vo.

Stephen, Leslie.—Byron. (*Dictionary of National Biography*, vol. viii., pp. 132-155.) London, 1886, 8vo.

Stowe, Harriet Elizabeth Beecher.—Lady Byron vindicated. A history of the Byron controversy, from its beginning in 1816 to the present time. Boston, 1870, 8vo.

——Another edition. London, 1870, 8vo.

Styles, John.—Lord Byron's works viewed in connexion with Christianity and the obligations of social life ; a sermon delivered at Kennington. London, 1824, 8vo.

Swinburne, Algernon C.—Miscellanies. London, 1886, 8vo.
Wordsworth and Byron, pp. 63-156.

Sydney, *pseud.*—Sydney's Letter to the King ; and other correspondence connected with the reported exclusion of Lord Byron's monument from Westminster Abbey. London, 1828, 8vo.

Taine, Hippolyte Adolphe. — Histoire de la Littérature Anglaise. 4 tom. Paris, 1863-64, 8vo.
Lord Byron, tom. iii., pp 522-613.

——History of English Literature. Translated by H. Van Laun. 4 vols. Edinburgh, 1873-4, 8vo.
Lord Byron, vol. iv., pp. 1-69.

Thomas, John Wesley. — An apology for [or rather a satire on Lord Byron's] Don Juan. Cantos I., II. [London] 1824, 8vo.

——Third edition. London, 1850, 8vo.

——New edition. London, 1855, 8vo.

Thomsen, G.—Om Lord Byron. Udgivet for Magistergraden af G. Thorgrimsson T. Kjobenhavn, 1845, 8vo.

Trelawny, Edward John.—Recollections of the last days of Shelley and Byron. London, 1858, 8vo.

——Another edition. Records of Shelley, Byron, and the author. [With portraits.] 2 vols. London, 1878, 8vo.

——New edition. London, 1887, 8vo.

Tuckerman, Henry T.—Thoughts on the Poets. Third edition. New York, 1848, 8vo.
Byron, pp 165-174.

Vyron, Lord.—The Age of Soap-suds, a satire. Bridgwater, 1839, 8vo.

Ward, Thomas H.—The English Poets; selections with critical introductions, etc. 4 vols. London, 1880, 8vo.
Lord Byron, by J. A. Symonds, vol. iv., pp 244-303.

Watkins, J.—Memoirs of the Life and Writings of Lord Byron; with anecdotes of some of his contemporaries. [By J. Watkins.] London, 1822, 8vo.

Weddigen, Friedrich H. O. — Lord Byron's Einfluss auf die europäischen Litteraturen der Neuzeit. Ein Beitrag zur Allgemeinen Litteraturgeschichte. Hanover, 1884, 8vo.

Welsh, Alfred H.—Development of English Literature and Language. 2 vols. Chicago, 1882, 8vo.
Lord Byron, pp 339-355.

Wetton, Harry W.—The termination of the sixteenth canto of Lord Byron's Don Juan. London, 1864, 8vo.

Whipple, Edwin P.—Essays and Reviews. 2 vols. Boston, 1856, 8vo.
Byron, pp. 267-293.

White, Mr.—The Calumnies of the "Athenæum" Journal exposed. Mr. White's Letter to Mr. Murray on the study of Byron, Shelley, and Keats' MSS. London, 1852, 8vo.

Wilkinson, Henry.—Cain, a poem, containing an antidote to the impiety and blasphemy of Lord Byron's Cain, etc. Pt. I. London, 1824, 8vo.
No more published.

SONGS, ETC., SET TO MUSIC.

The Bride of Abydos, founded upon the poems of Lord Byron, by M. Kelly, 1818.

Kain, für Solostimmen, Chor und Orchester, by Max Zenger.

The Corsair, a dramatic cantata, by F. C. Cowen, 1876.

Manfred. Dramatisches Gedicht, by Schumann, 1860.

Manfred, a dramatic poem in three acts, by Schumann, 1876.

The whole of the music in Byron's Tragedy of Sardanapalus, composed by J. L. Hatton, 1854.

Sardanapalus, Opera, by A. Duvernoy, 1883.

Hebräische Melodieen, by Karl Müller.

A Selection of Hebrew Melodies, Ancient and Modern, by I. Braham and I. Nathan.

Hebrew Melodies, by J. C. G. Loewe.

Hebrew Melodies, impressions of Byron's poems for tenor and pianoforte, by J. Joachim, 1855.

Three Canzonets, the words from Byron's Hebrew Melodies; the music by G. Pigott.

Vocal Sketches to words by Byron; music by E. Masson, 1848.

Lyric Illustrations of the Modern Poets; the poetry selected from Lord Byron, etc. Music by John Barnett.

Musical Riddles, by A. Voigt, words by Byron, 1820.

Twelve Songs, the poetry by Byron, music by E. Masson, 1843.

Six Canzonets, words by Byron, music by J. Lodge, 1826.

Sechs Lieder, etc. By E. Lassen (Nos. 5, 6, by Byron), 1880.

Six Songs; the words selected

· from the Poems of Lord Byron. Music by H. Fielding, 1843.

Four Songs, by F. Ries, poetry by Byron, 1835.

Three Songs for voice and piano, by S. Percival, poetry by Byron, 1851.

———

"Adieu! Adieu! my native shore" (from "Childe Harold"), by E. W. Buckingham, 1870; Miss Fowler, 1817; C. E. Horn, 1874; L. Jansen, 1820; E. Musgrave, 1863; C. Russell, 1850; C. A. Sippi, 1864.

"Adieu to thee, fair Rhine," by J. Barnett, 1860.

"Ah! love was never yet," by E. Masson, 1837.

"And dost thou ask what secret woe," by F. J. Klose, 1819.

"And wilt thou weep when I am low," by P. A. Carleton, 1855.

"As o'er the cold sepulchral stone," by F. von Woyrsch (*Drei Lieder*, Op. 3, No. 3), 1884.

"The Assyrian came down," by Miss Davis, 1867.

"Ave Maria, blessed be the hour," by T. Anderton, 1880; A. Bennett, 1852; C. Burt, 1882; E. Masson, 1840; E. Peruzzi, 1881; G. Roberti (*Six Trios*, No. 4.), 1864; A. Sampieri, 1860.

"Away, away, ye notes of woe," by W. Rogers, 1854.

"Away ye gay landscapes," by G. Linley, 1854.

"Aye! let me like the ocean patriarch roam," by T. F. Walmisley, 1835.

"Beware, beware of the black friar," by G. Linley, 1866.

"Bound where thou wilt, my barb," by G. Kiallmark, 1815; J. Nathan, 1820.

"Bright be the place of thy soul," by G. A. Barker, 1870; F. Bosen, 1845; J. Clarke, 1825; T. A. Matthay, 1878.

"The Castled crag of Drachenfels," by J. Nathan, 1821.

"The chain I gave was fair to view," by H. von Benzon, 1869; A. R. Logier, 1843; H. A. Robley, 1867.

"Come hither, hither, my little foot page," by R. Rogers, 1877.

"Deep in my soul," by R. A. Firth (*Six canzonets*, No. 6), 1825; G. F. Flowers, 1854; A. F. Harrison, 1878; E. A. Kellner, 1845; J. Thomas (*Six Songs*, No. 1), 1858; J. Tilley, 1820.

Dein Leben schied, dein Ruhm begann, by J. Tausch, 1876.

Di questo bacio ingenuo, by A. M. C. Patti, 1867.

Du in der Schönheit strahlendem Schein, by H. Bellermann (*Sechs Lieder*, Op. 10, No. 6), 1860.

"Fare thee well," by T. Bolton, 1816; A. D. Duvivier, 1877; G. Kiallmark, 1820; G. Lanza, 1820; T. Miles, 1816; Mozart, 1820; W. T. Parke, 1816; J. Pech, 1860; A. Phipps, 1876; C. Smith, 1817; S. Webbe, 1825.

"Farewell! if ever fondest prayer," by F. d'Alquen, 1876; A. E. Armstrong, 1873; F. C. Atkinson (*Six Songs*, No. 6), 1876; V. Bellini (*I Capuleti*), 1855; A. B. Burrington, 1868; I. Dawes; C. Dick, 1881; R. F. Harvey; J. D. Humphreys, 1840; H. Kearton, 1874; G. Linley, 1854; G. A. Macfarren, 1868; G. W. Martin, 1881; G. Muraton, 1873; S. von Neukomm, 1835; Sir H. S. Oakeley; T. H. Reed, 1871; C.

Salaman, 1843, and 1854 ; H. Salwey, 1878; A. Schulz, 1835; W. Shelmerdine, 1859 : Sir J. A. Stevenson, 1816 ; Hon. A. Stourton, 1862 ; A. J. Sutton (*Six Songs*, No. 4), 1858 ; G. Tartaglione, 1876 ; C. F. Webb, 1874 ; M. V. White, 1~74.

"Father of light," by J. Clarke, 1~30.

"Few are my years," 1880.

"Fill the Goblet again," by G. Hargreaves, 1835 ; I. de Solla, 1867.

"Forget this world," by J. Clarke, 1830.

"Hear me Astarte" (from "Manfred"), by L. W. Barker, 1849.

"Here once engaged," by G. Kiallmark, 1827.

"Hills of Annesley," by C. E. Horn, 1830.

"Ich sah dich weinen," by A. Winterberger (12 *Gesänge*, Op. 12, No. 11), 1865.

"I enter the garden of roses," by J. Nathan, 1825.

"If sometimes in the haunts of men," by W. L. Phillips, 1845.

"I had a dream," by J. Barnett (*Lyric Illustrations*, No. 8), 1837.

"I heard thy fate without a tear," by M. B. Hawes, 1856 ; J. W. Hobbs, 1855 ; J. T. Stone, 1856.

"I'll twine for thee a wreath of roses," by R. Hilton, 1870.

"I made a footing in the wall," by J. H. Gordon, 1881.

"I saw thee weep," 1845 ; J. Cheshire, 1874 ; G. V. Duval, 1830 ; C. Hause, 1868 ; H. J. Edwards, 1877 ; J. F. C. Goodeve, 1864 : M. B. Hawes, 1856 ; G. A. Hodson, 1827 ; A. C. Mackenzie, 1870 ; F. Naish, 1874 ; W. Shelmerdine, 1858 ;

J. de Solla, 1867 ; J. F. Stone, 1853 ; Hon. A. Stourton, 1861 ; G. Tartaglione, 1875 ; A. Walton, 1858. '

"I see before me the gladiator lie," by T. M. Mudie, 1870.

"The Isles of Greece," by J. Smith, 1879.

"It is the hour," by J. C Beuthin, 1857.

"I wish to tune my quiv'ring lyre," by T. F. Walmisley (*Cramer's Glees*, No. 42), 1874.

"I would I were a careless child," by J. W. Etherington, 1851.

"The kiss, dear Maid," by S. Anteri Manzocchi ; J. Beale, 1817 ; R. Guerini, 1878 ; Mendelssohn, 1855 ; B. Molique, 1866 ; A. Mullen, 1854 ; A. M. C. Patti, 1870 ; P. Rode, 1825 ; R. M. Williams, 1877 ; T. Williams, 1818.

"Know ye the land ?" by A. Bennett, 1~23.

"Long life to the grape," by W. Wilson, 1~47.

"Maid of Athens," by H. R. Allen, 1861 ; M. W. Balfe, 1869 ; G. V. Duval, 1830 ; B. Farebrother, 1873 ; C. F. Gounod, 1873 ; H. Kalliwoda, 1863 ; G. Kiallmark, 1830 ; G. Linley, 1854 ; J. Mount, 1880 ; S. Nelson, 1840 ; V. Pucitta, 1815 ; F. Vollrath, 1820 ; S. Waller, 1820 ; W. L. Williams, 1878 ; A. Winterberger.

"Must thou go ?" by A. M. Lawrence, 1838.

"My boat is on the shore," by Sir H. R. Bishop, 1818 ; W. Crathern, 1820.

"My days are in the yellow leaf," by F. Romer, 1849.

"My native land, good-night," by F. J. Klose, 1819.

"Mary, adieu," by E. Masson, 1837.

"The Moorish King rides up and down," by J. Lodge, 1830.

"My soul is dark," by T. D. Chatterton, 1869; T. Childs, 1860.

"No more the harp of Judah," by J. E'Astes (*Musical Sketches of Many Lands*), 1857.

"O'er the glad waters," by T. F. Walmisley, 1835.

"Oh! had my fate been joined to thine," by G. Linley, 1854.

"Oh, memory, torture me no more," by C. E. Horn, 1830.

"Oh! might I kiss those eyes of fire," by C. J. Wilson, 1864.

"Oh never talk again to me," by E. J. Nielson, 1838.

"Oh! snatched away," by G. V. Duval, 1830.

"Oh! weep for those that wept by Babel's stream," by G. Henschel, 1879; F. Hiller, 1885.

"Oh! would I were a careless child," by E. J. Loder (*Songs of the Poets*, No. 4), 1844.

"One struggle more" (from "Childe Harold"), by J. Clarke, 1816; W. M. Herbert, 1861.

"Peace to thee, Isle of the Ocean," by G. Cole, 1836.

"Remind me not, remind me not," by W. R. Bexfield (*Six Songs*, No. 5), 1847.

"River that rollest," by S. Drury, 1849.

"Roll on thou deep and dark blue ocean roll," by E. F. Fitzwilliam (*Set of Songs*, No. 9), 1853.

"The roses of love glad the garden of life," by J. J. Blockley, 1835; M. B. Hawes, 1856; E.

J. Loder, 1845; R. A. Ruest, 1858.

"She walks in beauty," by J. W. Elliott, 1870; W. Schulthes, 1855; H. Stanislaus, 1880; W. Staton, 1868; H. Temple, 1881.

"Sons of the Greeks, arise," by J. C. Bridge, 1877.

"A Spirit passed before me," by H. C. Deacon, 1865.

"Sun of the sleepless, melancholy star," by Mendelssohn, 1857; H. Rietsch (*Neun Lieder*, No. 2).

"There be none of Beauty's daughters," by E. J. Betterby; A. H. Brown, 1856; E. Bunnett, 1861; J. Carleton, 1870; W. Clayton, 1860; J. Downs, 1866; J. R. W. Harding, 1859; C. Hause, 1868; M. B. Hawes, 1856; A. Isly, 1867; P. Knapton, 1818; H. F. Limpus, 1880; Mendelssohn, 1857; T. M. Mudie, 1845; S. von Neukomm, 1835; J. E. Newell (12 two-part songs, No. 11), 1884; H. F. B. Reynardson, 1880; A. Sewell, 1881; C. V. Stanford, 1882; J. Thomson, 1840; B. Ward, 1859; M. V. White, 1885; T. H. Wright, 1837.

"There is a mystic thread," by J. M. Harris, 1828; M. Hinckesman, 1825.

"There is a voice," by B. M. de Solla, 1856.

"There's not a joy," by Sir J. A. Stevenson, 1815.

"There was a time," by W. Collins, 1848.

"They say that hope is happiness," by G. Arri, 1841; J. Thomson, 1834.

"This rose to calm my brother's cares," by L. Jansen, 1820; J. Nathan, 1825; C. K. Salaman, 1872.

" Those flaxen locks," by G. Kiallmark, 1827.

" Tho' the day of my destiny's over," by G. Kiallmark, 1820; A. Lee, 1830; G. Linley, 1854; F. Romer, 1849.

" Thou whose spell can raise the dead," by E. W. Simcox, 1876.

" 'Tis sweet to hear at midnight," by J. Lodge, 1835; E. Masson, 1851.

" 'Tis sweet to see the evening star," by J. Barnett, 1869.

" To horse, to horse," by G. Linley, 1854.

" To lonely grave," by T. Thorley, 1817.

" 'Twas whisper'd in Heaven," by Schumann (*Six Songs*, No. 5), 1853.

" We'll go no more a roving," by G. Kiallmark, 1827; J. Lodge, 1833.

" We sate down, and wept," by A. Lee, 1852; B. L. Mosely, 1875; N. E. Praeger, 1873.

" When all around grew drear and dark," by E. S. Mantz, 1857.

" When forced to part," by C. E. Horn, 1830.

" When friendship or love," by J. Nathan, 1824.

" When I dream that you love me," by F. B. Jewson, 1856.

" When I left thy shores, O Naxos," by J. R. W. Harding, 1854.

" When I roved a young highlander," by J. Nathan, 1824; H. Russell, 1835.

" When the last sunshine of expiring day," by A. E. S. Rae, 1881.

" When my soul wings her flight," by E. J. Nelson, 1844.

" When we two parted," by H. R. Allen, 1857; C. Armstrong, 1876; H. Cadogan; A. J. Caldicott, 1879; A. H. Comfort; G. V. Duval, 1830; R. F. Harvey, 1863; M. B. Hawes, 1856; P. Klapton, 1819; J. P. Knight, 1835; G. Linley, 1854; S. C. Lowry, 1879; G. A. Macfarren, 1859; J. Nathan, 1817; E. Rogers, 1876; C. Rudolphus, 1835; C. Thornton, 1869.

" Why should my anxious breast repine," by G. Kiallmark, 1827.

" The wild gazelle on Judah's hills," by H. Fielding (*Six Songs*, No. 1), 1860.

" The winds are high on Helle's wave," by S. Nelson.

" Without thine ear to listen to my lay," by C. Salaman, 1843.

" Ye Cupids droop each little head" (translation from Catullus), by M. V. White, 1882.

" Young Oak, when I planted thee," by G. Kiallmark, 1827.

MAGAZINE ARTICLES, ETC.

Byron, Lord.—Analytical Magazine, vol. 4, 1814, pp. 66-72.—New Monthly Magazine, vol. 3, 1815, pp. 527-530. — North American Review, by W. Phillips, vol. 5, 1817, pp. 98-110.—Blackwood's Edinburgh Magazine, vol. 11, 1822, pp. 212-217; vol. 17, pp. 131-151.—Knight's Quarterly Magazine, vol. 1, 1823, pp. 337-338.—British Review, vol. 22, 1824, 345-356.—Mirror of Literature, vol. 4, 1824, pp. 129-141.—North American Review, by A. H. Everett, vol. 11 N.S., 1825, pp. 1-47.—Southern Review, vol. 5, 1830, pp. 463-522.—Monthly Review, vol. 13 N.S., 1830, 217-237.—New Monthly Magazine, by T. Sheldrake, vol.

Byron, Lord.

29, 1830, pp. 294-303.—North American Review, by W. O. B. Peabody, vol. 31, 1830, pp. 167-199.—Edinburgh Review, by T. B. Macaulay, vol. 53, 1831, pp. 544-572. — Southern Literary Messenger, vol. 6, 1840, pp. 34-36; vol. 7, p. 32.—Democratic Review, vol. 10 N.S., 1842, pp. 225-238. — Knickerbocker, by Thomas Carlyle, vol. 21, 1843, pp. 199-212. — Tait's Edinburgh Magazine, by George Gilfillan, vol. 14, 1847, pp. 447-454; same article, Eclectic Magazine, vol. 11, 1847, pp. 556-565.—De Bow's Review, by G. Fitzhugh. vol. 29, 1860, pp. 430-440.—Revue des Deux Mondes, by H. Taine, tom. 41, 1862, pp. 908-948. — Blackwood's Edinburgh Magazine, vol. 106, 1869, pp. 24-33; vol. 107, pp. 123-138, 267-268.— Temple Bar, vol. 25, 1869, pp. 364-371; same article, Eclectic Magazine, vol. 9 N.S., pp. 547-553.—Dublin University Magazine, vol. 73, 1869, pp. 270-286. —Revue des Deux Mondes, by Louis Etienne, tom. 79, 1869, pp. 906-941.—Fortnightly Review, by John Morley, vol. 8 N.S., 1870, pp. 650-673.— Blackwood's Edinburgh Magazine, vol. 112, 1872, pp. 49-72; same article, Littell's Living Age, vol. 114, pp. 387-404; and Eclectic Magazine, vol. 79, pp. 385-403.—Macmillan's Magazine, by Matthew Arnold, vol. 43, 1880, pp. 367-377; same article, Littell's Living Age, vol. 149, pp. 131-139; Appleton's Journal, vol. 10 N.S., pp. 413-420.—Nineteenth Century, by John Ruskin, vol.

Byron, Lord.

8, 1880, pp. 394-410, 748-760. Critic, by E. S. Nadal, vol. 2, 1882, pp. 81-83, 95-97. ——*Address to the Ocean.* Blackwood's Edinburgh Magazine, vol. 64, 1848, pp. 499-514. ——*and Burns.* Southern Literary Messenger, vol. 15, 1849, pp. 165-170. — Portfolio, vol. 32, 1824, pp. 386-393.—London Magazine, vol. 10, 1824, pp. 117-122. ——*and Byronism.* Revue des Deux Mondes, by H. Blaze de Bury, tom. 101, 1872, pp. 513-550. ——*and Casimir Delavigne.* Foreign Quarterly Review, vol. 4, 1829, pp. 470-483. ——*and English Society.* Revue des Deux Mondes, by Nisard, tom. 8, 1850, pp. 413-418. ——*and his Biographers.* Fortnightly Review, by G. S. Venables, vol. 34 N.S., 1883, pp. 189-202. ——*and his Contemporaries, Leigh Hunt's.* Quarterly Review, by J. W. Croker, vol. 37, 1828, pp. 402-426. — Blackwood's Edinburgh Magazine, vol. 23, 1828, pp. 362-408.—Monthly Review, vol. 7 N.S., 1828, pp. 300-312. —New Monthly Magazine, vol. 22 N.S., 1828, pp. 84-96.— London Magazine, vol. 10 N.S., 1828, pp. 211-233. ——*and his Times.* Saint Paul's, by Roden Noel, vol. 13, 1873, pp. 555-577, 618-638. Reprinted in the Hon. Roden Noel's "Essays on Poetry and Poets," 1886. ——*and his Traducers.* American Monthly Magazine, vol. 2 N.S., 1836, pp. 491-498. ——*and Lady Blessington.* Irish

Byron, Lord.

Quarterly Review, vol. 2, 1852, pp. 782-792.

——and Lady Byron. Fraser's Magazine, vol. 1, 1830, pp. 484-488. — Revue des Deux Mondes, by A. Mézières, tom. 108, 1873, pp. 593-624.

——and Landor. Blackwood's Edinburgh Magazine, vol. 14, 1823. p. 99.

——and Mary Chaworth, Unpublished Story of. Lippencott's Magazine, vol. 18, 1876, pp. 637-639.

——and Mr. Kennedy. Fraser's Magazine, vol. 2, 1830, pp. 1-9.

——and Moore. Edinburgh Review, by F. Jeffrey, vol. 38, 1823, pp. 27-48.

——and Newstead Abbey. Athenæum, Aug. 30, 1884, pp. 275, 276, 305, 306.

——and Shelley. Fraser's Magazine, by Charles Kingsley, vol. 48, 1853, pp. 568-576.—Temple Bar, vol. 34, 1872, pp. 30-49. —Westminster Review, vol. 13 N.S., 1858, pp. 350-369 ; same article, Littell's Living Age, vol. 57, pp. 580-591.

—— ——and Shelley, Last Days of, Trelawny's. Athenæum, Feb. 27, 1858, pp. 267-269.

—— ——Shelley and Wordsworth. American Biblical Repository, vol. 1, 2nd Series, 1839, pp. 206-238.

—— —— ——Place of, in English Poetry. Temple Bar, vol. 40, 1874, pp. 478-494.

——and Southey. Blackwood's Edinburgh Magazine, vol. 16, 1824, pp. 711-715.—Portfolio, vol. 13, 1822, pp. 231-238.

——and Tennyson. Quarterly Review, vol. 131, 1871, pp. 354-392 ; same article, Eclectic

Byron, Lord.

Magazine, vol. 15 N.S., pp. 1-20.

——and the Countess Guiccioli. Belgravia, by W. Stigand, vol. 7, 1869, pp. 491-512.

——and Wordsworth. Imperial Magazine, vol. iv., 1822, pp. 416-439, 628-650.—Nineteenth Century, by A. C. Swinburne, vol. 15, 1884, pp. 583-609, 764-790.

—— ——and Wordsworth, Matthew Arnold on. Quarterly Review, vol. 154, 1882, pp. 53-82.

——as a Dramatic Poet. Selections from the Edinburgh Review, vol. 2, 1835, pp. 198-205.

——at Genoa. Blackwood's Edinburgh Magazine, vol. 15, 1824, pp. 696-701.

——at Newstead Abbey. Chambers's Journal, vol. 18, 1862, pp. 220-223.

——at work. Chambers's Journal, 1869, pp. 645-650 ; same article, Littell's Living Age, vol. 103, pp. 464-469.

——Beauties of. Charing Cross, by Fred Proctor, vol. 5 N.S., 1878, pp. 385-388.

——Beppo. Edinburgh Review, by F. Jeffrey, vol. 29, 1818, pp. 302-310. — Blackwood's Edinburgh Magazine, vol. 3, 1818, pp. 323-329.

——Lady Blessington's Conversations of. Monthly Review, vol. 1 N.S., 1834, pp. 97-109.

——Bride of Abydos. British Review, vol. 5, 1813, pp. 391-400.—Critical Review, vol. 4, 1813, pp. 653-658. — Monthly Review, vol. 73, 1814, pp. 55-63.—Analectic Magazine, vol. 3, 1814, pp. 334-344.—Portfolio, vol. 3, 3rd Series, 1814, pp.

Byron, Lord.

Jeaffreson, Sept. 1, 1883, pp. 273-275.

——*Galt's Life of.* Monthly Review, vol. 15 N.S., 1830, pp. 240-252.—Fraser's Magazine, vol. 2, 1830, pp. 347-370, 533-542. — Edinburgh Review, by H. Brougham, vol. 52, 1830, pp. 228-230.

——*Genius and Writings of.* Imperial Magazine, vol. 3, 1821, pp. 254-257, 978-983.

——*Giaour.* Edinburgh Review, by F. Jeffrey, vol. 21, 1813, pp. 299-309.—Analectic Magazine, vol. 2, 1813, pp. 380-391.— British Review, vol. 5, 1813, pp. 132-145.—Critical Review, vol. 4, 1813, pp. 56-68.— Monthly Review, vol. 71, 1813, pp. 202-207.—Quarterly Review, by G. Ellis, vol. 10, 1814, pp. 331-354. — Christian Observer, vol. 12. 1813, pp. 731-737.

——*Goethe and Matthew Arnold.* Contemporary Review, by W. H. White, vol. 40, 1881, pp. 179-185 ; same article, Appleton's Journal, vol. 11 N.S., 1881, pp. 335-339.

——*Heaven and Earth.* Edinburgh Review, by F. Jeffrey, vol. 38, 1823, pp. 27-48. — Blackwood's Edinburgh Magazine, vol. 13, 1823, pp. 72-77, 264-268.—New Monthly Magazine, vol. 7, 1823, pp. 353-358.

——*Hebrew Melodies.* Analectic Magazine, vol. 6, 1815, pp. 292-294.—Christian Observer, vol. 14, 1815, pp. 542-549.—British Review, vol. 6, 1815, pp. 200-208. — British Critic, vol. 3 N.S., 1815, pp. 602-611.— Critical Review, vol. 3, 1816, pp. 357-366.—Monthly Review, vol. 78, 1815, pp. 41-47.—

Byron, Lord.

Charing Cross, by R. Alston, vol. 5 N.S., 1877, pp. 135-140.

——*Home and Grave of.* Once a Week, by P. Skelton, vol. 2, 1860, pp. 539-542 ; same article, Harper's New Monthly Magazine, vol. 21, 1860, pp. 606-610.

——*Hours of Idleness.* Edinburgh Review, by H. Brougham, vol. 11, 1808, pp. 285-289 ; same article, Analectic Magazine, vol. 3, 1814, pp. 469-473. —Eclectic Review, vol. 3, 1807, pp. 989-993.—Monthly Literary Recreations, vol. 3, 1807, pp. 67-71.—Monthly Review, vol. 54, 1807, pp. 256-263.

——*Incident in the Life of.* Argosy, vol. 7, 1869, pp. 273-289.

——*in Greece.* Westminster Review, vol. 2, 1824, pp. 225-262.—Monthly Review, vol. 1, 1831, pp. 92-101.—Temple Bar, vol. 62, 1881, pp. 100-108.

—— ——*Dr. Millingen's Reminiscences of, in Greece.* New Englander, vol. 38, 1879, pp. 637-654.

——*in Venice.* Once-a-Week, vol. 2, 1868, pp. 287-290.

——*Jeaffreson's Real Lord.* Quarterly Review, vol. 156, 1883, pp. 90-131 ; same article, Littell's Living Age, vol. 158, pp. 451-473.—Nineteenth Century, by J. A. Froude, vol. 14, 1883, pp. 228-242. — Nation, by J. M. Hart, vol. 37, 1883, pp. 143-144. — Athenæum, May 12, 1883, pp. 595-597.—Saturday Review, vol. 55, 1883, pp. 773-774. — Academy, by T. H. Caine, vol. 23, 1883, pp. 357, 358.—Spectator, Nov. 10, 1883, pp. 1451, 1452. — Literary

Byron, Lord.

World (Boston), vol. 14, 1883, pp. 187, 326.

——*Journal of.* London Magazine, vol. 1. 1820, pp. 295, 296.

——*Judged by the Witnesses of his Life.* Athenæum, May 16, 1868, pp. 687-689.

——*Juvenile Poems.* Fraser's Magazine, vol. 6, 1832, pp. 183-204.

——*Lament of Tasso.* Blackwood's Edinburgh Magazine, vol. 2, 1817, pp. 142-144.

——*Lara.* Portfolio, vol. 6, 1815, pp. 33-56.

——*Last Days of.* Blackwood's Edinburgh Magazine, vol. 18, 1825, pp. 137-155.

——*Last Portrait of.* New Monthly Magazine, vol. 16 N.S., 1826, pp. 243-248.

——*Last Record of.* Chambers's Journal, March 27, 1869, pp. 198-202.

——*Lecture on.* Metropolitan Quarterly Magazine, vol. 1, 1826, pp. 457-479.

——*Letter on Pope.* North American Review, by W. H. Prescott, vol. 13, 1821, pp. 450-473.

——*Letter to Galt.* Blackwood's Edinburgh Magazine, vol. 18, 1825, p. 400.

——*Letters of.* Sharpe's London Magazine, vol. 34 N.S., 1869, pp. 10-14, 291-293; vol. 50, pp. 14-16, 70-73.—Westminster Review, vol. 12, 1830, pp. 269-304.

——*Letters to.* Pamphleteer, vol. 19, 1822, pp. 347-362.—Blackwood's Edinburgh Magazine, vol. 9, 1821, pp. 421-426.

——*Life and Genius of.* Pamphleteer, by Sir Cosmo Gordon, vol. 24, 1824, pp. 176-220.

Byron, Lord.

——*Life and Poetry of.* Selections from the Edinburgh Review, vol. 1, 1835, pp. 376-397.

——*Life of.* Mirror of Literature, vol. 3, 1824, pp. 337-350.

——*Lost Chapter of History of.* Lippincott's Magazine, by N. S. Dodge, vol. 3, 1869, pp. 666-673.

——*Manfred.* Edinburgh Review, by F. Jeffrey, vol. 28, 1817, pp. 418-431. — British Review, vol. 10, 1817, pp. 82-90.—British Critic, vol. 8 N.S., 1817, pp. 28-47.—Critical Review, vol. 5, 1817, pp. 622-629. —Blackwood's Edinburgh Magazine, vol. 1, 1817, pp. 289-295.—Monthly Review. vol. 83 N.S., 1817, pp. 300-307.—St. James's Magazine, by Julia Goddard, vol. 14 N.S., 1875, pp. 254-264.—Dublin University Magazine, by F. Parke, vol. 83, 1874, pp. 502-508.

——*Marino Faliero.* Monthly Review, vol. 95 N.S., 1821, pp. 41-50.—London Magazine, vol. 3, 1821, pp. 550-554.—British Review, vol. 17, 1821, pp. 439-452.—Eclectic Review, vol. 15 N.S., 1821, pp. 518-527. — Edinburgh Review, by F. Jeffrey, vol. 35, 1821, pp. 271-285.

——*Married Life of.* Temple Bar, vol. 26, 1869, pp. 364-393 ; vol. 28, pp. 61-91.

——*Mazeppa.* Blackwood's Edinburgh Magazine, vol. 5, 1819, pp. 429-432.—Analectic Magazine, vol. 14, 1819, pp. 405-410. —Monthly Review, vol. 89 N.S., 1819, pp. 309-321.— Eclectic Review, vol. 12 N.S., 1819, pp. 147-156.

——*Memorial of, Proposed.* Fraser's Magazine, vol. 13 N.S., 1876, pp. 246-260.

Byron, Lord.
——*Prophecy of Dante.* Western Review, vol. 4, 1821, pp. 321-328.
——*Quarto of* 1806. Athenæum, Dec. 5, 1885, pp. 731-733 ; Dec. 12, p. 769.—Athenæum, by R. Edgcumbe and F. Harvey, Jan. 16, 1886, pp. 101, 102.
——*Recent Criticism on.* International Review, by T. S. Perry, vol. 7, 1879, pp. 282-293.
——*Recollections of.* Westminster Review, vol. 3, 1825, pp. 1-35. — Blackwood's Edinburgh Magazine, vol. 15, 1824, pp. 696-701.—Mirror of Literature, vol. 3, 1824, pp. 417-423.
——*Religious Opinions of.* New England Magazine, vol. 1, 1831, pp. 63-68, 112-118.
——*Sardanapalus.* Blackwood's Edinburgh Magazine, vol. 11, 1822, pp. 90-94. — Portfolio, vol. 14, 4th Ser., 1822, pp. 487-492.
——*Separation from Lady Byron.* Blackwood's Edinburgh Magazine, vol. 17, 1825, pp. 131-151.
——*Shelley and English Poetry.* Revue des Deux Mondes, by E. de Guerle, tom. 19, 1859, pp. 69-88.
——*Siege of Corinth.* British Review, vol. 7, 1816, pp. 452-464.—Critical Review, vol. 3, 1816, pp. 146-154. — Monthly Review, vol. 79, 1816, pp. 196-208.
——*Swimming across the Hellespont.* London Magazine, vol. 3, 1821, pp. 363-365.

Byron, Lord.
——*Tragedies of.* Edinburgh Review, by Francis Jeffrey, vol. 36, 1822, pp. 413-452.—North American Review, by J. Everett, vol. 13, 1821, pp. 227-246.—British Review, vol. 19, 1822, pp. 72-102.—Monthly Review, vol. 97 N.S., 1822, pp. 83-98. —London Magazine, vol. 5, 1822, pp. 66-71.—Blackwood's Edinburgh Magazine, vol. 11, 1822, pp. 90-94.—British Critic, vol. 17 N.S., 1822, pp. 520-540.
——*Tributes to the Memory of.* Mirror of Literature, vol. 3, 1824, pp. 350-352, 357-358, 423-424 ; vol. 4, pp. 142-144.
——*Unpublished Letters of.* Athenæum, August 18th, 1883, pp. 206-211.
——*Vindicated.* Fraser's Magazine, vol. 80, 1869, pp. 598-617.
——*Vindication of Poetry of.* Imperial Magazine, vol. 3, 1821, pp. 810-812, 1016-1023, 1113-1124.
——*Voyage from Leghorn to Greece.* Blackwood's Edinburgh Magazine, by G. H. Browne, vol. 35, 1834, pp. 56-67 ; vol. 36, pp. 392-407.
——*Werner.* Blackwood's Edinburgh Magazine, by W. Maginn. vol. 12, 1822, pp. 710-719, 782-785. — Monthly Review, vol. 99. N.S., 1822, pp. 394-405.—Eclectic Review, vol. 19 N.S., 1823, pp. 136-155.—British Critic, vol. 19 N.S., 1823, pp. 242-250.

VII. CHRONOLOGICAL LIST OF WORKS.

Fugitive Pieces (Suppressed)	1806
Poems on Various Occasions	1807
Hours of Idleness	1807
English Bards and Scotch Reviewers	1809
Childe Harold's Pilgrimage Cantos i.-ii.	1812
Canto iii.	1816
Canto iv.	1818
Curse of Minerva	1812
Waltz	1813
The Giaour	1813
The Bride of Abydos	1813
The Corsair	1814
Ode to Napoleon Buonaparte	1814
Lara, a Tale [with Rogers' "Jacqueline"]	1814
Hebrew Melodies	1815
The Siege of Corinth and Parisina	1816
Poems on his Domestic Circumstances	1816
The Prisoner of Chillon	1816
Monody on the Death of Sheridan	1816
Manfred	1817

The Lament of Tasso	1817
Beppo, a Venetian Story	1818
Mazeppa	1819
Don Juan, Cantos i.-ii.	1819
,, ,, iii., iv., v.	1821
,, ,, vi., vii., viii.	1823
,, ,, ix., x., xi.	1823
,, ,, xii.,xiii.,xiv.	1823
,, ,, xv., xvi.	1824
Marino Faliero and the Prophecy of Dante	1821
Sardanapalus; The Two Foscari ; Cain	1821
Letter on the Rev. W. L. Bowles's Strictures on Pope	1821
The Vision of Judgment. [In Pt. i. of the *Liberal*]	1822
Heaven and Earth. [In Pt. ii. of the *Liberal.*]	1822
Morgante Maggiore. Translation from Pulci. [In Pt. iv. of the *Liberal.*]	1823
Werner	1823
The Age of Bronze	1823
The Island	1823
The Deformed Transformed	1824
Parliamentary Speeches	1824

Printed by WALTER SCOTT, *Felling, Newcastle-on-Tyne.*

Monthly Shilling Volumes.   *Cloth, cut or uncut edges.*

THE CAMELOT SERIES.

EDITED BY ERNEST RHYS.   VOLUMES ALREADY ISSUED—

ROMANCE OF KING ARTHUR.	Edited by Ernest Rhys.
THOREAU'S WALDEN.	Edited by Will H. Dircks.
ENGLISH OPIUM-EATER.	Edited by William Sharp.
LANDOR'S CONVERSATIONS.	Edited by H. Ellis.
PLUTARCH'S LIVES.	Edited by B. J. Snell, M.A.
RELIGIO MEDICI, &c.	Edited by J. A. Symonds.
SHELLEY'S LETTERS.	Edited by Ernest Rhys.
PROSE WRITINGS OF SWIFT.	Edited by W. Lewin.
MY STUDY WINDOWS.	Edited by R. Garnett, LL.D.
GREAT ENGLISH PAINTERS.	Edited by William Sharp.
LORD BYRON'S LETTERS.	Edited by M. Blind.
ESSAYS BY LEIGH HUNT.	Edited by A. Symons.
LONGFELLOW'S PROSE.	Edited by W. Tirebuck.
GREAT MUSICAL COMPOSERS.	Edited by E. Sharp.
MARCUS AURELIUS.	Edited by Alice Zimmern.
SPECIMEN DAYS IN AMERICA.	By Walt Whitman.
WHITE'S SELBORNE.	Edited by Richard Jefferies.
DEFOE'S SINGLETON.	Edited by H. Halliday Sparling.
MAZZINI'S ESSAYS.	Edited by William Clarke.
PROSE WRITINGS OF HEINE.	Edited by H. Ellis.
REYNOLDS' DISCOURSES.	Edited by Helen Zimmern.
PAPERS OF STEELE AND ADDISON.	Edited by W. Lewin.
BURNS'S LETTERS.	Edited by J. Logie Robertson, M.A.
VOLSUNGA SAGA.	Edited by H. H. Sparling.
SARTOR RESARTUS.	Edited by Ernest Rhys.
WRITINGS OF EMERSON.	Edited by Percival Chubb.
SENECA'S MORALS.	Edited by Walter Clode.
DEMOCRATIC VISTAS.	By Walt Whitman.
LIFE OF LORD HERBERT.	Edited by Will H. Dircks.
ENGLISH PROSE.	Edited by Arthur Galton.
IBSEN'S PILLARS OF SOCIETY.	Edited by H. Ellis.
FAIRY AND FOLK TALES.	Edited by W. B. Yeats.
EPICTETUS.	Edited by T. W. Rolleston.
THE ENGLISH POETS.	By James Russell Lowell.
ESSAYS OF DR. JOHNSON.	Edited by Stuart J. Reid.
ESSAYS OF WILLIAM HAZLITT.	Edited by Frank Carr.
LANDOR'S PENTAMERON, &c.	Edited by H. Ellis.
POE'S TALES AND ESSAYS.	Edited by Ernest Rhys.
VICAR OF WAKEFIELD.	Edited by Ernest Rhys.
POLITICAL ORATIONS.	Edited by William Clarke.
CHESTERFIELD'S LETTERS.	Selected by C. Sayle.
THOREAU'S WEEK.	Edited by Will H. Dircks.
STORIES FROM CARLETON.	Edited by W. B. Yeats.
AUTOCRAT OF THE BREAKFAST-TABLE.	By O. W. Holmes.
JANE EYRE.	Edited by Clement Shorter.
ELIZABETHAN ENGLAND.	Edited by Lothrop Withington.
WRITINGS OF THOMAS DAVIS.	Edited by T. W. Rolleston.
SPENCE'S ANECDOTES.	Edited by John Underhill.
MORE'S UTOPIA.	Edited by Maurice Adams.
SADI'S GULISTAN.	Edited by Charles Sayle.
ENGLISH FOLK AND FAIRY TALES.	Edited by E. S. Hartland.

London: WALTER SCOTT, 24 Warwick Lane, Paternoster Row.

IBSEN'S PROSE DRAMAS

EDITED BY WILLIAM ARCHER.

In Four Volumes.

CROWN 8vo, CLOTH, PRICE 3s. 6d. PER VOLUME.

The Norwegian dramatist, Henrik Ibsen, is at this moment one of the most widely-discussed of European writers. Throughout the English-speaking world his name has been made famous by the production of *A Doll's House*, in London, Boston, and Melbourne; in each of which cities it excited an almost unprecedented storm of controversy. As yet, however, there has existed no uniform and authoritative edition in English of the plays of which so much is being said and written. Mr. Walter Scott has concluded an arrangement with Henrik Ibsen, under which he will publish a uniform series of his prose plays. They will be carefully edited by Mr. William Archer, whose name will be a guarantee of the accuracy and literary excellence of the translations

---

Crown 8vo, Cloth, 3s. 6d. each.

VOL I.
"A DOLL'S HOUSE," "THE LEAGUE OF YOUTH," and "THE PILLARS OF SOCIETY."

VOL. II.
"GHOSTS," "AN ENEMY OF THE PEOPLE," AND "THE WILD DUCK."

VOL III.
"LADY INGER OF ÖSTRÅT," "THE VIKINGS AT HELGELAND," "THE PRETENDER." [*May 26*

London· Walter Scott, 24 Warwick Lane, Paternoster Row.

GREAT WRITERS.

A NEW SERIES OF CRITICAL BIOGRAPHIES.

Edited by Professor ERIC S. ROBERTSON, M.A.

MONTHLY SHILLING VOLUMES.

VOLUMES ALREADY ISSUED—

LIFE OF LONGFELLOW. By Prof. Eric S. Robertson.
"A most readable little work."—*Liverpool Mercury.*

LIFE OF COLERIDGE. By Hall Caine.
"Brief and vigorous, written throughout with spirit and great literary skill."—*Scotsman.*

LIFE OF DICKENS. By Frank T. Marzials.
"Notwithstanding the mass of matter that has been printed relating to Dickens and his works . . . we should, until we came across this volume, have been at a loss to recommend any popular life of England's most popular novelist as being really satisfactory. The difficulty is removed by Mr. Marzials's little book."—*Athenæum.*

LIFE OF DANTE GABRIEL ROSSETTI. By J. Knight.
"Mr. Knight's picture of the great poet and painter is the fullest and best yet presented to the public."—*The Graphic.*

LIFE OF SAMUEL JOHNSON. By Colonel F. Grant.
"Colonel Grant has performed his task with diligence, sound judgment, good taste, and accuracy."—*Illustrated London News.*

LIFE OF DARWIN. By G. T. Bettany.
"Mr. G. T. Bettany's *Life of Darwin* is a sound and conscientious work."
—*Saturday Review.*

LIFE OF CHARLOTTE BRONTË. By A. Birrell.
"Those who know much of Charlotte Brontë will learn more, and those who know nothing about her will find all that is best worth learning in Mr. Birrell's pleasant book."—*St. James' Gazette.*

LIFE OF THOMAS CARLYLE. By R. Garnett, LL.D.
"This is an admirable book. Nothing could be more felicitous and fairer than the way in which he takes us through Carlyle's life and works."—*Pall Mall Gazette.*

LIFE OF ADAM SMITH. By R. B. Haldane, M.P.
"Written with a perspicuity seldom exemplified when dealing with economic science."—*Scotsman.*

LIFE OF KEATS. By W. M. Rossetti.
"Valuable for the ample information which it contains."—*Cambridge Independent.*

LIFE OF SHELLEY. By William Sharp.
"The criticisms . . . entitle this capital monograph to be ranked with the best biographies of Shelley."—*Westminster Review.*

LIFE OF SMOLLETT. By David Hannay.
"A capable record of a writer who still remains one of the great masters of the English novel."—*Saturday Review.*

LIFE OF GOLDSMITH. By Austin Dobson.
"The story of his literary and social life in London, with all its humorous and pathetic vicissitudes, is here retold, as none could tell it better."—*Daily News.*

WORKS BY THE HON. RODEN NOEL.

A MODERN FAUST, AND OTHER POEMS.

(Kegan Paul & Co. 5/-.)

"With these words I quit what seems to me one of the most remarkable products of poetico-philosophical genius in the literature of our prolific century."—J. A. SYMONDS in the *Academy*.

"The poem appears to me to exhibit much power, with high moral aims."—RT. HON. W. E. GLADSTONE.

SONGS OF THE HEIGHTS AND DEEPS.

(Kegan Paul & Co. 6/-.)

"Il nous plait aussi d'entendre se prolonger les chants de l'ancienne lyre. de celle on si longtemps, de l'Edda à Shakspeare et à Byron, et de Byron à Browning et à M. Roden Noel vibrerent, et vibrent encore ces trois cordes alternantes, a notes profondes ou suaves, sentiment du sublime, sentiment du tragique, sentiment de la nature."—*Revue Contemporaire*, April, 1885.

THE HOUSE OF RAVENSBURG: A DRAMA.

(Kegan Paul & Co. 6/-.)

"Portions of the treatment are fine, we might almost say splendid, from the poetical standpoint."—*Athenæum*.

A LITTLE CHILD'S MONUMENT. (3RD EDITION.)

(Kegan Paul & Co. 3/6.)

"It may fairly take its place beside 'In Memoriam' as a book of consolation for the bereaved."—*Leeds Mercury*.

"*Lament*, qui, dans sa simplicité presque sacrée, est d'une incomparable beauté de forme."—*Le Parlement*, Paris.

BEATRICE AND OTHER POEMS.

(Kegan Paul & Co. 7/-.)

"Ce petit chef-d'œuvre de *Ganymede*."—SAINTE-BEUVE.

"Out of Coleridge it would not be easy to find any philosophical poetry finer than certain portions of Mr. Noel's 'Pan.'"—*Athenæum*

LIVINGSTONE IN AFRICA.

ILLUSTRATED BY HUME NISBET.

(Authors' Co-operative Publishing Co., St. Bride Street. 10/6.)

—— Passionate and catholic sympathy with human life, a power of seeing the romance of contemporary history, and a peculiar skill in the employment of strange and sonorous local names."—"Few poets have used scientific guesses or discoveries more felicitously than Mr. Noel in this passage." . . . "This is surely stately and admirable verse." . . . "Pictures of the greatest originality."—ANDREW LANG in *Academy*.

THE RED FLAG, AND OTHER POEMS.

(Kegan Paul & Co. 6/.)

"Perhaps one of the most solemn, awful poems of the present century is 'The Vision of the Desert.' . . . There are fine sympathies with the sorrows of London life, and wonderful knowledge of them."—*British Quarterly Review*.

"Nature is represented with the most minute and patient accuracy, yet each description is pervaded with a sense of the divine mysterious life that throbs throughout the world."—*Academy*.